"*Caroline...*"

Duke's voice held the unmistakable sound of patience wearing thin. "We couldn't think of each other as strangers if we wanted to."

"All I know," she said firmly, "is that whatever this is between us, it's moving too fast. And I don't like it."

"That's how it happened the first time, Caroline. That's how it is with us."

His tone was gentle, but that didn't help. He made everything sound too easy, and it wasn't. If there was one thing Caroline was positive of, it was that nothing between the two of them was ever easy.

"I'm sorry. I just don't think I can do it. Not again." Her words were quiet, but the emotions inside her were anything but.

She pulled free of his restraining arms and started to walk away, but Duke recovered from his surprise before she could go two steps. Catching her just above the elbow, he swung her back around to face him.

"I waited thirteen years to find you again, and I'm not letting you go that quickly."

Dear Reader,

Welcome to **Silhouette Special Edition** . . . welcome to romance. Each month, **Silhouette Special Edition** publishes six novels with you in mind—stories of love and life, tales that you can identify with—romance with that little "something special" added in.

And this month, we have a star-spangled surprise for you. To help celebrate the Fourth of July, we have two books that are dedicated to the Navy—and our country's valiant armed services. *Under Fire* by Lindsay McKenna is part of the thrilling WOMEN OF GLORY series—the hero and heroine are both naval pilots. *Navy Woman* by Debbie Macomber is set at a naval submarine base in the state of Washington—the hero is the commander of a vast fleet, and the heroine is a busy naval attorney. Three cheers for the red, white and blue—and the Navy! We're protected in the air as well as by sea! Happy Fourth of July.

Rounding out July are books by Ada Steward, Laura Leone and Carole Halston. And, as an added bonus, July brings the initial story of the compelling series SONNY'S GIRLS—*All Those Years Ago,* by Emilie Richards. The next installments in SONNY'S GIRLS due out in August and September, respectively, are *Don't Look Back* by Celeste Hamilton and *Longer Than* . . . by Erica Spindler. Don't miss these poignant tales!

In each **Silhouette Special Edition**, we're dedicated to bringing you the romances that you dream about—the type of stories that delight as well as bring a tear to the eye. And that's what **Silhouette Special Edition** is all about— special books by special authors for special readers!

I hope you enjoy this book and all of the stories to come.

Sincerely,

Tara Gavin
Senior Editor

ADA STEWARD
Even Better Than Before

Silhouette Special Edition

Published by Silhouette Books New York

America's Publisher of Contemporary Romance

SILHOUETTE BOOKS
300 East 42nd St., New York, N.Y. 10017

EVEN BETTER THAN BEFORE

ISBN: 0-373-09680-1

First Silhouette Books printing July 1991

Printed in the U.S.A.

Books by Ada Steward

Silhouette Special Edition

This Cherished Land #227
Love's Haunting Refrain #289
Misty Mornings, Magic Nights #319
A Walk in Paradise #343
Galahad's Bride #604
Even Better Than Before #680

ADA STEWARD

began writing a novel at the tender age of twelve, when romance and romance fiction were the farthest things from her mind. As a preteen, she favored the fast-paced action of Westerns, war stories, even science fiction. As she matured, however, she realized that what fascinated her most in life *and* in writing were people, and she turned her attention more fully to character. Since she was drawn to travel, the particular flavor and history of settings also became important. Romance fiction provided the perfect opportunity to combine the richness of place with the drama of people and possibilities. An Oklahoma resident, Ada Steward parcels most of her time into working, writing, traveling and exercising.

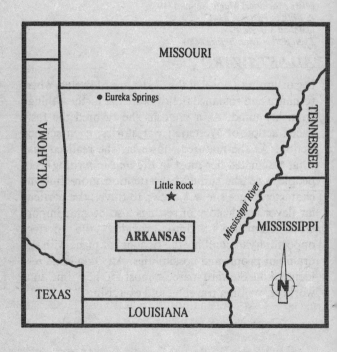

Chapter One

Caroline Adams stood at the parlor window and stared out into the blank, black night. She had been restless all day. Part of her was glad to be home again. Part of her was afraid she had made a big mistake. Almost all of her was just plain scared.

Outside, the wind clattered like a skeleton's bones through the ice-coated branches of the trees. Sleet pinged against the side of the house and skittered with a hollow ring across the wooden floor of the front porch. She should have been grateful to be inside, safe and cozy in the home where she grew up.

"Ooh, listen to that night," Viola Adams said, entering the room.

Caroline could almost hear the shiver in her grandmother's voice. The scene behind her was imperfectly reflected on the windowpane to her right, and she couldn't help the tug at her heart as she watched her grandmother, who had grown frail and stooped almost overnight after the sudden death of Caroline's grandfather a few months earlier.

"I wonder when it's going to stop," Caroline answered. "I've been in the mood to go for a drive all evening."

Her grandmother set a tray on the coffee table and straightened. The reflection of colored Christmas-tree lights flashed on and off in the windowpane, and the faint scent of pine freshened the cool, damp air that blew in around old windows.

Caroline released the curtain she had held crushed in her grasp, shutting out the scene reflected on the pane as the wisp of Irish lace slid back into place. She turned in time to see her grandmother's worried frown.

"You wouldn't really go out in that, would you, Caroline?"

Unable to resist teasing, Caroline answered, "But I've got my snow tires on."

Predictably, Viola took her seriously. "The rain's already turned to sleet, and there's going to be snow on top of that any minute now." When she saw that Caroline was laughing, her alarm evaporated in a smile and she patted the sofa cushion next to her. "You. I'm too old for you to tease me like that. Here, join me."

Caroline turned for one last wistful gaze over her shoulder through the lace curtain at the night outside the window. She wondered if it would really be so dangerous if she took just a short drive.

She longed to feel the freedom of the wind in her hair while she drove through the narrow, twisting streets of downtown. The old buildings there always made her feel as if she had stepped back in time to when life was a simpler, more graceful existence.

And after that, it wouldn't be too much farther to drive up into the mountains, just high enough to look down on the sleeping town, glittering under the blanket of its winter storm.

"Caroline? Are you hungry, dear?"

Breathing a deep sigh of contentment, Caroline reluctantly left her daydream and turned back to notice the tray of hot tea and pound cake her grandmother had set on the coffee table.

"What have you got there?" she asked with the beginnings of a smile.

"Oh, just a little snack." Viola leaned forward and began to pour the tea. "Supper's going to be leftovers, and I thought we could use a little something extra to perk us up until then."

"Gran." Caroline threw her hands up, laughing, and started toward the sofa. "I know the doctor told you to regain some of the weight you've lost, but you're going to have me looking like Porky Pig with all these little snacks."

Viola smiled warmly as Caroline settled onto the cushion next to her. "I know, dear, but it's just so nice to have you here with me."

The gentle lavender eyes that were fixed on Caroline suddenly misted over, and the delicate hand that patted Caroline's felt cold to the touch.

"I just hated going into that kitchen with nobody else to cook for," Viola said in a forceful, though husky, whisper.

Caroline could hear the pain and anger in her grandmother's voice and it tore at her. She knew how it felt and she knew how quickly the grief could materialize out of nowhere.

"It's just so hard sometimes," Viola said with a choked little sigh. "I hate eating alone. I hate being alone."

Reaching out to the woman who had been like a mother to her, Caroline wrapped her arms protectively around her grandmother's narrow shoulders and held her close. "I know," she crooned softly through the tears that burned suddenly in her own throat. "I know."

"When's it going to end?" Viola asked. "When am I going to feel right again?"

Caroline held her tighter, trying to offer the only comfort she could, and felt woefully inadequate. "I'm here," she said. "I can't take Grandpa's place, but I won't leave you alone."

"Oh, dear, I'm sorry." Viola separated herself gently from Caroline's arms and tried hard to smile. "I don't mean to be a burden. Sometimes it just hits me out of nowhere. Ooh." Again she suppressed a shiver. "Would you hand me my shawl, Caroline? Nights like this just seem to cut right through me."

"Of course." Eager to do anything that would help, Caroline lifted the shawl from the sidechair and draped it tenderly across her grandmother's shoulders. "Do you want me to light a fire?" she asked, and almost immediately realized her mistake.

Laying a fire in the fireplace had been one of her grandfather's evening rituals in the winter. After fifty years of marriage, her grandparents had still sat side by side, holding hands and watching the fire on long winter evenings.

Viola drew in a long, shaky breath and expelled it in a sigh. "I don't believe so, dear," she said in a voice that had gone hoarse again. "But thank you." She wrapped the shawl more tightly around her and rubbed her hands together. "It is cold, though, isn't it? I just seem to be cold all the time lately. Do you suppose our tea's still warm at all?"

Caroline took a sip and made a face at the tepid drink.

"I guess not," Viola said, smiling. "Why don't I just dump this down the sink?" She lifted their cups. "I'm sure what's in the teapot is still warm."

"I'll do it," Caroline offered, grateful for the chance to be alone for a moment. She couldn't quite put her finger on what, but something had been bothering her all day, and as the night wore on, her nerves were getting more frayed by the minute.

Taking a teacup in each hand, she left the parlor and crossed the dining room. At the swinging door into the kitchen, she turned sideways and nudged the door open with her shoulder just enough to slip through. The light was already on, and a radio played softly.

Caroline set the teacups next to the sink and dumped their contents. Then she walked to the end of the linoleum countertop, where an old radio sat tucked in the corner under the cabinets, out of the way. She reached to turn off the radio and then stopped, her hand frozen in midair as she realized what she had been hearing.

The song was an old one. It had been old even when she was young, but it was the kind of teenage lament to star-crossed love that withstood the passage of time. Bracing her hands against the countertop, she tried to fight the memories that came stealing quietly out of the past to tiptoe around her, but it was no use.

All day, a sepia-tinted image of Duke Hutchison, faded but persistent, had flickered at the edges of her mind. Now, against her will, she watched the mental image change to Technicolor clarity.

Duke—with his coal-black hair and misty gray eyes that could turn hard as steel or soft as the silvery sheen of a moonlit lake. Duke, the small-town bad boy from the wrong side of the tracks. He had been her first love, her only true love. Remembering him now made him seem almost more fairy tale than real: an authentic, leather-jacketed, motorcycle-riding leader of the pack.

But Caroline hadn't met him at the candy store, like in the song. Instead, she had been at the local Dairy Queen when he had first roared out of the dusk and into her life the summer she turned sixteen, in those long ago days when she had still been young enough to believe that wishing on a star really could make dreams come true.

"Caroline?"

Her grandmother's voice in the same room with her pulled Caroline abruptly back from the gray area of half-forgotten memories and haunting sorrows.

"I was afraid you'd gotten lost," Viola said with a hint of the good humor that had once been such a part of her. Taking another step into the room, she asked more seriously, "Are you all right, dear?"

"Yes," Caroline said, her heart still pounding like that of a criminal caught in the act. She turned off the radio and walked back to the sink to pick up the empty teacups. "I was just turning off the radio."

"Did I leave that thing on again?" Viola held the door open and then followed Caroline through the dining room. "I swear, my mind these days..." She shook her head. "I worry about me."

With her hands full, Caroline couldn't hug the older woman who trailed behind her, taking the small, uncertain steps of someone who was just recovering from a long illness. "Gran," she said gently with a smile that held all the love in her heart, "you're doing just fine. It's normal to forget little things during times of stress."

"Then I'm not just getting old?"

"Well, if you are, I'm your twin because I've been forgetting things like that for a long time."

"It's so nice to have you here with me." Viola walked past Caroline and sat contentedly on the sofa once again. "This house is just too big for one person. At least, it seems that way right now. But it is beginning to feel more like Christmas."

Caroline sat beside her and poured fresh cups of tea while her grandmother served them each a slice of pound cake. "It does, doesn't it?" She took a sip of tea and a bite of cake, and for an instant, she felt comforted by her surroundings.

"Do you think you should postpone your interview tomorrow?" Viola asked. "Those streets are going to be pretty slick in the morning."

The cup in Caroline's hand jerked, sloshing tea over the rim and onto the slice of pound cake that sat in the saucer on her lap.

Startled by Caroline's reaction, Viola asked, "Is something wrong, dear?"

Caroline choked down the pound cake that had turned to sawdust in her mouth, and she took a hasty drink of tea. "No." The word was more of a squeak than an answer.

"I didn't mean to upset you, dear. It was wonderful of you to give up your job in Chicago and move back here to keep me company. Really wonderful." Viola toyed with the fringe on her shawl and stared at the remaining pound cake on the coffee table.

Caroline closed her eyes and wished she had somewhere to hide. She didn't want to have this conversation.

"It's just…" Viola began hesitantly. "It's just that, well, are you sure this is the right job for you?"

"Oh, Gran." Caroline said with a sigh. She had managed to run from her own misgivings all day, but now there seemed to be nowhere left to go. Bowing to the inevitable, she said quietly, "It's the only one I've seen that I'm qualified for. It's exactly what I was doing before. I'm perfect for it."

"Oh, dear," Viola said with feeling.

"Gran, it's been thirteen years. Duke probably doesn't even remember me."

She had been telling herself that all day, but she still didn't really believe it. It may have been thirteen years since she'd seen him, but she remembered Duke. She remembered everything about him. She even remembered the color of the sky the first day they'd met.

"People don't forget their first loves, Caroline," Viola warned.

"Anyway," Caroline said, rushing on. "The interview isn't with him. It's with the director of human resources, a Mr. Harper." She took a deep breath and forced herself to slow down. "I'm sure I won't even see Duke."

"You will if you get the job."

Caroline resisted the urge to shout, took another deep breath, and said, "I know."

"You could get *another* job."

"Gran," Caroline said as patiently as she could, "I spent four years in college and another eight years with one company doing one job. I like what I do, and it's what I know how to do. I can't sell. I've never run a cash register. I don't even type very well. I'm a compensation-and-benefits analyst, and Hutchison Industries needs one."

"Your grandfather never liked that boy," Viola said a little sadly. "I was never too sure, myself. I always wondered if maybe we weren't just a little hasty."

Caroline wasn't prepared for the hot flush of anger and the hard pounding of her heart as her grandmother spoke. If it were anyone else but her grandmother and any other time but now, she would probably vent some of that anger. But the time for recriminations was long past and she just wanted to get away before she said something she couldn't take back.

With shaking hands, she set down her cup and saucer. "I think I'm going to turn in early," she said quietly.

Viola looked stricken. "I've upset you."

"This is a hard time for us all," Caroline said, still forcing a calm she didn't feel. She stood, then leaned down and kissed her grandmother's forehead. "Don't plan on me for breakfast in the morning. I'll probably be leaving early."

"Caroline," Viola protested as her granddaughter started toward the hallway and her upstairs bedroom.

At the foot of the staircase, Caroline looked back and tried to smile. "Good night, Gran. I love you."

"Very well. Do what you think best," Viola called after her and, as clearly as if she were still in the parlor, Caroline could visualize the halfhearted shrug that went with the phrase.

Suddenly, her anger didn't seem nearly so unjustified when she remembered all the times she had fallen victim to her grandmother's innocent-sounding battle cry. "Do what you think best" translated literally to "I have just begun to fight," and it was deadly for the unwary.

On the landing at the top of the stairs, Caroline paused to rub her temples, trying to ease the beginning pressure of a headache. When she had decided to move back home, it had seemed so reasonable, almost inevitable. Now it was beginning to seem hopeless.

She thought she had forgotten Duke, or at least learned to cope with the memories. She thought after thirteen years, her grandmother would have been ready to let her live her own life, even if it meant making mistakes.

At the doorway of her bedroom, she stopped and took in the awful, pink ruffledness of it. The bed was the same white, canopied twin-size one she had had all her life. Dolls still filled the armoire, where they had been put when she turned fourteen and stuffed animals had replaced them on her bed. The stuffed animals were now in a trunk at the foot of the bed.

All the things that had been left behind thirteen years earlier were there still. Her youth had been frozen in time, awaiting her return. Inwardly, she felt herself crumbling under the weight of too many memories and too much hurt that she had foolishly thought was behind her.

Her head was beginning to throb as she made her way to the window and opened it just enough to let the cold, wet air blow over her while the tune that had been on the radio began to play again in her head.

The song had been a piece of nostalgia already on that warm summer evening so long ago when she first fell under the spell of a man who had seemed out of step with his time.

The year was one of hope and upheaval. Vietnam was ending, and Northern Ireland was just beginning. Miniskirts were still hot, and hot pants were still shocking. It was a time of change and a summer made for memories.

Tricia Nixon had just given the White House a June wedding. Romance was in the air. And it was a Friday night when it all began.

The day had softened and grown old, lingering as it drowsed through the long, warm twilight hours while the pace of the day slowed and the excitement of the nighttime edged ever closer. And when the children came out to play in those early evening hours, it was with old thoughts on their minds and restless feelings in their hearts. . . .

"I really should get home soon," Caroline said reluctantly.

"It's not dark yet," Ariel argued. She leaned across the back of the convertible's front seat and tapped her brother, Joey, on the shoulder. "Caroline's getting nervous, Joey. Tell her it's all right."

Joey turned lazily in the seat and draped his left arm across the top of the steering wheel. He looked bored, as only an eighteen-year-old can look when his younger sister becomes a nuisance. He focused on Ariel. "What?"

Tank, who was Joey's best friend and Ariel's steady, turned in the passenger's side of the front seat and gave Caroline his best benevolent smile. "Your granddad raised your curfew to ten o'clock on weekends, and it's nowhere near that yet."

Joey twisted around further and smiled at Caroline. "Don't worry, Caroline, we won't get you into trouble." He laughed suddenly. "Boy, I'll never forget last summer, when we kept you out too late that one lousy time. I didn't think your grandfather was ever going to let you out again."

Caroline tried to smile, but the memory wasn't very funny to her. What little freedom she had was hard won and she couldn't afford to take it for granted.

Ariel's round, freckled face leaned nearer. "Feel better now?"

Sighing, Caroline rested her head on the back of the seat and stared up at the pink-and-mauve sky. She felt embarrassed, actually, and she wished she hadn't opened her mouth.

"Great," she said without much enthusiasm.

"Good," Ariel answered with all the enthusiasm Caroline had been lacking. "Isn't this fun?"

Caroline looked sideways at the girl who had been her best friend since kindergarten and who was like a sister to her. Ariel had a good heart and was a lot of fun, but she didn't have a subtle bone in her body. Caroline thought briefly of trying to explain to her that something as simple as sitting around the Dairy Queen, watching the other cars cruise past, was like a bite of forbidden fruit, that what was ordinary to Ariel was still exotic to Caroline.

She settled on a smile instead. "Yeah, this is fun. This is a lot of fun."

And it was. She liked the town of Eureka Springs. It was small enough to feel cozy and yet big enough to still hold surprises. Its familiar surroundings were a welcome comfort, and yet the possibilities of the unknown held an excitement that was almost tangible. And as night crept into the shadows around them, she could feel the first stirrings of that excitement.

"Hey, Joey, you know what I just realized?" Tank said, startling Caroline out of her reverie.

"What?" Joey asked without moving.

"No," Tank said impatiently. "Turn around. You've got to look at this."

Joey and Caroline turned at the same time to look behind them. Caroline saw only the highway that led around the town and on up to the lake. She and Joey both swung back to face Tank.

"What?" Joey demanded.

Tank, whose broad build and deliberate mind earned him his nickname, spread his hands and beamed. "Look at these two gorgeous girls we're with," he crowed as Caroline felt bone-deep embarrassment slowly spread through her.

Joey looked at Tank as if he'd lost his mind and then turned to scrutinize Ariel with a cold, hard eye.

Caroline felt her own discomfort blossom into a blush that could set off fire alarms as she waited for Joey's gaze to reach her. In her opinion, only a man as much in love as Tank was could call either one of them gorgeous. At the moment, Ariel's pretty, beet-red face was clashing fiercely with her carrot-red hair while her dark brown eyes skewered Tank with a look that could at least maim.

Without warning, Joey's appraisal moved to Caroline, and she knew how Ariel felt.

"Now, this one," Joey said after an endless minute of silent torture, "this one shows definite promise."

As his bold eyes roamed her length, Caroline was painfully conscious of her bare legs that were longer than last summer and her neatly cuffed shorts that were shorter than last summer. Even the starched, sleeveless blouse her grandmother approved of couldn't hide a body that was far shapelier than it had been just a year ago.

The clearer Joey's admiration grew, the more Caroline's embarrassment turned to anger. "Joey Mason," she finally ground out between clenched teeth, "I've known you since grade school."

His gaze didn't falter. "Tank's known Ariel since grade school, too."

He didn't have to say any more. Caroline looked away, staring off to the side and blushing furiously again while her mind spun with a jumble of uncomfortable sensations.

This summer was shaping up differently from other summers. Tank and Ariel were still kids, and yet, they weren't. Joey had always been as much a big brother to Caroline as he was to Ariel, and now he wasn't anymore.

"Hey," Joey said gently. His long arm reached over the back of the seat and he caught Caroline's hand in his. "I was kidding."

When she finally got up the nerve to look at him, his brown eyes were soft and apologetic.

"I didn't mean to upset you. Hey," he said again, laughing, "you remember me. I'm never serious."

Caroline nodded. "Yeah, I remember you. I'm okay."

But she knew things were different, no matter what he said. They were all growing up, whether they wanted to or not, and nothing was ever going to be quite the same again.

Just then, the low rumble of a motorcycle mixed with the revving of car engines that cruised the highway behind the Dairy Queen. Gravel crunched as each new car turned into the parking lot, circling the building and slowing while they studied the cars already parked under the double metal awnings at the side of the building. Newcomers squeezed into a ragged third row on the graveled expanse next to the highway.

The sound of the lone motorcycle deepened as it slowed and then came to a halt on the highway, caught in the string of traffic waiting to turn into the Dairy Queen.

Tank turned to check out the sound and his face lit up. "Hey, Joey, it's Duke."

"All *right*," Joey said, excited. "This is where the night gets interesting."

He turned to watch and, intrigued, Caroline looked over her shoulder in time to see the motorcycle kick up the dust along the side of the road. She watched it roar past the sluggish line of cars and disappear over the hill.

"Damn," Joey and Tank exclaimed in unison, their disappointment obvious.

"Oh, yeah," Caroline said under her breath as she glanced once more at the hilltop and the slowly settling dust, "that was really interesting."

Ignoring Ariel's glare, Caroline snuggled into the corner of the convertible's back seat and tried to dismiss her brief glimpse of black leather on black metal.

"He'll be back," Joey said confidently.

Another irreverent remark was dying to be free, but Caroline held it in check. She glanced once more toward the hilltop, almost hoping to see the motorcycle and its rider reappear, and was vaguely irritated to realize that her heart was pounding at the thought.

"That was Duke Hutchison," Ariel said in a stage whisper.

"Oh, now I'm impressed," Caroline said. She could feel her irritation turning to anger. She had never heard of this person, and she didn't understand why everyone was getting so worked up over someone who looked like he'd just stepped out of an old Brando movie.

"Don't you know who he is?" Ariel continued to whisper loudly.

"No, I don't," Caroline whispered back just as loudly. "Why don't you tell me?"

"He's the one they say got Patsy Miller pregnant."

Shocked, Caroline sat straighter. "I didn't know Patsy Miller was pregnant."

"She's not," Tank said quietly, leaning over the back of the seat to join their conversation. "What Ariel's driving at is that Duke's the kind of guy that gets rumors like that started about him."

"Poor Patsy," Caroline said with feeling. "How did she get involved?"

"They say she went out with him once," Ariel offered, not bothering to whisper anymore.

"Did she?" Caroline asked. She couldn't help thinking how horrible it would be to have a rumor like that started about her. And she couldn't help being thankful that this Duke person had gone by.

"Very doubtful," Joey said. "I've never actually seen Duke out with anyone. I think he confines his attentions to people whose reputations can't be ruined, if you know what I mean."

"Joey," Ariel hissed.

"What?" He defended himself. "That's no worse than what you were saying. Besides, Caroline's almost sixteen. She's not a baby anymore."

"He's coming back," Tank said quietly.

In unison, they all turned and Caroline saw a dark figure against the faded sky. Then the long, lean motorcycle slowed in a graceful arc from the highway into the parking lot. The light was too dim to see more than Duke's outline as he followed the drive that would circle out of sight on the far side of the Dairy Queen.

In the short time she could study him, he seemed at home in the bike's deep seat. She couldn't see his face, just the dark hair that blew in the wind, the even darker jacket that shrouded his body in mystery and the stiff, new, thigh-hugging jeans that suggested the mystery would be worth investigating.

From a distance, he conjured up images as romantic as they were dangerous, and Caroline couldn't help wondering how many Patsy Millers there had been and how many more wished they could have been. The bike glided out of view as she realized where her mind had wandered and, embarrassed, she felt the beginnings of a furious blush.

"What we didn't get around to saying," Ariel whispered, quietly this time, "is that he's really a nice guy. What Joey was saying was just more rumors. I've never seen Duke be anything but a perfect gentleman."

"Seriously, Caroline," Joey turned around and stared at her with dark brown eyes that were just like Ariel's. "Duke's one of my best friends. But he's had a hard life, and he's kind of a loner, so he gets a bad rap from a lot of people."

Caroline scanned the three earnest faces that were turned toward her. "What did I say?" she asked, spreading her hands innocently.

"It's what you've been known to say," Ariel said with her big, brown, pleading eyes drilling a hole through Caroline.

Joey began slowly, "Sometimes, you can be just a little bit—"

"Sarcastic," Tank finished.

"Sharp," Ariel said.

"This boy must be really sensitive." Feeling backed into a corner, Caroline leaned away from them.

"Look, he doesn't have a dad, and he had to drop out of school to help support his mother and two sisters. So just be nice to him, okay?" Ariel asked.

"Good grief, you were the ones talking about him. Look!" Caroline pointed, trying to get their attention off her. "He's coming this way."

The motorcycle threaded its way between two cars and headed toward them. When the bike passed under the harsh yellow light of the first awning, Caroline could feel anticipation begin to tingle through her.

From a distance she could tell only that the rider's dark hair was combed back from his face, fifties style. His eyes were deeply shadowed by stern, dark brows. While she watched, a gust of wind caught his battered leather jacket and billowed it open. Underneath, a stark white T-shirt hugged a broad, strong chest.

Her eyes were still trained on the white, muscled expanse of his chest when Duke pulled to a halt next to their car and cut the engine of his motorcycle. In the awesome quiet that followed, Caroline's gaze slowly crept from his chest to his face in time to watch while he nodded first to Joey, then to Tank and Ariel, greeting them each with a slow smile that grew wider as he seemed to relax.

Up close, his eyes were beautiful—large and liquid—beneath the straight mantel of his brows. But the warmth in his gaze faded quickly when it fell on Caroline, and his smile wavered and then slowly reversed itself.

He dipped his head in a half nod, and he held it there, watching her through those beautiful eyes that could have been any color. They were a constant play of shadow and light. At the moment, they were as serious as thunderclouds, dark and knowing, and they studied her with quiet assurance until Caroline's pounding heart threatened to dance right out of her chest.

As if he could read her mind, Duke smiled finally, a slow, lazy smile that started on one side of his face and gradually spread to the other side, warming her as it grew. His voice was deep and surprisingly soft when he asked, "Are you new here?"

Caroline drew in an unsteady breath. "No," she said in a whispery voice that was as unfamiliar to her as the feelings he was stirring in her. "I've lived here all my life."

His jaw shifted, drawing her eyes to his mouth. Fascinated, she watched his lips—firm, well-formed and generous—and their changing shapes as he spoke.

"I can't believe I've never seen you before," he said, studying her as closely as she was him.

"Caroline doesn't get out much," Joey offered unexpectedly.

Caroline jumped at the sound of his voice. She had forgotten the others were there.

"Doesn't get out much, huh?" Duke's eyes never left hers, and he smiled while he repeated the words, as if their sound pleased him.

"I'm out now," Caroline said, feeling very bold. But her voice seemed faraway, drowned out by the sound of the racing pulse inside her head.

Duke's smile widened, just for her, and his voice softened. "You are, aren't you?"

"Her grandparents keep pretty close tabs on her," Joey added helpfully.

Caroline crushed her milkshake cup to keep from hitting him.

Duke just nodded. Without looking away from Caroline, he smoothed strong blunt fingers through his windblown hair. There was a quiet power about him that came through in the simplest action. It was there in his wide-legged stance, heels dug in to use the strength of his legs to hold the bike steady under him.

And it was there in the way he looked at her, as if they were the only two people in the world, until Caroline wanted to shudder from the goose bumps that crawled along her bare arms.

"I'm still surprised I haven't seen you before," he said finally. "I think you'd be pretty hard to miss."

There was an intensity in his wide, almond-shaped eyes that made him seem very serious even when he smiled, as he did then, looking slightly embarrassed while he reached for her hand. "By the way, it's nice to meet you, Caroline. My name's Duke."

Caroline's hand slid into his, and at the warm, strong touch of his fingers, the shudder she had been fighting coursed its way up her back, over her shoulders and down her arms into the hand that was held in his.

Duke slipped his hand out of hers and, in a smooth, unbroken movement, shrugged out of his jacket. "Still gets kind of chilly when the sun goes down, doesn't it?" A lot of understanding was compressed into those few, soft words as he leaned forward and slipped his jacket around her shoulders.

Cologne, leather and a warm, male scent that was all his own wrapped itself around her with the jacket that still held Duke's body heat.

"Silly me," Ariel said, pointedly interrupting. "And I was afraid you two weren't going to get along."

There was an awkward silence while Caroline alternated between wanting to melt into the earth and wishing she could drop-kick Ariel into the next county. She stole a glance at Duke and found him waiting for her with a conspiratorial grin and a wink.

"Now why would you think a thing like that, Ariel?" he asked lightly.

Caroline closed her eyes and prayed. She couldn't remember everything she had said before Duke pulled up next to them, but she knew Ariel would.

Ariel's hand brushed Caroline's arm reassuringly and she heard Ariel say, "No reason really. I was just looking for some way to break the spell you were weaving over my innocent little friend here."

Caroline almost groaned aloud, and the crumpled milk-shake cup began to leak its sticky remnants over her clenched fingers. Ariel's tone had been joking, but she was partly serious, and anyone who knew her could tell it.

When Caroline opened her eyes again, Duke wasn't laughing anymore. The storm clouds were back in the eyes that she could suddenly see were gray. "I guess they forgot to warn you that I'm the big bad wolf," he said with an icy calm.

"Aw, Duke..."—"She didn't..."—"It's not..." Joey, Tank and Ariel all spoke at once.

Duke lifted his hand and waved them quiet. His silent, smoky gaze was for Caroline alone, wordlessly sharing feelings that were too tender to voice. "How old are you, Caroline?"

It was a simple question that meant a lot. Joey was eighteen. So was Tank. She knew Duke was older, not by much, but by enough to make a difference.

"Sixteen," she said in a voice that was barely audible. "Almost."

He winced slightly, then asked, "Do you and Joey date?"

His expressive eyes were sad and glitteringly hard at the same time. The muscles at the side of his jaw seemed to clench with each word. Caroline was too caught up in the way he made her feel to be surprised at his question, but she couldn't miss the faint gasp from the others.

She shook her head no and tried to swallow away the sudden dryness in her mouth. She had never felt this way before. Hot and cold. Cotton dry and clammy wet. Not with anyone else.

"But you *do* date?" he asked in a voice too soft for the steely gaze that waited for her answer.

His jaw set with his last word, and his full bottom lip took on a sultry prominence that riveted her attention and sent her swimming into emotions that were over her head.

Again she shook her head and then answered in a husky rasp that was as strange to her as the way she was feeling. "My grandparents won't let me. Not yet."

If he had touched her at that moment, she would have been lost. Maybe he knew it. Or maybe he was just as lost in the same deep waters and feeling just as confused.

Duke let out the breath he had been holding and dropped his head, then slowly lifted it again. The shadow of a smile flickered over his face when he asked, "Don't you just hate it the way Ariel's always right?"

The echo of his words, almost as husky as Caroline's had been, was cut short by the stunning roar of his bike's engine. Leaning close enough to be heard, he whispered, "Take care, little one." He brushed the backs of his fingers over her cheek, and then he was gone, out of the parking lot and over the hilltop without ever looking back.

"Well, I didn't mean to cause all that," Ariel said in exasperation.

"Just shut up, Ariel. Okay?" Joey snapped as he turned the key in the ignition and put the car in reverse.

Caroline closed her eyes and rubbed her cheek against the soft collar that smelled of leather and Duke. She hadn't known she could feel this way, that she could hurt so bad and feel so good all at once. She listened to the quiet pounding of her heart and remembered the touch of his hand on her cheek, and she wondered if she would ever feel this way again.

Chapter Two

Daniel "Duke" Hutchison stood alone in the empty living room of Hurley House, his newly purchased home. Sun streamed through the tall windows behind him, sparkling like polished gold on the wood floor of the room and glittering like diamond dust against the marble facade of the fireplace next to the front door.

Unconsciously, he massaged his fingertips into the small of his back while he turned in a semicircle and frowned at the massive bare windows in the corner of the living room. The house was overwhelming. Not for the first time, he wondered if he had been out of his mind to move back to Eureka Springs, to uproot his daughter, buy this place and face all the memories once again.

He shook his head and laughed. He had forgotten to be careful of what he wished for. And now that his wishes had come true, he was finding them difficult to live with.

"Sounds like I found you in a good mood," a familiar voice called from behind him. "Mind if I come in?"

Duke turned to find Joey Mason standing on the front porch, peering in through the screen door.

"Joey, hi. Come on in. You here as friend or Realtor?" Unconsciously the frown returned to his face.

The screen door creaked when Joey opened it and stepped cautiously inside. "A little of both. Am I interrupting?"

"No. Uh-uh," Duke said shaking his head and frowning harder.

Joey took another cautious step forward. "You seem a little tense. You're not sorry you bought this place, are you?"

Duke's mouth twisted sourly, and when he didn't answer, Joey exclaimed in surprise, "You are! You had a standing offer in for three years until they gave in and sold, and now you're sorry?"

"Crazy, huh?" Duke ran his fingers through his hair, rumpling it. Then he chuckled softly once again at the foolishness of it all.

Joey scowled, then shrugged and slipped on the mantle of Realtor. "We shouldn't have any trouble finding you another place, but unloading this one isn't going to be easy. Not everybody has that kind of money."

"Can't do that," Duke said, shaking his head. "Kimi loves it. She thinks she's died and gone to heaven every time she walks through here. She can't wait till we move in."

Visibly torn between his professional and personal feelings, Joey asked, "What's the problem?"

Heaving something very close to a sigh, Duke looked away. His gaze passed over the heavy, dark wood steps that led up to a landing, then turned and disappeared behind a wall paneled in a matching dark wood. His survey continued down the wall to the massive, leaded glass windows in the far corner of the living room.

Beyond the windows was a garden filled with tall, lush shrubs that had seen a long and hearty life. In his mind's eye, he envisioned the ivy that climbed three stories high across the gray limestone blocks of the home's exterior. On the second and third stories, stained-glass windows faced the street. The main entry at the side of the house and its large, square porch faced a shaded green lawn.

He understood why Kimi had fallen in love with it. To a young girl, it must look just like something out of a fairy tale. Caroline had once described it to him as a place where a princess should live. Peering through the wrought-iron gate as a little girl, she had fallen in love with the house, but she had never seen the inside.

Pulling himself back from his thoughts, Duke looked once more around the room Caroline had never seen, and he couldn't help feeling like a thief. The house had been Caroline's dream, and he had stolen it.

Maybe in time, he would feel right living here without her. Maybe in time, her memory wouldn't wait for him in every corner and around every turn. Maybe in time, the awful, aching loneliness would go away again.

"Yo, Duke. You okay, buddy?"

Duke refocused to find Joey standing a few feet away, making semaphores with his arms.

"Memories, Joey," he said quietly. "I just didn't think there'd be so many memories."

Joey's eyes glazed with panic while his face twisted painfully in an effort to find something to say, and Duke realized he'd created one of those awkward emotional moments that left so many men paralyzed.

He had wanted to ask if Joey had heard anything about Caroline lately, but he couldn't bring himself to say the words now. "What brings you out in weather like this, anyway?" he asked instead, and was rewarded by the look of immense relief on his friend's face.

"Business as usual," Joey said, smiling in his eagerness to embrace the mundane. "Can't let a little snow and ice slow me down."

Duke nodded, remembering the winter wonderland outside. "I'd forgotten how steep these streets were until I slid my way over here this morning."

He glanced at the window next to the fireplace. Sunlight reflected almost painfully bright against the snow-covered landscape.

"It should melt off fast though," Joey said. "It's supposed to be back up into the fifties today."

Still staring at the window, Duke nodded distractedly. It had been an equally bright day in August when he had returned from a trip East and heard that Frederick Adams had died and that Caroline had been in town for the funeral.

He would never forget the hot pain that had sliced through him when he learned he had missed seeing her by a day. He wouldn't have gone to the funeral even if he'd been in town, but he would have seen Caroline. He knew what her grandfather meant to her, and he knew how deep her pain must have been.

"So," Joey said loudly enough to shatter the heavy silence, "you want to start looking for a new house or not?"

"Forget it." Duke shook his head and smiled as he turned his thoughts away from the past. "The love of my life would never allow it."

"Daddy!"

At the sound of his daughter's eager, happy voice, a warm surge of contentment and joy flowed through him. "Ah, there she is now."

"You stop right there, young miss, and wipe your feet," a stern, motherly voice commanded. "Don't you go tracking snow in on that hardwood floor."

"And Martha." Duke's smile broadened, and he called loud enough to be heard outside. "I'm in here, sweetheart."

The door flew open and a petite, dark-haired whirlwind blew in, followed by a stout, gray-haired storm cloud.

"Daddy, it's just beautiful outside." Kimi clasped her hands together and graced the world at large with a beatific smile.

"We're lucky to have made it here alive, sir," Martha announced dourly. "I'm shaking like a leaf."

Duke beamed at them both. "I'm sorry, Martha. You look very pretty today, pumpkin. You remember Mr. Mason, don't you?"

"How do you do, Mr. Mason?" Kimi extended her hand and clasped Joey's larger hand firmly in her small grasp. "It's nice to see you again. Thank you for finding this house for us." She released her handshake and leaned toward him confidentially. "I just love it."

"Your father was just telling me. I'm glad."

"If only it wasn't halfway up one of the steepest hills in town," Martha added.

"Ah, but, Martha, think of the cardiovascular benefits of living in a town like Eureka," Duke said, unable, as always, to resist teasing her.

Martha crossed her arms and looked at him somberly. "In better weather, maybe, sir. But I'm not driving or walking on those streets again until that ice melts." She punctuated her statement with an abrupt nod of her head that seemed to say "so there."

Kimi glanced at her father through thick, dark lashes and then stared at the floor while forbidden laughter twitched at the corners of her mouth.

"It's supposed to get into the fifties today," Joey said helpfully. "Most of it should be melted by this evening."

"I have to go by the office to pick up some papers, but I'll be free all afternoon to take you anywhere you need to go," Duke said.

"That hotel is getting kind of boring, Daddy," Kimi said wistfully. "When can we move in here?"

Duke glanced to Joey for help and got another look of blank panic in return. Feeling a little panicked himself, he regarded the women in his life. Kimi, who needed a home and yard, returned his look patiently.

Martha, who needed a kitchen of her own and a house to look after while her young charge was in school, said, "I have been wondering that myself, sir, but didn't want to be so bold as to ask."

"I thought you might enjoy staying in a hotel for a while," he said lamely. He looked at his daughter, still hoping to find support. "If you don't like that suite, we could try another one."

"I had kind of hoped we could spend Christmas in our new house," Kimi said.

"But we don't have any furniture."

She looked past him at the large, barren living room, and her eyes began to sparkle. "But we have sleeping bags." Eagerness danced across her face when she turned her gaze back to him. "And a tent. We could pretend we're camping out. Here." Her slender arm swept the air toward the living room.

Duke turned to Martha for help and could tell from the defiant set of her jaw and the subtle shift of her body toward Kimi that she had joined the enemy camp. He looked at Joey in defeat. "Do you know a good decorator?"

Joey hesitated, then with a half-embarrassed shrug said, "Ariel's done a little decorating."

"Great." Duke forced a smile he didn't feel. "I'll call her today."

Kimi gave a squeal of delight accompanied by a small leap into the air. Then she ran to her father and wrapped her arms tightly around his waist.

"Oh, Daddy, thank you." She gazed up at him with her chin pointing into his stomach.

Besotted, Duke smoothed his hand down her long, dark hair and looked into the loving gratitude in her brown eyes. "Anything for you, sweetheart."

He smiled softly and studied her, lost in wonder at the changes each year brought. At ten, she was still a child, and yet there were moments when she seemed so much older. In seven short years and two months, she would be eighteen and grown. He reminded himself of that often these days, but it still wasn't real to him, not yet.

It seemed only yesterday that she'd been a chubby, scowling baby with so little hair he'd had to tape the bows to her head to get them to stay in. And now she was a heartbreaker in the making.

The half of her that was Oriental was barely visible, except in the faintly honeyed tones of her skin and in the softly rounded features that added an exotic delicacy to her beauty.

And the other half of her, well, it really didn't matter. Maybe she was his and maybe she wasn't. But she had given him a reason to go on living at a time when he had begun to doubt there was a reason.

"Hey, Dad." Her voice nudged him gently, and when he refocused, he found himself facing her bored look.

"You know how I hate it when you drift off into space like that," she said reprovingly.

"Sorry."

"You weren't thinking about that Caroline person again, were you?" She ignored a sudden glare that had stopped grown men dead in their tracks and went blithely on. "You've been thinking about her an awful lot since we got here."

"Caroline?" Joey asked in a stunned whisper.

Kimi snapped her head around and pinned him with a gaze that could rival her father's. "Do you know this Caroline person?"

The glare that Duke had wasted on his daughter was now focused on Joey, and it was doing its job.

"Huh..." Joey took a step backward, shook his head and opened his arms helplessly. "Hey. There are a million Carolines. I'm sure everybody's known one or two."

"Wow, look at the time," Duke said holding his arm out for everyone to see the watch on his wrist. "We're going to have to get going or we're not going to have any time this afternoon to run those errands.''

''We'll talk later,'' Joey said, walking backward toward the door.

''Sounds good.'' Duke tried to smile, but the wooden muscles of his face didn't move. He looked at Martha. ''If you want to wait in my car while I lock up here, I'll take you all back to the hotel.''

''Very good, sir. Come along, Kimi.''

He watched them leave, watched the door close behind them, then closed his eyes and took a deep breath, the first one he had taken since Caroline's name had come into the conversation.

When he had decided to move back, he hadn't realized that reminders of Caroline would be everywhere. He hadn't realized he could still want her so much and that not having her could still be so painful.

He must have been out of his mind, opening the new offices here. It was too late to turn back now, but if he'd known how totally she could dominate the memories that were stirring, he would never have come back. Never.

Caroline smiled and held herself well back in her chair, feigning a relaxation she didn't feel while Jonathan Harper, director of human resources, studied her résumé in silence.

''Your résumé is quite impressive.'' Mr. Harper glanced at her briefly, then quickly scanned the pages in front of him once again and frowned just slightly. ''You've taken into account that we can't offer you what you were making in Chicago?''

''Yes.'' Caroline sprang forward automatically as she spoke. She caught herself halfway and tried to relax in her chair once more as unobtrusively as possible. ''But the cost of living here is so much lower that it shouldn't be a factor.''

Mr. Harper nodded in agreement and set the résumé aside. Steepling his fingers in front of him, he looked her in the eye with practiced but friendly sincerity. "If you don't mind my asking, what prompted your move back to Eureka Springs?"

"Uh." Caroline had no trouble staying well back in her chair. In fact, she felt pinned to it.

The question was expected and she had spent the last week preparing an answer. But at the moment, she couldn't remember a word that she had planned to say.

So she took a deep breath, gripped the arms of the chair and spoke from her heart. "My grandfather died in August," she said slowly, in a voice that was shakier than she had intended.

"Oh, I'm so sorry to hear that," Mr. Harper offered sympathetically.

"Thank you." She could feel the tiny shards of pain inside her. Even after four months, it was still almost impossible for her to say the words aloud.

She kept thinking that if she said it often enough, *My grandfather died,* it might not hurt so badly, but so far, it hadn't worked. It was still a shock each time she heard the words.

"Would that be Dr. Frederick Adams?" Mr. Harper asked.

Caroline nodded. "Yes." Her voice was almost a whisper, but the dam she had constructed around her tears didn't give way.

"I didn't know him personally, but I know that the entire town felt his loss greatly."

Nodding again, Caroline took another deep breath. Her grandfather had been a town leader, as his father before him had been. And as the felling of a great tree shakes the forest, so did the passing of Frederick Adams shake the town of Eureka Springs. Her grandmother seemed to find consolation in that fact, but to Caroline, it meant nothing.

She appreciated the caring of others, but her own personal sorrow remained untouched.

"My grandmother..." she began, then stopped and cleared her throat. "My grandmother wasn't adjusting very well to living alone. She wouldn't eat and couldn't sleep, and she was losing weight every week. I couldn't stand the thought of losing her, too, and so..." Caroline shrugged, and her words stopped abruptly before her tears could betray her.

Mr. Harper nodded understandingly. "And so you moved home to take care of her. I agree totally. And now I'm going to ask you something that may seem a little harsh, but I hope you can understand that I'm only doing my job."

"Of course," Caroline agreed, hoping he would change the subject.

She had started the day in an excellent mood, optimistic and determined. Now she felt as if she was struggling through an obstacle course, and the obstacle course was winning.

"Well, in all honesty," Mr. Harper said, leaning back in his chair and spreading his arms expansively, "this is a small town. And generally in towns of this size, the young people, the people with promise, and especially the people with your kind of training and experience, move away, not back home."

He leaned forward again, bracing his forearms against the edge of his desk and steepling his fingers once more as he gazed at her earnestly. "Now what I want to know is why you aren't going to return to Chicago as soon as your grandmother no longer needs you."

Caroline thought briefly of trying to conjure up a glib, politically expedient answer, couched in careful office-speak, but she was too tired. What little emotional reserves she possessed had been used up.

She looked him straight in the eye and said, "There is nothing in Chicago for me to return to, Mr. Harper. And I hope that it's a very long time before my grandmother no longer needs me."

He flattened his palms on his desk and smiled. "Well, ordinarily I would discuss this with Mr. Hutchison, the owner and president of the company, but he's on vacation with his family this week, and he told me to have the position filled by the time he came back. So, Caroline," he said, and extended his hand across his desk, "welcome to Hutchison Industries. I hope you like hard work."

After the ordeal of the interview, Caroline was stunned by the suddenness of his decision. She stood and took his hand, trying to smile. She had the job and she wouldn't have to come face-to-face with Duke for at least another week. By any standard, the morning was a success.

"Come on out to Veronica's desk and we'll get the paperwork started," Mr. Harper said, coming around his desk to lead her to the door. "Then I'll show you around."

Halfway across the office, Caroline realized that Mr. Harper had said Duke was on vacation with his family. None of the local newspaper or magazine articles she had read over the past few months had mentioned Duke's having a family.

A sudden ache blossomed inside her, as if someone had just kicked her in the chest, and she felt lonelier than she had in a long, long time. After thirteen years, it shouldn't have been such a blow to discover that Duke had a wife and children, but it was. After all the time that had passed, she shouldn't have felt so betrayed, but she did. And in one week, she was going to have to face him and find some way to put the past behind her, once and for all.

Duke pulled into his parking space and stomped on the brakes, bringing the car to a squealing halt. Then, instantly embarrassed at his actions, he glanced around to see if anyone had noticed. He was relieved to see nothing but empty cars.

"What an idiot," he muttered as he got out of his car, slammed the door shut behind him and stalked into the building.

"Why, good morning, Mr. Hutchison." The receptionist greeted him with a sunny smile. "I didn't think we'd be seeing you this week. Do you want your messages?"

Barely slowing down, Duke waved his hand in reply. "No, thanks. I just came to take care of some paperwork."

"Your mail should be on Donna's desk, if you'd like to look through it," she called after him.

"Thank you."

Taking the back corridor that led straight to his office, Duke avoided the main work areas. The day was beginning to seem like one disaster after another, and he just didn't feel like making conversation, polite or otherwise.

He was still reeling from the incident that had occurred in the hotel parking lot after he had dropped off Kimi and Martha. In his rearview mirror he had caught sight of a slender girl with long, pale blond hair, and without even thinking, he had slammed on his brakes, sending his car into a sideways skid on the ice. It came to a halt inches from a parked car, and the last he had seen of the girl, she was running for safety in the other direction.

"Idiot," he muttered again as he opened the outer door of his office suite. Even worse than the anger and embarrassment he felt at his actions was the grinding disappointment at the realization that the girl wasn't Caroline.

Duke picked up the stack of mail from his secretary's desk, went through the door into his office and slumped into his desk chair. He stared at the fistful of envelopes he held clenched in his hand.

Caroline was gone. No amount of remembering and wishing could bring her back.

He tossed the envelopes onto his desk and stared at the closed door across the room. He didn't even know what he'd do if he saw her again. She was just a memory now, a memory with white-blond hair and lavender eyes, a memory that was indelibly etched in his mind for all time.

He'd given up even trying to forget that first night they were alone together, the night he had whisked her away from a town dance, right from under her grandfather's nose, and carried her to a hilltop above town.

From the hilltop, the lights of the town below had twinkled like stars in an upside-down sky. And a hot, August breeze had rustled past, turning the velvet night electric....

"Caroline." Duke whispered her name and smoothed her wind-tossed hair from her face. A stray curl slipped through his fingers and lifted on the shifting breeze to wrap around his wrist.

The summer shades of white sand and sunlight that danced through her hair by day turned to diamond dust in the light of the full moon, covering each strand with a sheen of silver.

At the sound of her name, Caroline looked up at him with the most beautiful eyes he had ever seen—wide eyes that were lavender blue.

Her eyes, so filled with innocence in the sunlight, became midnight pools of need and wonder and misplaced trust in the magical light of the full moon. Mesmerized, Duke brushed the backs of his fingers across the powder-soft skin of her cheek.

Her beauty had the dew-kissed glow of a rosebud at dawn, and he wanted her so badly he could hardly breathe, but she was barely seventeen. He had already waited over a year, and he could wait a little longer. Tonight, he just wanted to talk.

"I wasn't sure you'd come with me," he said in a voice that was growing hoarse with the need he could neither satisfy nor control.

Caroline lowered her gaze. Her dark lashes rested on her cheeks as she seemed to sway toward him in the barest of movements.

"I wasn't sure you'd ever ask me," she said quietly.

Duke felt his heart turn over with a gut-wrenching lurch and wondered if he hadn't overestimated his shaky self-control. They had never been totally alone before. Since he had first met her, he had maintained a chaste distance between them, afraid to trust himself.

Now the only thing between them was his willpower, and that seemed to be fading fast.

"I thought you might be afraid," he said, thinking of his own fears, and of emotions that had been too long denied.

"Of you?" she asked softly, and touched his cheek with her small, warm hand. "I'd never be afraid of you."

She gazed into his eyes with a shy, trusting innocence that drove him wild and held him at arm's length at the same time. Blindly, Duke felt behind him for the rock wall that rimmed the overlook.

His fingers brushed the rough stone and he took a step backward and sat down with the last of the strength left in his trembling legs. His body was one huge ache. If a year of staying away from her had been bad, one night of being near her was worse.

Reaching out, he guided her toward him until she stood in the open vee of his legs, close but not touching. "Maybe you should be afraid." His voice was rasping badly, and he knew his resolve was crumbling.

"Why?"

"You don't know?"

Caroline took a step backward and stood there, almost out of reach, watching him with a challenge in her eyes. For the first time, Duke wondered if the waiting might not have been as hard for her as it had been for him.

"No," she said in a defiant voice that was almost as husky as his was. "I don't know. I want you to explain it to me."

As she spoke, the wind lifted a lock of her hair and feathered it across her face. Duke reached to brush it back and Caroline cupped his palm against her cheek.

All the longing that had been in her eyes through a thousand stolen glances was there now, and where his hand touched her cheek, he was on fire. As the fire spread through him, Duke closed his eyes and thought how easy it would be to save the talking for later, how easy it would be never to talk at all.

He drew a deep, ragged breath and pulled her into his arms. He never knew heaven could hurt so much, but he wouldn't trade it for anything. Her softness cradled against him in an exquisite torture.

Finally, when he could speak, he said, "You have to know how I feel about you, Caroline. Hell, everybody in town knows how I feel about you."

She stared straight at him, her eyes filled with challenge and need. "Tell me," she said.

Duke tightened his arms around her waist and leaned his forehead against hers. He breathed the scent of lilac that she always wore. He breathed the warm, moist closeness of her while his whole body throbbed with desires that were at the breaking point. He had held in too much for too long.

"I love you," he said simply. "I love you so much, I don't know what to do about it."

Caroline was quiet for a long time. While he waited for her answer, an almost overpowering urge to make love to her where they stood made it hard for him to concentrate on anything else.

"I was afraid to hope," she said finally. "You never…"

She stopped in midsentence. Her face was happy, bewildered and infinitely beautiful. She looked like a china doll, painted in soft pinks, lavenders and creams.

Duke wanted to kiss her. He knew she was waiting for him to, and he knew that if he did, he might never stop.

"Caroline." He clasped her waist in his hands and held her farther away from him, still close, but not touching.

There were things he had to say. "I know you've heard some things about me."

"Yes."

He felt her tense and had a fleeting image of her turning and running away. He steeled himself for the possibility and plunged ahead. "Have you heard the rumors that I have a child?"

Caroline drew in her breath in a soft gasp and wouldn't look at him. "I don't think I want to talk about it," she said barely above a whisper.

He cupped her chin in one hand and lifted her head until she was at least facing in his direction. "I don't have any children."

She looked at him then, and her eyelids fluttered as she blinked back a glittering of tears.

"You *are* afraid," Duke said gently, almost wanting to cry himself. He had watched her for a year, and he knew her innocence was real. She was too young and too fragile for someone like him who had nothing to offer her but a love that was nearly out of control.

"No. No, I'm not afraid." In spite of his restraining hands, her arms encircled his neck and she tried to move closer.

"Wait! I'm not through." His hands tightened on her waist, holding her away from him in desperation. "Just because I don't have any children doesn't mean it couldn't have happened. Ariel was right when she warned me away 'from you. And I've cared enough to stay away. Or at least try."

His voice died away as she leaned her body into the cradle of his thighs. Her soft lips, warm and seeking, touched his in a tentative, feathery caress. She was eager, willing and wanting, and every last ounce of self-control Duke possessed drained away into the ground beneath his feet.

He spread his legs wider and molded her to him, returning her kiss, taking in her sweetness until he felt drunk with the taste of her. Instinctively, his hand slid up from her waist until his thumb brushed the edge of her breast. Not daring to go further, he let the warmth of her seep into him while he tried to rein in his rampant desires.

Their lips parted for an instant, and Caroline's breath caught in a quick, hard gasp. She twisted, offering herself to him, and he cupped the lush fullness of her breast in his palm. Surprised by her ardent response, Duke felt himself harden to an aching throb in reaction.

From the moment he first saw her, he had dreamed of how Caroline would feel in his arms, and now he knew. She was soft and warm and sweet, and in her innocence, she was more woman than he had ever known.

His passion tempered with a rush of tenderness, Duke trailed kisses over her face while he caressed the rounded weight of her breast in his hand. His breath came in catches as he stroked his thumb upward over its peak, feeling the aroused tip through the thin layers of cotton and lace that separated his flesh from hers.

Caroline moaned softly, and in the next instant, the hot tip of her tongue flicked at his neck in a light caress that quickly grew bolder until her open mouth reached his throat in a kiss that brought every nerve ending in his body screaming to life.

His control was a ragged remnant and his breath came in gasps as Duke raked his free hand down the small of her back. He cupped the swell of her firmly rounded derriere in the palm of his hand and pulled her hard against his wildly enflamed body.

Caroline moaned again softly, and willingly welded herself to him, and Duke knew he was lost. Her lips met his in a kiss that was as out of control as their passion. While he held her so close they could have been one person, she moved against him in small, instinctive undulations that drove him almost mindless with desire.

Arching into him, she whimpered, shuddered and seemed to melt in his arms. Dazed by a love like he had never felt before, Duke held her in surprised wonder, their breathing becoming a chorus of gasps until an explosion rocked him from the inside out and he joined her in a moment of stunned silence.

Gradually, Caroline lifted her head from his shoulder and gazed up at him in amazement. "I love you," she said in a dazed whisper.

"I love you, too," he answered.

Her lips reached up to his and he kissed her in return, as moved as she was by what had happened.

His arms ached from holding her so tightly, but he didn't want to let go. He wanted to give her the world. He wanted to spend the rest of his life making love to her, the way it was supposed to be, with a ring on her finger and a house of their own. He wanted it so much it scared him.

But she was only seventeen and what he wanted most from her wasn't even legal. He couldn't marry her, even if her grandparents would allow it, because he had nothing to offer her. He was just a garage mechanic with no diploma and no future, and he already had more responsibilities than he had money.

Headlights swept past them, and Duke quickly hid Caroline's face against his shoulder until the car was gone. When they were alone again, sanity slowly stole back into the night.

The overlook was too public a place for the things he still had to say and for the feelings that were already rebuilding inside of him.

"You want to go someplace a little more private?" he asked tenderly.

She lifted her head from his shoulder and looked up at him with eyes as starry as the night. "Anywhere with you."

Anywhere with you. Duke leaned his elbows on his desk and pressed his forehead against his clenched fists. Caroline's voice still rang inside his head, her soft, sweet voice speaking promises that meant nothing. Less than six months after that night, she had disappeared without an explanation or even a goodbye, and until her grandfather's funeral, she had never come back.

And he still couldn't get her out of his mind. The house he was afraid to live in was Caroline's house. The town he had foolishly moved back to was Caroline's town. Everything was Caroline's. He couldn't look at a tree or a building or a cloud that didn't have some memory of her burned into it.

The only refuge he had was his office, and now he was bringing her with him into it. Duke lifted his head and unclenched his fists. He'd spent a lot of years putting his life back together again after Caroline left, and he wasn't going to go through that again.

He picked up an envelope in one hand and a letter opener in the other. "Caroline is gone," he said aloud, and slit the envelope open.

"She's been gone for a lot of years." He slid the opener under the flap of another envelope and ripped it cleanly. "And no amount of remembering or wishing—" he picked up another "—is going to bring her back."

He slit the envelope and added it to the mounting stack. "Some things just aren't meant to be." He reached for the last letter. "And for you—" his voice became a whisper of regret, and he stared at the envelope without really seeing it "—Caroline is one thing that just isn't meant to be."

"And this is our accounting department," Mr. Harper said. "We have a pretty even division of people we hired locally and those who relocated from our old corporate office. Mr. Hutchison likes to be the one to introduce new people around, so we're just going to hit the highlights today."

He smiled at her over his shoulder, and Caroline tried very hard to smile back at him, but it wasn't easy. On her tour through the building, she had begun to realize just how insane she had been to take a job at a company owned by Duke Hutchison.

Even worse, she had begun to realize that her grandmother had been right. Taking a lesser job, even retraining totally, would have made a lot more sense than the mess she had just committed herself to.

Next week, she thought, not knowing whether to laugh or cry, she would meet Duke and he would show her around the company. If she had ever been in a more awkward position in her life, she had obviously blocked the incident from her memory.

"And this is sales," Mr. Harper said, continuing down the corridor of six-foot-high office partitions. "In there are the payroll and computer areas." He gestured toward the core of solid walls in the center of the building.

A woman came out of an office just ahead, turned toward them and came to a standstill in the middle of the aisle.

"Caroline," the woman exclaimed. "Caroline Adams."

Caroline stared at the streamlined blonde who looked in no way small town. Finally, a vague image of stringy brown hair, braces and a figure like a stick imprinted itself on her brain.

"Barbara...?" she asked hesitantly, not really believing that Barbara Clark could have made such a transformation.

"I've changed a little, haven't I?" Barbara held out her arms and laughed. "What in the world are you doing here?"

"Caroline has just joined us as our benefits-and-compensation analyst," Mr. Harper said. "Barbara is one of our leading salespeople, Caroline."

Barbara's mouth dropped open just slightly before she caught herself and closed it. Caroline felt a serious urge to wheel and run in the other direction while Barbara's eyes bored into her with a thousand questions.

"You're working here?" Barbara asked simply in a show of masterful self-control.

Caroline forced her lips into a nervous smile and nodded. She could feel Barbara's curiosity warring with her discretion and hastened to add, "Maybe we could have lunch one day next week."

"Oh, yes." Barbara's relieved smile lit up her face. "That would be nice."

With a nod of dismissal to Barbara, Mr. Harper led Caroline on down the hall and around a corner. Obviously glad to be moving again, he ushered her through an open area that led to a snack room in one direction and the receptionist and lobby in the other.

Growing winded from their sudden dash through the remainder of the building, Caroline idly wondered if Mr. Harper was a jogger in his spare time. She was relieved when they reentered the personnel area and he slowed their tour to a trot.

"This section of the building is less populated and a lot quieter." He gestured to a door as they passed it. "That will be your office."

Caroline broke formation and backed up a step to peer into the cubicle that would be her new home. She almost wished she hadn't.

It contained a standard office-issue desk, a chair, a credenza and two visitors' side chairs covered in an unappealing mustard yellow. Blinds covered the windows, and she didn't have the heart to investigate the view that lay behind them.

When she trudged on down the hall toward Mr. Harper, she found him patiently waiting. His expression was sympathetic.

"My wife took one look at my office and gasped. Then she started hauling in plants," he said in a genuine show of understanding. "You'll be amazed at what a little greenery can do to make a place look more cheerful."

Caroline couldn't help laughing. "Did I look that distressed?"

"Well, I know it must have been a pretty hard morning for you. But it's almost over now."

At the end of the short hallway, he stopped in front of a set of double doors. "Mr. Hutchison's secretary, Donna, is taking the week off, too, since he won't be in." Mr. Harper opened the door and ushered Caroline in.

She felt like she was walking on a marshmallow as her high heels sank into the plush carpet with every cautious step she took beyond the threshold. To one side of the room was a large desk of dark, highly polished wood. The credenza and filing cabinets were in the same wood.

On the other side of the room was a chesterfield davenport covered in navy leather. An oil painting of a hunt scene was on the paneled wall behind the sofa.

"This is Donna's office?" Caroline asked, almost whispering. As intimidating as the room seemed while empty, she couldn't imagine what it would be like when it was occupied.

Maybe because the room was so quiet, Mr. Harper lowered his voice to match Caroline's. "Donna's been with Mr. Hutchison since the beginning. Her husband was retiring anyway, so they decided to relocate with the company to Arkansas."

Just as he pointed to them, Caroline noticed the second set of double doors on the other side of the room.

"That's Mr. Hutchison's office," Mr. Harper said quietly. "Would you like me to check inside, just in case he's in?"

"No," she answered forcefully and took a quick, instinctive step backward. A little less vehemently, she added, "No, thank you. That's just fine."

The very thought of coming face-to-face with Duke unexpectedly was enough to send her into a panic. Keeping her eyes on the set of double doors across the room, she took another step backward.

"In fact, I think I've probably seen enough...."

Her voice died in her throat and her heart started a drumroll inside her chest as one of the double doors clicked and slowly began to open.

Chapter Three

Caroline watched helplessly as a fog of panic descended upon her and welded her feet to the spongy carpet. Like a scene in slow motion, the door inched its way open while half of her twisted in anguish, looking for a way out, and the other half of her waited in breathless anticipation, heedlessly eager to see him again.

There had been pictures, blurred, grainy newspaper prints that Ariel had mailed her, of a man who was tall, with dark hair and frowning eyes. But in her mind, she still carried a thirteen-year-old image of the blue-jeaned, leather-jacketed youth who haunted her dreams.

She could hardly breathe with the waiting. Her legs trembled, and her hands clenched and unclenched nervously at her sides.

When Duke finally walked through the half-open door, he was wearing jeans and a crewneck sweater. Carrying a fistful of envelopes in one hand and a stack of file folders cradled in his other arm, he took two brisk steps into the room before he looked up and came to a surprised halt.

"Hello," he said, barely raking them with his eyes before he continued toward Donna's desk.

His neatly clipped black hair was swept smoothly away from his face, and in the instant that she had to study him, Caroline could see that he was all she had remembered and more. Duke had grown to manhood taller, broader, stronger and better. He wasn't a boy anymore.

His back to them, he leaned over the desk and deposited the mail. The small weave of the sweater revealed every ripple of the muscles across his shoulders and down his back.

Longing for what she could never have rose up in Caroline as she wondered if his wife was the one who starched and pressed the jeans that hugged him so snugly.

"I was just catching up on a little work while no one was around," Duke said, turning slowly back to face them.

Mr. Harper chuckled and leaned confidingly toward Caroline. "Mr. Hutchison tends to spend large portions of his vacation time hiding in his office," he said in an undertone that was not meant to escape Duke's hearing.

Smiling, Duke leaned against the desk with his ankles crossed and his arms folded across his chest. He looked from Mr. Harper to Caroline, truly seeing her at last, and for the first time in her life, Caroline understood the real meaning of the term *thunderstruck.*

She could almost smell the sulfurous odor of lightning striking as she watched the smile slowly bleed from Duke's face. The wonderful dark eyes that she remembered so well looked at her with shocked disbelief.

Over the years, she had fantasized endlessly about seeing Duke again. She had imagined how they would look, what they would say, how they would feel. In an instant, she could see in Duke's face all the emotions she had imagined through the years—happiness, hurt, anger, betrayal. They were all there so briefly they could easily have been just in her imagination once again. In a flash, they had come and gone leaving only what she had never though she would see in Duke's eyes—indifference.

Slowly, he smiled in a politely distant way, as if he had never seen her before, as if he had never held her in the moonlight and promised to love her for as long as he lived.

"Well, Jonathan," Duke said, "aren't you going to introduce me to this lovely young lady?"

Caroline struggled to breathe past the lump in her chest while Mr. Harper said, "This is Caroline Adams, our new compensation-and-benefits analyst."

In horror, she watched Duke untangle his arms and legs and walk toward her with his hand extended. Numb, she slipped her hand into his and returned his enthusiastic handshake.

"Caroline Adams," he said. Duke's eyes narrowed and he studied her, still holding her hand. Finally, he broke into a broad smile of remembrance. "Why, it's little Caroline Adams, all grown up." His friendly handshake grew even more enthusiastic. "Well, how are you doing these days, Caroline?"

Caroline stared at him, beyond thunderstruck, beyond numb. She felt as though she were in a nightmare. She had told her grandmother that Duke had probably forgotten all about her, but never in her wildest dreams did she really think he could have.

"I'm just fine, Duke," she answered, hoping she could just get away before she made a total fool of herself. "And how are you doing?"

Her voice sounded like a whisper in a tunnel, but there was nothing she could do about it. She had always wondered what it took to make a person faint. She thought she might be about to find out.

"I'm doing just fine. Really good."

He sounded incredibly hearty. Caroline didn't realize she still had his hand clutched in her own white fist until he gently began to work himself loose.

"Imagine that," he said, flexing his fingers and not sounding quite so hearty, "you're going to be working right here. Just down the hall from me." His smile began to look pasted on. "All the time."

Caroline clenched her tingling hand shut around a fistful of her full, dusty-rose corduroy skirt and fought down the aching rush of tears in her throat.

"Yes," she said, twisting her mouth into what she hoped was a smile. "Imagine that."

Struggling to maintain at least her outward composure, she released her skirt and surreptitiously smoothed it against the side of her leg. She forced herself to confront his gaze and said, "It was certainly nice to see you again, Duke."

And in spite of everything, it was. He was the first man she had ever loved and the one man she had never been able to forget.

"It was," he agreed enthusiastically. "It really was."

He raised his arm, and afraid that he wanted to shake her hand in parting, Caroline stepped back quickly.

"I really do have to go now."

With her last ounce of strength, she turned and walked from the room, holding her frayed dignity tightly around her. Her chest ached with the awful pain of tears she wouldn't allow herself to shed while she fumbled blindly through the hallway, searching for a way out.

Clenching her jaw in determination, she blinked away the tears that continued to gather like dew drops in her lashes. Heartache rolled over her in waves as she realized that all her romantic dreams of a reunion with Duke had just been reduced to a bad joke she had played on herself.

She could almost hear her grandfather's voice from so long ago, warning her about boys like Duke, boys who only wanted one thing from girls, boys who forgot you once they had what they wanted.

She hadn't believed her grandfather, not then and not for the thirteen years she had carried Duke's memory in her heart. And if she hadn't been forced to live through the humiliation she had just gone through in his office, she would never have believed that the man who haunted her dreams had been nothing but a fake and a fraud all along.

Her face burned with shame and her head roared from the effort of self-control when Caroline finally found the reception area and escaped to the blue skies and fresh air of the parking lot.

Hurt and angry, she yearned to burn rubber and kick up gravel all the way back to the highway, but she couldn't do it. Patches of ice still dotted the road, and even with the frustration that was churning inside her, she couldn't be that stupid. She had already been stupid enough for one day.

By the time she slowed to a rolling stop and then fish-tailed onto the highway, reality had begun to burn through the haze in her mind. Silent tears trailed down her cheeks and dripped from her chin onto the paisley bolero jacket of her suit.

She didn't know what she was going to do or how she would face Duke again. She had gotten the job and lost everything, even the memories she held so dear, in the process.

All she wanted to do was to go home and hide, but she couldn't even do that. She couldn't let her grandmother see her like this. She didn't want the pity of the I-told-you-so's that would be waiting.

With nowhere left to go, Caroline lifted her foot from the accelerator and coasted to a stop on the shoulder of the road. Alone and heartbroken, she sat numbly contemplating the disaster that had become her life.

Feeling like he'd been kicked in the stomach, Duke didn't take the time to think. He pointed to the door that stood ajar after Caroline's departure and said, "Maybe you'd better close that, Jonathan."

"On my way out?"

"No, I want you to stay a minute. I think there's something I need to say." He couldn't believe he had been so stupid. The only excuse he could think of was that he had temporarily lost his mind at the shock of seeing Caroline so suddenly standing in his outer office.

Obediently, Jonathan shut the door and then turned back to face Duke. "Yes, sir?"

Duke heaved a sigh and wished he could sit down, but that wouldn't make it any easier to do what he had to do. "Uh, this isn't going to be easy to say." He ran his fingers restlessly through his hair.

Jonathan's face blanched slightly. "Yes, sir."

"I just lied to you and to that girl—excuse me—woman who just left."

"Yes, sir." Jonathan's voice held a barely audible sigh of relief and the color began to return to his face.

Dredging the confession up from the pit of his stomach, Duke continued in a clear, steady tone, "I knew her very well at one time and I remember her clearly."

"Yes, sir?"

"I don't know why I tried to hide that fact, just now, from you and from her." He realized that Jonathan probably thought he was crazy, but there was nothing he could do about it now. "Our past is something the whole town knows about. And it's something you would have eventually heard about, one way or another. I thought it was best that it come from me."

Jonathan's expression was carefully noncommittal. "Yes, sir. I understand."

"Do you? I don't." Disgusted with himself, Duke sighed again. "Well, I guess that's all. I just wanted you to know."

Jonathan eased toward the door. "There's nothing else, then?"

"No. Have a Merry Christmas. I probably won't be back in until after then."

When the door finally closed behind Jonathan Harper, Duke sagged into a chair in front of Donna's desk. Holding his hand in front of him, he was relieved to see that he wasn't visibly shaking, even though he was trembling on the inside.

"You idiot," he muttered in disbelief, and leaned forward, propping his elbows on his knees while he held his head in his hands.

All he had thought about for months was Caroline. After years of trying to forget her, she had practically consumed his thoughts since he had moved back to Eureka.

She had been on his mind all morning, and when he had walked out of his office and found her standing there, what had he done? He had pretended he didn't know her.

Duke shook his head and groaned. He felt like a fool and a coward. Leaning back in his chair, he stared at the wall behind the desk, lost for a moment in the memory. The Caroline he had carried in his mind was someone so fragile, so delicate, he had almost been afraid to touch her.

But the Caroline he had met today was stronger and more stunningly beautiful than he would have believed possible. Her hair was the same startlingly pale blond that he remembered. Her eyes were the same clear delicate lavender, and her skin was still like rich cream and rose petals.

He had lost count of the nights he had lain awake remembering the feel of her skin against his, the whisper of her hair against his cheek. He breathed deeply and drew in the scent of lilac that lingered in the air. After so many years, he couldn't believe she still wore the same scent. After so many years, he couldn't believe she could still go straight to his heart.

Today when he had seen her standing there in her pink skirt, her high-heeled shoes and high-buttoned collar, the impact had been almost physical. With her hair pulled back from her face and a few soft curls escaping, God help him, it was as though he was seeing her all over again for the first time.

Fifteen years ago, she had struck him like a bolt of lightning. For her, he had become an awkward boy, afraid to reach out for what he wanted, afraid of the power of his own feelings. And today he had done it again.

Out of fear, he had rejected her. At the look of hurt and confusion in her eyes, he had longed to take her into his arms and comfort her. But Jonathan had been there looking on, watching without understanding anything of what he was seeing.

After she was gone, it was the memory of Caroline's gallant attempt to play along with his stupidity that was hardest to take. And he couldn't rest until he found her and explained. He didn't really expect her to forgive him, but he had to at least apologize if he was ever going to get her look of pain out of his mind.

No matter how much heartbreak Caroline had caused him in the past, he couldn't stand to hurt her. She still meant too much to him. And he couldn't let her think that he had forgotten her, not after what they had once meant to each other.

Leaving his office, Duke tried to stay calm. Now that he had decided to go after her, he realized how little chance he had of actually finding her and he dreaded having to go to her grandmother's house. One icy look from the proud, disdainful Viola Adams had always been enough to reduce his ego to ashes, and he wasn't sure he would live long enough to overcome that feeling.

Driven by urgency, Duke sped back toward town, heedless of the patches of ice that stubbornly clung to the road. He almost missed the convertible that was pulled onto the shoulder of the road.

His heart pounding, he slowed and pulled to the edge of the highway just in front of the car in which a girl with platinum hair sat behind the steering wheel with her head bowed in thought.

In all the years since he last saw Caroline, the two things Duke could never get out of his mind were the soft lavender blue of her eyes and the way the sun turned her hair to the shimmering silver of white-sand beaches.

With no idea of what he was about to say, he got out of his car and started the long walk back to Caroline.

At the sound of crunching gravel, Caroline looked up from her misery and saw Duke walking toward her. She tossed a wadded tissue into a paper bag on the floorboard and pulled a fresh one from the box on the seat beside her.

Since her emotions had become so undependable, she was never without a handy tissue supply. For some reason, she always seemed to think of her grandfather when she was driving.

"Hello," Duke said, stopping next to her door.

Caroline glanced up, remembered that her eyes would be red and puffy from crying and looked back down again.

"Hello." She could already feel herself growing fragile in his presence. If he stayed more than a few minutes, she didn't know how she was going to get through it without bursting into tears again. She didn't have any strength left for pretending.

"I came to apologize for being such a jerk."

Taken aback, Caroline lifted her head and looked at him. In her surprise, she forgot to worry about the damage her tears might have done.

"I really don't have any excuse for what I did," Duke continued in a deep, steady voice, "except that when I saw you standing there, I just lost every bit of good sense I ever had."

His apology barely registered. All Caroline heard was that he remembered her. She wasn't just another meaningless conquest, after all. She waited for happiness to engulf her, but all she felt was relief—relief that the Duke she carried in her memories was genuine. But the one who stood beside her now was still a stranger.

"Caroline." He put his hand on the car door and leaned toward her. "This is really hard. Do you think we could go someplace? Just to talk?"

Caroline looked him full in the face and didn't bother to hide her apprehension. He had just put her through hell and she wasn't sure she wanted to go anywhere with him for any reason.

"We've got so much to catch up on," Duke coaxed. "There's a diner just down the road that serves great coffee. It would be a good place to talk."

His voice was gentle and his dove-gray eyes were sincere. He was older. His features were leaner and more defined, but at that moment he looked so much like the young Duke she remembered that she would have done anything for him.

She began to smile, a yes on her lips. Then a bitter taste rose in her throat and reality hit her with a numbing force. Duke was a married man.

It was one thing to have good feelings about the past, but it was another thing entirely to share a cup of coffee and a cozy trip down memory lane with a man who could still make her knees weak with a glance. To do that would be just another form of self-torture.

"I'm not sure that's such a good idea," she said.

Duke put his other hand on the door and leaned nearer. "Look, Caroline," he said softly, "we can't change the past. And pretending that it never happened doesn't work, either. I just tried it. And I ended up looking stupid and feeling rotten."

Caroline could feel him looming over her, his chest almost brushing her shoulder. Being this close to him and hearing his voice almost a whisper in her ear hurt so bad and felt so good that she never wanted it to end.

She didn't know how she was going to survive working around him every day, but she might as well start finding out now.

"I'll meet you there," she said.

"What?"

She looked up at him and turned the key in the ignition, raising her voice over the sound of the engine. "I said I'll meet you there."

"Great."

He backed away smiling and then turned and started toward his car at a jog. She waited for him to buckle up before she drove off.

All the way to the diner, his car was in her rearview mirror, maintaining a steady distance behind her. Caroline wondered if he really felt as matter-of-fact as he seemed, or if, inside, his emotions were churning as badly as hers were. He had hidden his feelings well in his office. Maybe he was still hiding them.

The thought stung her all over again. A simple apology wasn't really enough to make up for what he had put her through, but he was right about one thing. The past wasn't going to go away, not for them and not for anybody else, if her grandmother and Barbara Clark were any indication.

She pulled into the parking lot and waited nervously for him to arrive. When he did, the transition into the diner was awkward.

Duke held the door for her and Caroline walked ahead of him, consciously avoiding contact. His hand hovered near the small of her back and stirred her into a brisk walk to the nearest booth. She slid in, leaving no room for him to sit beside her.

Duke sat facing her, and they ordered coffees, then sat in silence. Caroline poured powdered creamer into her coffee and stirred it. She contemplated adding sugar, just to keep her hands busy, but finally rejected the idea.

Alone with Duke, she felt so shy she was almost paralyzed. She didn't even know why she had agreed to come. It frightened her to think that she just wasn't ready to let go of him yet. Duke might be a married man now, but once he had been hers in a way no one else could ever be. That was a hard thing for any woman to forget.

"I was sorry to hear about your grandfather," Duke said finally. "I would have come to see you then, but I was out of town."

Caroline stopped fiddling with her coffee and looked at him, surprised. "That's very nice of you. Thank you."

"How's your grandmother doing?"

Even more surprised, she said, "Better now. I think she'll be all right." Considering that there had never been any love lost between Duke and her grandparents, Caroline found it touching that he would ask.

"I was talking to Reverend O'Malley. Have you met him yet?"

"Not actually. He performed the funeral service, but we weren't introduced. Gran talks about him quite a bit, though." Caroline took a sip of coffee and looked at him.

"He was pretty concerned about her for a while." Duke lifted his cup and cradled it in both hands while he stared at it, lost in thought.

Until now, Caroline had had difficulty separating the boy of her memories from the man who was with her now, but the hurt, angry youth that Duke had once been would never have shown such compassion for a sad, lonely old lady.

"I thought about going to see her after the funeral," he said. His elbows propped on the table, Duke toyed with the coffee cup he held aloft and watched Caroline as he talked. "But I wasn't sure how your grandmother would feel about a visit from me, so I sent Martha instead."

In the flash of an instant, all the good feelings that had been building in Caroline were gone. Once Duke had made her feel loved in a way she had never felt loved. Now he made her feel like someone who was on the outside looking in at all the things she'd never have.

"Martha," she said, trying to sound more gracious than she felt. "Your wife?"

"Wife?" Duke was taken aback.

"Wife," Caroline repeated. She hoped he wasn't one of those men who liked to play at being single. "You *are* married, aren't you?"

"Did someone tell you I was married?" he asked with a frown.

Caroline shifted uncomfortably. She was beginning to feel as though she was the one on the defensive and she resented it. "Jonathan Harper," she answered, and her quick temper began to rise.

"Told you I was married?" Duke asked as if he was having trouble believing it.

He leaned forward and set down his cup while his dark eyes seemed to look right through her.

Caroline pressed her back against the high, padded back of the booth. "Well, who *is* Martha?" she snapped.

"My housekeeper."

She lifted her chin and stared at him. "Your housekeeper?"

"My housekeeper," he said again, relaxing his aggressive posture enough to take a drink of his coffee.

Caroline's eyes narrowed with suspicion. "But you *are* married?"

Duke shook his head. "Nope."

She glared at him and let her breath out in an exasperated huff. "Then what did Jonathan Harper mean?"

"I don't know. I wasn't there."

Unable to decide between apology and anger, Caroline asked, "You're not lying to me?"

Duke's full, expressive lips curved in a coaxing smile and he put down his coffee cup again. "I guess I can't really expect you to believe me, but . . ." He laid his hand on the table next to hers. "I've done enough lying to you for one day. I have no wife. I do have a daughter, though. I don't know how anyone starched as stiff as Jonathan could confuse a wife with a daughter, but I guess he must have."

Caroline winced. "Actually, he said 'family.' I just assumed…" She shrugged, opting for apology. "How do you have a daughter without a wife?"

"It's a long story," Duke said. His smile retreated and seemed to take him with it.

"I've got time," she urged gently, intrigued by the faraway look in his eyes.

A minute earlier, she wouldn't have pressed, but now she wanted to know. Thirteen years was a long time, and Duke had come a long way from the penniless grease monkey he had once been.

"It's a *very* long story," he warned.

The waitress came by and Caroline held out her cup for a refill. "I believe the sign on the window advertises a bottomless cup of coffee," she said when they were alone again. "And I've got all day."

Grudging but not resentful, Duke said, "Okay, you asked for it, but don't say I didn't warn you."

"Several times," Caroline agreed.

"Well…" He took a deep breath. "Not wanting to dredge up the past, but it all started when this girl I was in love with left town suddenly. I waited around for about a year, thinking she might show up again, and then when she didn't, I went out and got drunk for a couple of weeks. After that, I looked around for something else to do instead because I didn't think I'd hurt enough yet, and that's how I ended up in the air force."

He took a sip of coffee and looked at her. "Are you tired of this yet?"

"You don't have a daughter yet."

"That part's coming."

Caroline nodded. "Call me a glutton for punishment. I want to hear it."

"Okay. I tried," Duke said with a sigh, then continued his story. "Well, they taught me how to work on planes and sent me to Korea, and it wasn't really all that bad, so I had to keep looking."

"For something that would hurt?" she asked, interrupting the fast history.

Duke glanced up with a halfhearted lopsided grin. "Crazy, huh? So, anyway, I finally found this bar girl. She was really beautiful, a Eurasian, which made her an outcast, too, sort of, so we had something in common."

Caroline could feel herself shrinking inside. She wanted to hear the story, and yet every word and the images they conjured, hurt. She had had nightmares over the years of Duke with someone else, and now the nightmares had come true.

"But I wasn't the only G.I. dating her. There were two others that I knew of. And one of them had just been transferred out when she found out she was pregnant. The other one wouldn't even talk to her after she told him."

Duke stopped and looked directly at Caroline.

"You have to understand, she was a sweet girl. Life had just been really hard for her."

Caroline nodded automatically. She wanted to be understanding. She had asked him to tell her the story, and it wasn't his fault that it was tearing her up inside to hear it. He hadn't said yet that the child was his. He sounded as if it could easily have been one of the other men's.

"But it was important to her that her child have a better life," Duke said quietly, staring at Caroline intently. "And it was important to me to have a reason to live again. The baby might have been mine and it might not have been. It really didn't matter."

There, he had said it, Caroline thought, oddly happy with such a small crumb. The child might not have been his. For an instant, she almost wanted to cry from the relief, and then in the next instant, she wanted to cry for an entirely different reason.

Without even knowing, he cared enough to call the child his own. Caroline had thought she knew him, and yet just a few years after she had seen him last, he had done this.

"So," Duke continued, "I married her and lived with her, and when the baby came, I was the father. And when my tour was up, I took the baby and left the mother. She wanted something better for her child, but she didn't want to leave her home."

"You left her there?" In spite of the jealousy that burned inside her, Caroline felt an even deeper sadness for the lonely woman who was left behind. In her mind, nothing could have been worse than to have had Duke and to have lost him. She knew, because it had happened to her.

"We were never in love. We were just two unhappy people who were able to do one good thing together."

Caroline pulled out a tissue and dabbed at the tears that had pooled in spite of her efforts. "What happened to her?"

Duke shook his head. "Let's talk about happier things. I have a beautiful daughter. Want to see her picture?"

"Sure."

Sniffing, Caroline put the tissue away again and smiled as she took the wallet Duke held out to her. She saw the picture of the little girl instantly. She was a jewel, with dark hair and bright eyes and a sweet face. It was easy to see how a little girl like that could have captured so much of Duke's heart that there was nothing left for the mother.

"What's her name?"

"Kimi."

"She's beautiful, Duke. You must love her very much."

"She's my life."

Something in the way he said it left Caroline feeling as left out as the child's mother must have felt. It was strange to feel jealous of a child, and yet she did.

She looked at the wallet again and her eyes wandered to the picture below the one of Kimi. It was of a tall, regal-looking woman with black hair past her waist and softened Oriental features of delicate, heartbreaking beauty.

"This is your wife, isn't it?" she asked softly, feeling renewed sympathy for the woman.

Duke shifted uncomfortably and Caroline realized that he never thought of her as his wife, only as Kimi's mother.

"For a while," he said.

Caroline wondered if that was the way Duke felt about *her* now, if she was just an uncomfortable memory from his past like that poor, tragic woman in the picture. She found it hard to understand how a man couldn't love a woman who was that beautiful, but the fact that Duke hadn't somehow just made the story that much sadder.

"What happened to her?" she asked again, still lingering over the faded photograph.

"She died a few years after we left."

"Oh." Unexpected tears welled up, spilling onto her cheeks before she could catch them.

"Caroline, honey, please. Don't cry." Duke reached across the table and caught her free hand in his. "Damn it, I knew I shouldn't have told you that story."

"It's okay, really." She looked at him and tried to smile while she batted her eyelashes to free the tears that clung to them. "I'm just very emotional right now."

"I know. I'm sorry. It's my fault."

"No, it's not. It's . . ."

Her words died in her throat as she realized how near he was to her. His hands held hers, making it impossible for her to pull away even if she wanted to as he leaned across the table toward her. His face was concerned and open and so very close. His eyes found hers and held her locked in his mesmerizing gaze.

"God, I've missed you," he said with feeling.

Trapped by her own desire, Caroline stared into his eyes and wondered where they would go from here.

Chapter Four

"I'm sorry," Duke said, releasing her hand. "I shouldn't have said that."

"No—I mean..." Caroline laughed uncomfortably, relieved and disappointed at the same time.

Taking a mental deep breath to regain her composure, she started again, speaking softly. "I know what you mean, and I've missed you, too. It's really good to see you again, Duke. I can't tell you how much I've thought about you over the years, and wondered what you were doing."

She ran out of words and sat there missing the touch of his hands on hers. A part of her still couldn't believe she was sitting across the table from him, talking as if it were the most normal thing in the world when only that morning, she had been driving herself crazy with worry at the thought of seeing him again.

"I guess I lost more than a girlfriend when you left," Duke said quietly. "I lost my best friend. I suppose, someday, we're still going to have to talk about all that."

Caroline nodded. In time, maybe she could stand to re-live that day, but not now. "Someday," she agreed. Then, turning the subject away from something that was still painful to her, she asked, "And your mother, your family, how are they?"

Duke frowned and shifted uncomfortably. "My, uh, mom passed away just before I left." He drew in a deep breath and went on quickly. "My sisters were out of school by then. One of them had just gotten married and moved to Kansas when Mom died. And Betsy, the youngest one, went to work down in Little Rock. She's married now, too. They're both doing just fine."

"I'm so sorry, Duke, about your mother. I hadn't heard." He had never talked about his mother or any of his family, and yet Caroline felt callous for not having known.

"It's okay," he said with a shake of his head that fore-stalled further discussion. "That was a lot of years ago. Do you think we could talk about you for a minute?"

Surprised, she looked up. "What about me?"

He shrugged. "You know what a soft heart Ariel has. A lonely soldier, faraway. She wrote me the whole time I was overseas."

"Oh." Her voice came out in a breathless wheeze. She knew what was coming. The whole time she was in col-lege, she and Ariel had stayed in touch. "Funny. She never mentioned you to me."

"I guess you didn't have Joey threatening to write if she didn't."

"I guess not." She felt like a butterfly trapped in a spi-der's web. Talking about Duke's past was one thing, but dredging up her own was something else entirely.

"It really hurt me when you got married," Duke said quietly. "Until then, I kept hoping there was still a chance we could get together again."

The air seeped out of Caroline in a devastated sigh. "There wasn't much to it," she said, hoping he wouldn't really want to hear about it.

"There was enough."

His eyes were the smoky gray of thunderclouds, and their steady gaze said clearly that he would have no more mercy on her than she had had on him.

Giving in, Caroline asked, "Where do you want me to begin?"

"Who was he?" Duke reeled off the questions as if he had a mental list ready and waiting. "Did you really love him? And what happened?"

She stared at the table and rolled her half-empty cup between her hands. Her voice shook just slightly as she began. "He was an upper classman I met at the end of my freshman year. Possibly the worst year of my life. He was a friend when I really needed one, and after a while, I talked myself into thinking that I really cared about him."

She lifted her gaze to Duke and didn't bother to hide the pain that remembering caused. "It didn't take long after the marriage for us to both realize I was just lonely and unhappy and that we really had nothing to build a marriage on. My stepfather arranged a discreet annulment, and that was that."

Duke winced in sympathy. "Damn."

Caroline pushed on. Even if she didn't like talking about it, she could at least be honest. "He remarried the next year to a very nice woman. They have a big home in the suburbs and a handful of kids, and I imagine he's very happy he didn't end up with me."

"I doubt that."

"I don't," she said with conviction. "Those were four very long, hard months we were married."

"But you're still friends?"

"He's a nice man. At least we had that. And he got me through a very bad year. I don't know what would have happened if I hadn't found a friend."

Gentle but persistent in his probing, Duke asked, "Are you sorry it didn't work out?"

"No." Caroline looked at him in surprise that he would have to ask. "I married a life jacket. But by the time we finally married, I didn't really need one anymore." Her courage began to fail her and her tone dipped to just above a whisper. "And there were other problems."

"I was wondering why you got an annulment instead of a divorce." Duke's voice held hopeful speculation. "He had problems?"

"I had problems." Caroline gathered up her purse and moved to the outside of the booth. "This has been a very long morning for me, Duke." The look she gave him asked for mercy. "I think we should save some of this for another time."

Duke rose instantly, fished in his pocket and dropped several bills on the table. He put his hand lightly on her arm and fell into step beside her.

Outside, he tightened his grasp and held her still for a moment. "I didn't mean to upset you."

She looked into his eyes and wished she could accept the safe harbor he seemed to offer. Her battered emotions needed a rest, and there had been a time when Duke's broad shoulders had been all she ever hoped for.

"I guess those were rough years for both of us," she said, keeping her real thoughts to herself.

"I guess."

They walked on and, at her car, Caroline hesitated. "I'm sorry for jumping up like that."

"I'm sorry I pressed you."

His hands slid up her arms and for an instant, she thought he was going to pull her closer. Then he released her and took half a step back.

"I'll try to be more patient in the future." His deep, velvety voice vibrated with feeling. "It hasn't been that long since your grandfather died and I know you still have to be hurting a great deal inside."

Caroline started to shrug off his sympathy, then stopped herself. "It comes and goes," she admitted. "The tough part is that it makes me so much more sensitive to anything that's even remotely upsetting." Laughing, she added, "*Commercials* can make me cry. It's like a case of raging hormones."

Duke smiled. "So we're friends again?"

"That sounds nice, doesn't it? Friends." She tried the word out and liked the way if felt.

"It certainly does. I'll see you tomorrow?"

Switching instantly into a more businesslike mood, she said, "I didn't think I was supposed to start until next week."

He slipped a hand into the pocket of his snug-fitting jeans and lifted a shoulder in a shrug. "If it's no problem for you to start tomorrow, I think I have a project you could help me with."

"You're the boss. I'll see you tomorrow."

He left her at her car, waited for her to leave and followed her into town. Once there, Duke honked his horn in parting and turned down a side road. Caroline was sorry to feel the connection break. For just a while, it was as if thirteen years had never passed.

From something that had had such a horrible beginning, it was hard to believe that their meeting today had turned into something so... She groped for words as she pulled up in front of her grandmother's house. So friendly, she finally decided.

For a little while, the encounter had almost been something more, but in the end, it had been just friendly, nothing more. After so many years of waiting, she wondered if that would ever be enough for either of them.

All through her nap and during the drive to Ariel's for supper, thoughts of Duke floated into Caroline's mind, causing tingles of excitement to flutter through her. The more she thought about it, the more it seemed that the time she spent with him that morning was merely something she had dreamed.

She was torn between telling Ariel everything and reliving every minute in the telling, or holding the memories close and sharing nothing. As she closed her car door behind her and started up the front walk of Ariel's house, Caroline wondered which she would do when the time came.

Janie, aged six, and Susie, aged eight, were playing on the front-porch steps. Charmed by their seemingly effortless happiness, Caroline stopped to talk and, for a moment, she thought of Kimi and wondered what Duke's daughter was like. She hadn't even thought to ask how old she was.

"Hi," Janie greeted Caroline, all smiles, "know what we're having for supper?"

"No, what?"

Janie's freckled face fell. "Oh."

"We were kinda hoping you knew," Susie said, scooting over to make room for Caroline to pass. "Mom's making us stay out of the house until she's through. The last time she did that, we were having eggplant."

Janie shuddered at the memory, and all the freckles on her face seemed to run together when she puckered.

"Let's hope it's not something like that," Caroline said with real sympathy.

Little Janie had her mother's coloring and her father's features. Together, they looked very cute on her, but Caroline couldn't help envisioning a redheaded Tank when Janie grew up.

With Susie, it was the other way around. She had her mother's features and her father's brown hair and olive complexion. Susie had every promise of being a real beauty someday. Somehow the thought opened Caroline's heart and let little Janie slip inside.

"Maybe you can talk to her," Janie suggested. Her big brown eyes were filled with pleading.

"She listens to you," Susie said.

"I'll do my best," Caroline promised. "I just hope it's not too late."

Holding her smile until she was past them, she opened the screen door and went into the house and toward the kitchen. "Yoo-hoo, Ariel."

"You're late," Tank called back.

Caroline pushed open the kitchen door and entered a scene of controlled chaos. "I'm early."

"Only technically," Tank said. "You're always *very* early. Today, you're only a little early. We were counting on you to be here fifteen minutes ago."

"I was detained by two terrified urchins. They think you might be cooking eggplant."

Tank darted a glance at Ariel, who ignored him. With a knife in one hand and a head of lettuce in the other, she kissed Caroline on the cheek.

Ariel stepped back, smiled significantly and said, "I can't wait to hear all about this morning." Then she thrust the knife and lettuce into Caroline's hands. "Chop," she said, pointing to a section of the counter containing a cutting board and salad bowl.

"You chop your lettuce?" Caroline queried. "Don't you read any magazines. You're supposed to tear. And what do you know about this morning?"

"Kids won't eat lettuce that's been torn," Ariel explained patiently. "It doesn't feel right when they chew it."

Obediently, Caroline went to the cutting board and proceeded to chop the lettuce. "You're avoiding my question."

"Which question?"

"What do you know about this morning?"

"First things first." Ariel handed her a cucumber and a bell pepper.

Caroline raked part of the lettuce from the cutting board into the salad bowl and went back to chopping the rest. It really was a lot faster than tearing.

"Okay, so what are we having for dinner?" she asked, deciding not to worry yet. Ariel couldn't possibly know that she had come face-to-face with Duke that morning.

"Eggplant casserole and spinach soufflé," Ariel said with pride.

Ah, the wisdom of children, Caroline thought. Aloud, she said, "I think Janie may cry."

"Not to worry." Ariel pulled a tray of hamburger patties and hot dogs from the refrigerator and handed them to Tank, who saluted and exited to the backyard.

Caroline raked the rest of the lettuce into the salad bowl and started slicing the cucumber. "You're such a wise mother."

Ariel set bunches of green onions and radishes on the counter next to the cutting board. "Thank you. Now tell me everything that happened this morning—and don't leave anything out."

Caroline stared at her with her mouth agape. "What?"

"Don't bother to play dumb." Ariel lifted her shoulder and gave her head a smug toss. "Duke called me this afternoon."

"He called you? I don't believe it. We had coffee. We *just* had coffee." Caroline put down her knife and glared. "Why would he tell you?"

"Just the teensiest bit defensive, aren't we?" Ariel asked, obviously enjoying herself.

"We only had coffee." Caroline made short work of the pepper and started on the green onions. "I just don't understand why he had to call and give you a report, that's all."

"He wants me to help him get his house ready to move into by Christmas," Ariel said soothingly. "He mentioned that you were going to work for his company, and try as I might, all I could pull out of him was that the two of you just had coffee."

Ariel made a familiar funny face and held out her hands innocently. Caroline slowed in her massacre of the radishes. "That's it?"

"That's it."

"Then why did you make me think—"

"All I said was that Duke had called. You jumped to all the conclusions by yourself. And if I helped you along a little, it's just because it's so much fun to watch you once your temper gets going."

Caroline drew the knife slowly through the remainder of the radishes. "Well, I feel so silly now."

Ariel giggled and hugged Caroline around the shoulders. "Just tell me what happened, okay?" she demanded. "I know you didn't just have coffee, not after thirteen years and—" she threw back her head and drew her forearm dramatically across her brow "—all the tragedy of your past." She straightened up and wiggled her fingers in front of Caroline. "Give."

Caroline pointed toward the stove with her knife. "Don't you have to check your dishes?"

"They're on a timer."

Giving up, Caroline laid down her knife and gave Ariel a detailed description of the morning. As she talked, Ariel's frown grew until Caroline finished. Then Ariel said, "Gee, it sounds like you just had coffee. Gosh, Caroline, I'm sorry. You must be so disappointed."

"Ariel, what had you expected?"

"Well, after thirteen years, more than that."

"After thirteen years, how much more could there be? Lives move on."

"Don't give me that old song and dance, Caroline Adams. I happen to know you're still nuts about him, and until today, I thought he was nuts about you, too."

"Thanks a lot," Caroline said coldly. "Besides, I don't know what gave you the idea I'm still nuts about him."

"Oh, maybe the fact that you've never been in love with anybody else. Or maybe the fact that you still have dreams about him. Or..."

"What I dream about happened thirteen years ago, Ariel. You can't go back and time doesn't wait for you."

"Oh, honey." Ariel put her arms around Caroline's shoulders and pulled her close. "Gee, Caroline, you really do feel bad, don't you? I hate it when you talk like that."

"Well, actually, Ariel, I was feeling pretty good when I got here." She extracted herself from Ariel's comforting arms and began to toss the salad. "It's just that whatever Duke and I had at one time doesn't really exist anymore. We just have to put that behind us and start over."

"But you still love him," Ariel protested.

Caroline looked at her and tried not to show the pain she felt. "The Duke I love is twenty-one years old and he's just a memory. The Duke I met this morning is another man, and I don't know what's going to happen. I don't even know what I want."

Ariel looked uncomfortable. "I suppose, for starters, you want me to butt out."

Tank came through the back door in time to catch Ariel's last words. "Of course, that's what she wants, sweetheart. That's what we've all wanted for a long time, but we've never gotten it."

He set a platter of steaming burgers and hot dogs on the kitchen table just as the timer on the built-in oven across the room pinged. Tank winked at Caroline and continued as Ariel turned and went to the oven. "I'm sure Caroline would be tickled if you'd mind your own business. But I doubt that she seriously expects you to. I know I don't."

Peter, Ariel and Tank's eleven-year-old son, appeared in the doorway, leading his younger brother Eugene, aged three, by the hand.

"Supper ready?" Peter asked eagerly.

The front screen door slammed and the tap-tap of hurrying feet grew closer. "Burgers, burgers," Susie and Janie chorused. "We can smell 'em."

A second timer pinged. Ariel looked at Caroline and said, "Microwave." Then she continued to the doorway and said, "Janie, you watch Eugene. Peter, you and Susie set the table."

Just like everyone else, Caroline obeyed without question. The microwave dish appeared to be the dreaded eggplant casserole. She lifted it out with potholders and then stood holding it, waiting for further orders.

Noticing her, Tank picked up his platter and said, "Follow me."

He led the way to the dining room, where they both deposited their burdens on the sideboard and then stood back, out of the way. Janie joined them, with Eugene's tiny hand clutched firmly in her own.

"Good work, Aunt Caroline," she said, cupping her hand to the side of her mouth and whispering in a voice that could be heard throughout the room.

"I'm afraid we're having eggplant anyway," Caroline warned her. She wasn't going to tell her about the soufflé. Some things were better left to surprise.

Janie shrugged philosophically. "But I only have to eat a little bit," she said, holding up her thumb and index finger a fraction of an inch apart. "Then I get to eat hamburgers and hot dogs."

"A hamburger and a hot dog," Ariel corrected, arriving to collect Eugene. "Okay, everybody, sit." She rolled her eyes at Caroline and dropped her voice. "And let the games begin."

It was late when Caroline finally left. The children had been tucked in. Tank had lighted the fire and the three of them had sat remembering old times when they had been the same ages that Susie and Peter were now.

Caroline had watched as Ariel had slowly leaned toward Tank and he had unconsciously wrapped his arm around her shoulders and tucked her against his side. And when the warmth and happiness that seemed to radiate from the very walls of the house began to make her feel a little too sad and lonely, Caroline knew it was time for her to go.

She loved Ariel dearly. She loved Tank and the children she had watched grow through Christmas cards and school pictures through the years. She loved almost every minute she spent with them, right up until the cozy family scene began to hurt too much.

When Caroline excused herself, Tank and Ariel walked her to the door, protesting her exit. Their arms slung familiarly around each other's waists, they waved goodbye, unable to hide the doe-eyed looks of expectation they gave each other as they closed the door behind her.

She looked back once and saw their porch light go dark, and a pang of longing for a life she had never known rose up in Caroline so strongly that it took her breath away.

She gripped the steering wheel hard and waited for the wave of sadness to ease. Christmas was less than a week away, and she had a grandmother she loved and resented in almost equal measure, a mother she hardly knew, a stepfather she cared nothing for and a father she had never known. She didn't even know his name. Sometimes she wondered if her mother even knew his name.

She shifted into first gear and drove slowly away. The balmy day had extended into the night. Whipping through the narrow streets, she followed a dizzying labyrinth of sharp curves, steep climbs and steeper descents into the downtown of Eureka Springs.

In her memories, it was a place of magic, of stained glass windows and limestone walls, of Victorian homes and gingerbread trim, a place where the past was still alive in the present. Letting her breath out with a contented sigh, she eased through the town and felt the ache inside her begin to ease.

The lonely days of her childhood were behind her, but even now, the feelings lingered. Driving through the same streets where she used to ride her bicycle, she couldn't help remembering the shame of growing up illegitimate in a small town.

When Caroline was seven, her mother, Marion, had moved to Kansas City to work and left Caroline in the care of her grandmother and grandfather. Caroline had waited a year for her mother to send for her. Then her mother had married a wealthy older man she had met in Kansas City, and Caroline waited another year before she realized her mother was never going to send for her.

It hadn't been an easy time, but she held her pain inside and tried very hard to be happy and good and never to make anyone mad, hoping that she wouldn't lose the only home she had left.

Almost shuddering at the thoughts that had suddenly surrounded her, Caroline picked up speed again and within minutes the sleeping shops of the downtown were behind her. She headed out of the valley and up the mountain, past promontories, wooded hollows and dripping springs.

Combing her fingers through her wind-whipped hair, she took a deep breath and felt free of the oppressive memories that seemed so much a part of the town.

At a deserted intersection in the middle of nowhere, she lifted her foot from the gas pedal to coast through a flashing yellow caution light. The filling station at the side of the road was shut up tight.

The rock station she had been listening to signed off the air, and stray snatches of mariachi music began floating across the empty air waves. Keeping one hand on the steering wheel and her eyes trained on the serpentine, tree-shadowed highway, she fumbled blindly with the radio's tuner.

Crackling, spitting wisps of music leapfrogged stretches of silence until finally, a warm, clear baritone filled the night with a country-and-western lament about lost love and two-timing women.

Caroline unzipped her leather jacket, rearranged her long, cramped legs and cuddled deeper into the bucket seat of her convertible. Country wasn't exactly her first choice in music, but the hour was late and the road was eerily empty.

The song ended and the deejay gave the time as 12:05 a.m. and said the temperature in Springdale, on the hour, was fifty-four degrees. "Isn't that something, folks, for this time of year. Looks like Santa won't be bringing us a white Christmas *this* year. And now a song for all you lovers out there listenin' on this fine, spring-like night.''

Caroline groaned and almost turned off the radio, but she dreaded the silence. The song came and went while a vagabond eighteen-wheeler blasted by her, going in the opposite direction, first blinding her with its headlights, then rocking her car with the concussion of its passing.

Once it was gone, darkness engulfed her and she was alone with the night once again. And inevitably, with the wind ruffling through her hair and the moon and stars lighting the night, Duke was suddenly beside her, so close and so real, she could almost hear him breathe.

The radio helped the mood along with one more love song, a really sad song about lost chances and wrong choices and memories that wouldn't go away.

Why, Caroline wondered, did country love songs have to be so sad? She turned up the volume and sniffed as a wayward tear cooled her cheek. Maybe because they were real, she thought. Maybe because some loves were a gift you were only given once. Maybe because magic wasn't something you got a second chance at.

Even after thirteen years, the memory of Duke's arms around her, his lips on hers, his whispered words, could still weaken her knees and send her stomach tumbling. Lately, she had begun to doubt that fifty years would be enough to deaden the feelings that memories of what they had once had could arouse—especially when those memories were of a wild motorcycle ride in search of seclusion.

With her arms clasped tightly around Duke's waist and her head resting against his back, she had clung to him while her heart had pounded with the thrill of the ride and the knowledge that soon, she would truly be Duke's girl. Whatever else happened, she knew she would always have that night....

* * *

A heavy canopy of trees shut out the light of the moon as Duke coasted to a stop and turned off the motorcycle. It was close to midnight and past her curfew, and Caroline was intensely aware of the dark and the deep quiet that was broken only by the sound of crickets and the wind through the trees.

"Caroline?" Like the wind, Duke's voice was a deep, soft sigh. His hands covered hers, then slid up her arms, holding her tightly against him. "You okay back there?"

She lifted her cheek from its resting place on his back and propped her chin on his shoulder. Laughter bubbled in her eyes. "Yes. Very okay."

Duke turned his head to the side and nuzzled her cheek. "Very okay, huh? You want to walk down to the lake?" he asked, planting a row of soft kisses across her chin, nose and the corner of her mouth.

Growing shy, Caroline buried her face against his shoulder and nodded. This was what she had wanted, what she had dreamed of, and yet, she was suddenly uncertain. She looked everywhere but at Duke while he helped her from the bike. Her pulse pounded and her face burned, and she began to walk away, not even sure of what direction she was heading.

"Ah, Caroline," Duke said in that same softly sighing voice. Reaching out, he caught her by the shoulders and turned her around to face him. He slid his hands down her back and pulled her tight against him. "Are you afraid of me now, baby?"

He sounded so sad, and Caroline almost thought she could feel him tremble. But she knew it was just her imagination and nothing more. It was she who was trembling, and all the rest was only a trick of the night, with its hidden moon and the hot August wind wrapping them in its embrace.

"I'd never hurt you, Caroline."

He lifted her chin and stared down at her. The gray of his eyes was soft and shining, like molten silver in the shadowed light. "What I feel for you is like nothing I've ever felt before," he said slowly, willing her to believe him. "This past year has been like living in hell. There were so many things I wanted to say to you, and I knew I couldn't."

Just the way she had envisioned it a thousand times in her dreams, Caroline watched while Duke's lips slowly lowered toward her. Gently, they brushed hers, warm and firm and better than anything she could have imagined.

His hands cupped the back of her head, holding her close while his mouth began to move on hers, drawing her to him, demanding, promising, coaxing and teaching until her head spun and her arms clung to him for strength and she discovered how pale dreams could be.

When their lips finally parted, Caroline caught her breath in quick, jerky gasps while Duke buried his face in her hair and whispered in her ear, "If you don't want to, I'll understand. It can end right here and I'll take you home."

The ragged sound of his breathing sent her stomach tumbling madly. Her knees grew weak at the memory of the passion he had already ignited in her earlier. Instinctively, Caroline tightened her arms around him.

"I don't want to go home," she said. Her words were breathless with love, wonder and need she had never imagined she could feel.

"God, I love you," Duke whispered in a voice tight with desire.

His hands moved restlessly over her, exploring the curves and planes of her body as he kissed her again, harder than before, until Caroline thought she would faint from the wild emotions he set loose in her.

Breaking off the kiss, he said, "Let's go while we can still walk."

He let go of her with one arm. Keeping the other around her waist, he held her tightly against his side all the way down the rocky path to the lake.

At the edge of the sand, he let her go just long enough to take off his T-shirt and spread it on the ground. Then his fingers slid through her hair while he guided her tenderly onto her back and lay down beside her.

"Are you scared?" he asked gently.

Her heart was pounding so loud she thought he had to hear it, but it wasn't from fear. "No." Her voice was thick and throaty in a way she had never heard it before.

He looked down at her. His eyes glittered like silver in the moonlight; his hair was dark as coal. He had never looked more wonderful.

"I'll never stop loving you," he promised.

His kiss was deep and lingering, and when he lifted himself on one elbow to unbutton the front of her dress, his gentleness stilled her doubts and left her bold with desire.

Tantalized by the soft, dark curls that covered his chest, Caroline stroked her fingertips lightly over the springy cushion of hair. While Duke spread her dress apart and unfastened the front closure of her bra, her fingers slid deeper into the mat of curls and over the hard muscles of his chest.

His breath came in catches as Duke smoothed the lacy bra aside. As he looked down at her, Caroline felt her desire surge.

"You're so beautiful," he said softly. His fingertips traced the curve of one breast and then the other. "So smooth. So firm."

Caroline caught her breath in a gasp, then released it in a soft moan as his thumb grazed the aroused tip of her breast. Twisting with pleasure that was almost too intense, she raked her fingers through the soft dusk of his hair and guided his mouth down to cover hers in a hard kiss.

While his tongue slowly parted her lips, his hand closed over her breast and squeezed gently, sending desire pulsing through her, growing stronger with every beat of her heart.

She had wanted him for so long, for so many years. And now he was in her arms, holding her, touching her. She had never dreamed it could be like this. She had never known she could feel this way.

Pulling away suddenly, Duke rolled onto his back beside her and let his breath out in a shudder.

"We've got to slow this thing down," he said through labored breaths.

Half dazed by the powerful emotions still sweeping through her, Caroline turned her head to the side and gazed at him from under eyelids that were almost too heavy to keep open.

"Why?"

"A lot of reasons."

Caroline rolled toward him. Her bare breasts cradled against his arm as she watched his chest rising and falling with each gasping breath.

"I want you," she said softly. "I know what I'm doing."

He pulled her into his arms and held her, bare chest to bare chest. "No, you don't," he said sadly. "Not really."

"I want to be your girl, Duke." Her voice was close to tears.

"You are my girl, Caroline." He crushed her against him. Weaving his fingers through her hair, he lifted her head from his shoulder and stared tenderly into her eyes. "You're the only girl I've ever loved, and you're the only girl I'll ever want. From now until the end of time, you belong to me, just like I belong to you."

He kissed her urgently. "Oh, baby, don't you see, that's why I'm waiting. It's not because I don't love you, sweetheart. It's because I love you so much. I want it to be right when we do it. I want it to be forever."

"Promise?"

"Solemnly. Now let's get you home before your grandparents start getting suspicious about who you were really with tonight."

Yellow streetlights glared on wet, empty streets. A fine, steady mist fell, mingling with her tears. She staggered down the street past dark storefronts, alone in the night while the town slept. There was no one to hear her or see her or comfort her. She carried her burden alone, running from the night, hurrying toward an elusive shelter.

She turned a corner and there, under a streetlight, stood Mrs. Rochester, her arm stiff, her finger pointing straight at Caroline.

A smothered sob escaped her and Caroline turned the other way to find Mabel Collins standing in the doorway next to her. Her eyes glaring, her teeth bared, she pointed, too, straight at Caroline.

Whirling away, Caroline saw dawn bleeding across the gray sky and suddenly there were people everywhere, standing in the street, blocking the sidewalk, coming out of the stores, all raising their arms to point, all staring straight at her.

Panicked, she began to back away, to go back the way she had come, to go back to what she was running away from. As she turned, she saw her reflection in a store window. Her long braids hung over her shoulders and down to her waist across a hugely swollen stomach that strained at the seams of her little-girl dress.

She stared at her reflection in horror as her hands clutched at her melon-ripe belly, and she screamed and screamed and screamed and...

"Caroline, wake up."

Her heart pounding and her gown sticking to her with sweat, Caroline jerked awake at the rough shaking from her grandmother.

"Is she all right?" her grandfather's voice asked.

Caroline opened her eyes and saw her grandmother's face leaning over her. Her grandfather stood in the light of the door. He wore pajamas and one side of his hair stood straight up. He smoothed it down as she watched.

She sat up, wiping tears from her face. "I'm okay."

"Were you dreaming?" her grandmother demanded.

"Yes." Her heart still pounded as if she had been running for hours. "I was just dreaming. I'm sorry." She looked past her grandmother to the figure standing in the doorway. "I'm sorry, Grandpa."

"Can you go back to sleep now?" he asked.

"Yes." She laid back down and pulled the sheet up to her chin. "I'm sorry."

Her grandfather turned and left the doorway. Her grandmother patted her hand.

"Are you sure you're all right?" she asked gently.

"Yes."

"That must have been some dream." Her grandmother still sounded worried.

"I'm so sorry."

"That's all right, sweetheart, you can't help it." Her grandmother smoothed Caroline's wet hair back from her face. "You get some sleep now."

"Good night."

When her grandmother had left the room and the hall light had been doused, Caroline lay alone in the dark, staring at the ceiling, her heart still pounding as shame rolled over her in hot waves.

She longed for Duke's arms to hold her and comfort her and, at the same time, she trembled in fear of the consequences. She couldn't end up like her mother. She just couldn't. She didn't think she could live if her nightmare ever came true.

Chapter Five

Gravel crunched under the wheels of Caroline's car as it climbed the short drive and pulled to a halt on the semicircular overlook nestled in the trees on a hillside above the town. Caroline turned off the engine and the radio and sat there in silence, listening to the wind in the trees.

Her heartbeat was rapid, and she could almost feel the cold sweat on her skin, so real was the memory of the nightmare that had haunted her since her childhood. The first dream had been soon after her mother had married. It had been a short dream, just a hint of the nightmares that were to come.

It was after she met Duke that the nightmares became so much worse. They weren't always the same, but the terror that she felt never changed.

She was always alone, abandoned and cast out into a world of whispers and pointing fingers, suffering from a shame that weighed her down and left her begging for forgiveness. Sometimes she was a child; sometimes she was grown. Sometimes she had her mother's face; sometimes her own. She always awoke from the dreams crying and drenched with sweat, her heart pounding as she gasped for breath.

She had never seen Duke on an evening without awakening at dawn from another nightmare. The more deeply she had loved him and the closer they came to consummating their love, the more intense the nightmares became, but she had never told him.

Caroline clenched her fingers around the steering wheel and stiffened her arms, fighting off the memories. It had been years since she had had one of the nightmares. Now she was afraid she was going to trigger them all over again just by worrying, when all she really wanted to think about was tomorrow when she would see Duke again.

She leaned her head against the back of the seat and stared up at the clear, star-studded sky. She felt restless and eager and, in spite of everything, happy. Maybe it was just nostalgia and maybe it was real, but she was still half in love with Duke.

Getting out of the car and slamming the door behind her, Caroline walked to the rock wall along the rim of the overlook. She stared down at the darkened town below and asked herself who she thought she was kidding. She was more than half in love with him, whether she wanted to be or not.

And standing there in the moonlight with the cool night breeze blowing through her hair, loving him didn't seem so wrong and happy endings didn't seem so impossible.

Caroline continued to thumb through the backlog of paperwork on her desk while she held the phone wedged between her shoulder and her tilted head.

"Mrs. Jenkins just left," her grandmother was saying in her ear. "She wants me to go to the mall in Fayetteville with her tomorrow, but I just don't know...." Her voice died away in indecision.

"Don't know what, Gran?" Caroline asked. She finished looking through the pile and started over again, separating the paperwork into smaller stacks by category.

"Well, whether I want to go all that distance or not. I might get too tired out."

"You could tell Mrs. Jenkins that you can go but you can't stay too long because you still get tired easily," Caroline suggested.

"I guess I could do that," Viola said, sounding relieved. "Are you busy, dear?"

"A little. Some of this work got pretty far behind while they were waiting to fill this position."

"Well, that's nice. What time do you think you'll be home?"

Caroline stared at the stacks fanning out across her desk. Organization had only succeeded in making it look like a worse mess.

"That's hard to say, Gran. I may be working longer hours at first, until I get some of this caught up."

"Oh."

Her grandmother sounded so crestfallen that Caroline wished she hadn't been so honest. She wondered if it was too late to sugarcoat her reply.

"Did you need me?" she asked.

"It's just that it's the holidays and I had hoped we could spend more time together for the next week or two."

"Well, maybe I can—" A knock on Caroline's door interrupted her. "Just a second, Gran," she said as Duke looked in and flashed a big smile.

"Hi. Mind if I come in?" Without waiting for a reply, he slipped inside and closed the door behind him.

"I know you weren't really planning to start work until next week," Viola continued, as if she hadn't heard Caroline.

"No, fine, come in," Caroline said to Duke. "Just a minute, Gran," she said into the phone.

At the same time, her grandmother practically shouted, "What?"

"Just a minute," Caroline repeated louder than before. "Someone just came in."

"Sorry." Duke held up his hands and retreated a step. "I didn't know you were on the phone."

"It's okay," Caroline said, lowering her voice again. She motioned him forward. "It's my grandmother."

"Are you talking to me, Caroline?" Viola yelled into the phone.

"No, Gran," Caroline said, "Duke just came in. I think he needs to talk to me."

"Oh," Viola said, her tone cooling off. "Well, what time are you coming home?"

"It's kind of hard to say right now," Caroline explained patiently while she watched Duke pull out the chair in front of her desk and sit down. "I'll call you this afternoon when I have a better idea of what my schedule will be like."

"Oh, all right," her grandmother said with a sigh. "I just won't take my nap today so I won't miss your call."

Caroline could feel her patience wearing thin. "Why don't you just call me when you get up from your nap, Gran?"

"Well, I guess I could do that."

"Okay, that's what we'll do, then. You have a nice day, and I'll talk to you this afternoon. Love you, Gran."

Before her grandmother could say anything else, Caroline hung up the phone.

"I guess the house must seem pretty empty again with you gone all day," Duke said sympathetically.

Caroline drew in a deep breath and caught herself just before she released it in a heavy sigh. Carefully, she let the air out in a long, slow, quiet exhalation. "I guess."

"I do that sometimes," Duke said.

"What?"

"Deep breathing. To relax. Usually I do it more than once, though."

"Oh." Caroline realized that she did feel better. Her voice had lost some of its frayed edge of exasperation. "It works, doesn't it?"

"Pretty well," Duke agreed. "So, how are you settling in?"

"Hard to tell, so far." She waved her hands over the mountain of paperwork on her desk. "All I've done is shuffle papers from pile to pile."

"Well, most of that's already been waiting for a couple of months. So don't feel like you have to get it all caught up overnight. Jonathan's already handled anything that couldn't wait."

Caroline did sigh this time, with relief. "Thank you. I think I *was* beginning to feel a little overwhelmed."

Duke smiled. "I was afraid of that. That's one of the reasons I dropped by." He tilted his head to the side and studied her. "You know, I really do like that suit. What is that?"

He caught her so off guard, she had to look to see what she was wearing. It was a simple two-piece suit, collarless and cream colored, with a lacy, crocheted trim around the neck and sleeves. "You mean the fabric? It's raw silk, I think."

"I really like that," he said, nodding. "You know, one of the things that impressed me when I first met you was that you always dressed just a little different from the other girls."

Caroline remembered the same thing, and it had been just one more private shame. "You can thank my grand-mother for that."

"It looked nice on you. I liked it. But I guess I never told you that, did I?"

"No."

"Having a daughter, it's something I've learned to do. To notice clothes. To give compliments."

He smiled, a slow, relaxed smile, and Caroline found herself joining him. "She certainly seems to be training you right," she said laughing.

"She's doing her best."

"How old is Kimi? I forgot to ask yesterday."

"Ten years and ten months. We have a countdown going to the big eleven. She considers that a very serious age."

Caroline laughed again. "She sounds pretty terrific. I hope I get to meet her soon."

"I think she'd like that. She's very curious about you."

"About me?"

Duke shrugged. "She's heard your name once or twice."

This time, Caroline didn't know whether to laugh or cry. "Oh, no. Even the children are talking about us now?"

He spread his hands helplessly. "I never set out to be notorious. It just happened."

Caroline leaned forward and propped her elbows on the desk. "Duke," she said, getting serious, "do you think it's going to be a problem, my working here? I have to tell you, my grandmother was very opposed, and I'm beginning to wonder if she wasn't right."

"No," Duke said firmly. His jaw was set and his eyes flashed. "You were hired on your merits, and I won't let our personal lives, past or present, interfere. And I will never again let a bunch of small-town gossips run my life—or yours."

Something about the way he said what he said and the way he looked at her when he said it sent flutters through Caroline's stomach and shivers up her back. It reminded her of the night she truly became Duke's girl and he swore to love her forever.

Maybe Duke felt some of the same sensations, because he suddenly became quiet. When he spoke again, he sounded less personal and more businesslike, as if he were retreating.

"The other reason I came in here was to ask for your help on a company project. It's the sort of thing Jonathan's no good at, and we've been waiting until this position was filled to proceed. You might like to know that I've also asked Ariel to help."

"Decorate your house?" Caroline asked incredulously.

"No," Duke said, looking puzzled. "Where do you come up with these things?"

He seemed to be waiting for an answer, so Caroline explained, "I had dinner at Ariel's last night and she told me you'd asked her to decorate your house."

"Your powers of deduction are stupefying. And almost always way off target." A reluctant grin spread over his face. "What I want *your* help with is organizing a party."

"A party?" Suddenly apprehensive, Caroline thought she would probably have more luck decorating his house, but at this point, she didn't dare say so.

"Yes, for New Year's Eve. I know it's awfully short notice, but until Jonathan hired you, I couldn't think of anybody in the company who could pull it off."

"What makes you think I can pull it off?" She hadn't given many parties in her lifetime, and none of them had been much of a success.

Duke smiled confidently. "Because Ariel said you could. She said the two of you wouldn't have any problem."

"How important is this party?"

He leaned forward in his chair, and his expression took on a look of extreme earnestness. "From a public-relations standpoint, it's something the company needs right now. I want us to be accepted as part of the community. I want Eureka to be glad we're here."

From the intensity in his voice and the silver flashes in his eyes, Caroline knew this party really mattered to him. It wasn't just a question of doing her job. It was a question of personally disappointing Duke, and she didn't think that was something she could be a part of again.

His voice softened, and he became even more serious. "Ordinarily, that's something that takes years, but I haven't got years. My daughter's ten. This is her home and

I want her to be happy here. I want her to be accepted. That's not something I'd tell just anybody.''

Caroline nodded, knowing there was nothing else she could do. "All right. I'll do it.''

Duke relaxed in his chair, obviously relieved. "Thank you, Caroline. This means a lot to me.''

"I know. I just hope you're happy with the results.''

He stood. "I will be. Let me know if there's anything you need from me.''

The door shut behind him, and Caroline stared at the closed door until her vision began to blur. So this was what it was like to work with Duke. How long, she wondered, before the memories began to blur with the present, before she couldn't tell the difference anymore? How long before her dreams turned to nightmares, before the past once again destroyed the future?

"I can't help feeling like I'm playing hooky,'' Caroline said.

"Relax,'' Ariel answered. "We've already had to cancel this shindig once because Duke couldn't find anyone at the office to help coordinate it. Nobody resents the time you're spending on this.''

"Are you sure?''

"Positive.''

"Good,'' Caroline said with a laugh. "Because I've waited my whole life to walk into this house.''

"So, what do you think?''

"It's bare. How can we have a party here?''

"Well, I've already talked to Duke's housekeeper, Martha.'' Ariel cut her eyes sideways to Caroline. "Wait till you meet her.''

"Why?''

"You'll see. Anyway, she's going to do the catering. I made the mistake of asking if she'd ever done anything like this before, and she gave me a look that could've frozen Beaver Lake, so I guess she has.''

"Have you told him yet what we discussed?"

"Duke?"

"Yes, Duke," Caroline said, not buying Ariel's expression of wide-eyed innocence.

"I thought maybe you should be the one."

"You coward."

"He likes you better."

"This is strictly a business relationship."

"In a pig's eye," Ariel shot back good-naturedly, and then shrugged. "Anyway, you should still be the one. I'm just the community liaison. You work for him."

Caroline relented. She didn't like to admit it, but she was almost beginning to like the idea of working for him. Deep down inside of her, the teenager who had been thrilled to be called Duke's girl still seemed to exist. "Is there a phone here?"

"Gee, I don't know."

"Don't know what?" Duke asked.

He appeared on the staircase, wearing gym shorts with a towel wrapped around his neck. The ends of the towel draped down over his bare chest.

"If there's a phone here," Ariel answered, turning toward the sound of his voice.

"Upstairs in my bedroom." He lifted one end of the towel and wiped the sweat from his forehead. "And there may be one in the kitchen. You're free to use them if they're working. Service should be on some time today."

"That's okay," Ariel said. "You're the one we were going to call."

"Oh?" He looked from Ariel to Caroline. "Is there a problem?"

Ariel looked at Caroline and after a sinking moment Caroline said, "Well, not really. It's just that we were talking, and..." She took a deep breath and gathered her thoughts. "As we understand it, the object of this party is to introduce the people of the company to the people of the town, correct?"

"Right." He sat on the staircase. One leg was bent, his foot braced on the second step. The other leg was straight with the back of his heel resting on the floor. His forearm was draped across his upraised knee. He was beginning to frown.

"And that means several hundred people, plus spouses or dates, from the company," Caroline continued.

Duke nodded.

"And the whole town? Not just selected individuals, but the whole town? Here?" Caroline spread her arms. "In this house?"

He idly stroked his chest with the end of the towel while he looked around the room. "Well, I *had* envisioned an intimate gathering."

"Assuming that only a small percentage of the townspeople actually attend, you're still looking at maybe a thousand people, possibly more," Caroline said, trying hard to ignore the bare chest he was toweling dry.

Duke looked around the room one more time. "They're not going to fit, are they?" he asked quietly.

"Not here."

She couldn't tell if he was disappointed or amused by her news. Uncertainly, she glanced at Ariel, who motioned for her to go on.

Steeling herself, Caroline said, "So what we thought might work better is a picnic."

Duke dropped the end of the towel and looked at her as if he hadn't heard her right. "It's winter."

"But it's unusually mild for this time of year," Caroline said, thankful that she had checked with every weather expert she could track down. "And it's expected to stay that way for several weeks at least. There's a very large front that stalled over us, and next week should be identical to this week, sweater weather and sunshine. We could have the picnic on Saturday, just before New Year's."

Emboldened by Duke's silence, Ariel added, "I have a committee ready to go. We're just waiting for your okay."

Duke looked from Ariel to Caroline. "A picnic?"

"Could it really be any worse than standing around in the sweltering heat of August?" Caroline coaxed. "And people do that all the time."

"I must be out of my mind." He looked toward the ceiling and raised his hands helplessly. When he lowered his gaze again, his expression said clearly that he wasn't kidding. "This had better be good or the whole town's going to think I'm the one who's nuts."

"Trust us," Ariel said, ready to take charge again.

Duke shrugged in submission. "Okay. Do it."

Ariel beamed. "Great. Well, I've got things to do if we're going to pull this off. Do you need a ride back to the office, Caroline?"

"Uh, actually," Duke said quickly, "I had hoped to borrow Caroline for a while." He looked from Ariel to Caroline. "I can give her a ride to the office if she needs one. If it's okay?" The question was directed to Caroline.

"We really have a lot to do if we're going to get this done on time," she hedged.

What had seemed possible the night before now seemed like just so much moonlight madness. The last time she had dreamed of a happily-ever-after with Duke, her life had gone down in flames. It had taken her thirteen years to reach a point where she was reconciled with the past and ready to look to the future.

More than that, she just plain didn't trust herself to be alone with Duke in an empty house.

"This won't take long," he said with a determination that made arguing useless.

Duke drew the damp towel from his neck and stood, leaving the towel laying on the step. Then he walked to the front door and opened it for Ariel. "Don't worry," he assured her. "I'll take Caroline back to the office."

Ariel looked from Duke to Caroline, uncertain of what to do.

"It's all right," Caroline said to avoid a scene. "I'll talk to you later."

Ariel frowned but turned obediently and left. Duke shut the door behind her. When he looked at Caroline again his expression was less confident.

"Are you angry?"

"I don't know if that's the word. I feel a little like I've just been kidnapped," she said stiffly.

"You didn't have to stay."

"No. I could have made a scene and forced Ariel to choose sides. That would have made everything very pleasant for the next week or so."

"Hmm. You are mad, aren't you?"

"I think your actions were a little high-handed."

"There was a time when I wasn't firm enough about what I wanted, and I ended up losing the most important thing in the world to me. But I didn't mean to offend you. I'm sorry. If you like, I'll take you back now."

"Oh, Duke," Caroline snapped. "If you're going to make me mad, don't turn around and apologize in the next breath. I'd at least like to stay mad at you for a little while."

"So, you're not mad at me anymore?" He sounded hopeful.

"Well, since you went to so much trouble to keep me here, the least you can do is tell me what you wanted," she said grudgingly.

"I wanted to show you the house."

A dead calm engulfed her and with a shudder and huff, her sails went slack. "How sweet," she said, all her anger gone.

"I remember how much you used to love this place. I thought you'd like a tour."

"You remember that?" She was deeply touched, and it was more than a little disconcerting.

"You were eight when you first fell in love with this house. You used to stare at it from the gate and pretend that you lived here."

Caroline laughed to keep from crying. "You remember my dreams."

He looked at her with eyes that were full of meaning. Then, again, as he had earlier in the day, he seemed to retreat.

"Ready?" He smiled and held out his arm to her.

She stared at his arm, tan even in December. Sleek, hard muscles beckoned. Bare skin tantalized, glistening still from his workout.

Caroline backed away a step and motioned to her suit, as handy an excuse as any. "It's silk."

He smiled apologetically. "My clothes are upstairs."

"That's nice."

"Let's go up the back way. The dining room's through there." He motioned this time, not offering his arm.

The downstairs didn't take much time. Beyond the dining room was the kitchen, which looked very much like the one in Caroline's grandmother's house.

"I'll have to have this redone. I'd like to do it now, but they're in a hurry to move in, so I guess we'll just have to live through remodeling later."

"Why? It looks just fine. A little old-fashioned, maybe, but I'll bet everything works."

Duke laughed. "Caroline, I own a custom-cabinetry firm. I'm going to have to have a Hutchison custom kitchen eventually. Even if it wasn't good business, Martha would insist. She's been spoiled."

"Do you realize that I work for you and I've never even seen your product?"

"We can fix that. I'll arrange a tour of the factory for you."

"Thank you. I wonder how many other employees are just like me? Have you considered upgrading your orientation program?"

"That's a very good idea, Miss Adams," Duke said, hurrying her through the kitchen. "But I would like to point out that I'm on vacation this week. This is the powder room, which could also stand to be remodeled."

"It looks fine to me."

"We do bathrooms, too. We've got built-ins you never even knew you needed. This is the back staircase." He stood aside. "After you."

The stairs were narrow, with no handrail, in dark, uncarpeted wood. They went straight up and emerged on a landing between two bedrooms. Neither was furnished. A simple bathroom was tucked into the corner.

Through another doorway was a room that was also the passageway to the room beyond. The first room was empty except for a tall, complex weight machine. Benches and arm rests and pulleys jutted from it at all angles. The jeans and sweater that Duke had worn earlier were in a neat pile on top of a folded towel.

"This is the only furnishing I've seen in this house," Caroline said, surprised by his priorities.

"It's the only thing I've moved in so far. Ariel's supposed to take care of the rest."

"Don't you even want to pick your own furniture?"

"No."

"Professional decorators are nice and I'm sure Ariel will do a wonderful job," Caroline argued. "But you're the one who's going to have to live here."

Duke stopped walking and looked at her closely. "You still care about this house, don't you?"

Caroline frowned. "Some." She wasn't sure she liked being so transparent to him.

"Then I'll tell Ariel to clear everything through you. Anything you want in this house, you can have."

"Duke!" Exasperated, Caroline left him standing in the weight room and went through the door that led into the next room.

This room was larger. At one end was a fireplace between two windows. At the other end was a single window and another bathroom. In the wall beside the bathroom was a doorway with a step-up into the next room.

"What did I say?" Duke asked, catching up to her as she stood surveying the room.

"What is this room?"

Against his will, he answered her question first. "It's going to be our family room. The living room downstairs will be formal, but I want this one to be cozy. Now, what did I say that upset you?"

"This is your house, not mine," she said, wondering how he could have such insight one minute and be so obtuse the next. "You're going to live here, not me. I don't want to pick your furniture."

"I'm sorry. Obviously I was insensitive once again. I was just trying to do something that would please you."

"Oh, damn it."

Again she left him and walked angrily on to the next room. It was a divided room identical to the foyer and living room downstairs. There was a fireplace next to a door that led onto a porch. On the far side of the larger section of the room a set of French doors opened onto a balcony.

From the smaller area where she now stood, another delicately curving staircase led to the third floor.

"What was wrong with what I said that time?" Duke demanded when he caught up with her again.

"You didn't even know what you were apologizing for."

"Well, that's true," he agreed without hesitation. "And I was pretty sure I wouldn't really understand even if you explained it to me. But I still meant what I said. Without meaning to, I upset you and I'm sorry."

Caroline glanced up at him finally, standing there looking so tall, dark and handsome. And sincere. He looked really sincere.

"No, I'm sorry," she said, relenting partially. "I shouldn't have gotten angry. It's just that if this house were mine, I would care so much about everything in it. And you don't seem to care at all."

Duke shook his head and walked past her into the larger room. He stood there with his legs spread and his back to her, massaging the back of his neck with his hand.

He still hadn't changed clothes, and the jersey gym shorts that he wore outlined the tight muscles of his behind like a second skin. Caroline tried to look around the room, but like magnets, her eyes were drawn back to him.

His legs were long and tanned, the muscles smooth and well formed. Her gaze traveled to his slim, tapered waist, then on up the widening vee of his back to his broad shoulders. Caroline watched, fascinated by the play of his muscles as Duke lowered his arm and slowly turned around to face her.

"It's not that I don't care," he said quietly. "It's just that I can't get over the feeling that I'm living in your house. Ever since I bought it, I've felt like I've taken something that should have been yours." He was quiet for a second, and then continued in a voice soft as a whisper. "Or ours."

Lost chances, broken dreams and shattered promises suddenly swirled around her like sad, lonely ghosts, and Caroline turned and began to walk away. Before she had gone half a dozen steps, Duke caught up to her.

His strong hands closed over her shoulders and pulled her gently back toward him.

"Caroline, don't go. Not again. Not now."

Too weak to fight, she held back tears while his hands slid down her arms and across her waist, drawing her closer, until her back was pressed to his bare chest and her head rested against the hollow of his throat.

"I can't seem to do much that doesn't hurt you," he said tenderly. "And that's the last thing in the world I want to do."

Caroline drew in an uneven breath and felt her chest ache with the pain of endless regret. "Oh, Duke," she whispered, "ours is such a tangled web."

"It doesn't have to be. We can fix it. Or we can put it all behind us and start over again. We can still make it work, Caroline."

"Can we? Can we ever do that? There's still so much that's unfinished."

"Then let's finish it," he urged with rising intensity, "and get on with our lives."

"I don't know if I can right now."

"Damn it, Caroline." Duke whirled her around to face him. His strong hands held her by the shoulders as he glared down at her.

Caroline opened her mouth to say something and her mind went blank. His lips, full and tempting, leaned toward her and her heart began to pound. She had never wanted anything more in her life than she wanted at that moment to feel his lips on hers.

Her fingers touched his ribs and she felt him flinch. His warm breath brushed her cheek in a sigh, and he pulled her into his arms while her hands slid around his sides and over his back.

"Oh, Caroline," he whispered, and his mouth touched hers gently, quickly, and then withdrew a fraction of an inch.

The phone in the next room began to ring. Lifting his head, Duke glanced toward the sound for an instant before he turned back to Caroline and lowered his mouth to hers once again.

This time, his kiss was slow and thorough. His lips gave hers his undivided attention and demanded the same response. His arms tightened, pressing her breathlessly against his chest, while his heartbeat raced with hers.

Caroline felt the powerful muscles of his back move under her hands, and her knees went weak with the emotions that were spinning out of control inside her. "Daddy, it's for you," a little voice said from behind them.

Duke froze, and an icy rush of shock went through Caroline so suddenly that for an instant, the room seemed to spin. Gasping for breath, hearts still pounding, Duke and Caroline looked at each other through eyes that were only inches apart.

"Have you met my daughter?" he asked weakly.

"No."

Her voice was barely more than a startled squeak, and Duke kept his arm protectively around her waist as he moved to her side.

Standing in the middle of the broad opening to the adjoining area, looking very small, was a little girl with long, black hair pulled back neatly in a barrette. She wore a white velour jogging suit with pink trim and pink jogging shoes. The telephone receiver dangled from one delicate hand while her large, dark eyes looked from Caroline to Duke and back to Caroline.

"They're waiting," she said, holding out the receiver to her father. "It's long distance."

"Oh." Duke hastily slipped his arm from Caroline's waist and crossed the room.

Kimi's eyes never left Caroline as Duke took the receiver from her and disappeared into a corner of the smaller room that was hidden. Once her father was busy, the little girl walked slowly toward Caroline.

"You're Caroline, aren't you?" she asked quietly. "I've been waiting to meet you."

The innate strength and self-confidence that had gotten Caroline through a traumatic adolescence failed her in the face of this intimidating child who seemed to see straight through to the heart of her. She wanted very much to hide until Duke came back to protect her from his intense little daughter.

"You have?"

"Yes." With a solemn face, she lifted her hand and held it out to Caroline. "I'm Kimi Hutchison, and I'm very pleased to meet you. But I don't know your last name."

"Adams." Caroline took the small hand and shook it as solemnly as it was offered. Somewhere deep in the heart of those piercing brown eyes Caroline began to see a little part of herself, and in that moment, she felt herself begin to melt. "Caroline Adams. And I'm very pleased to meet you, too."

As if Kimi sensed the change in Caroline, a smile slowly lit the girl's face. "Have you seen my room?" she asked shyly.

"I don't know. Which one is it?"

Kimi turned her index finger straight up.

Caroline looked at the ceiling and then at the curving staircase that seemed to disappear into the wall. "Is it up those stairs?"

The little girl nodded and slipped her hand into Caroline's. "Want to see it? He'll be a while on the phone."

"Sure."

With a clarity that made her heart pound in anticipation, Caroline could remember when she used to stand outside the wrought-iron gate that protected Hurley House from intruders like her and dream of the world inside. The things that had always stood out in her mind were the three white porches that were stacked one on top of the other like the layers of a wedding cake. The top porch opened off of what looked like a turret, and the room inside that turret was the one thing Caroline had always wanted most to see.

Carefully, she followed Kimi up the staircase, which exited in the corner of a nearly circular room. The door that opened onto the porch was in the center of a group of windows. The side of the room by the windows was built up one step from the rest of the room, creating a nook that added interest and charm to an already magical place. It was a little girl's fantasy come true.

Kimi's hand squeezed Caroline's. "Isn't it great?" she asked, gazing around her with awe. Together, they walked deeper into the room.

"Where are you going to put your bed?" Caroline asked. She didn't bother to conceal her excitement. With Kimi, she knew instinctively that she didn't have to play the adult or hide the emotions that other people might not understand.

"There." Kimi pointed to the wall opposite the door and windows. Then she released Caroline's hand and seemed to float across the floor to the nook.

"Here," she said, gesturing dramatically with her arms, "I'm going to have a table and chairs. For tea." She held the leg of her pants out to the side while she curtsied and rose again, and her voice became very proper. "I *do* hope you'll join me sometime, Miss Adams. I *do* hope we can be friends."

Joining the spirit of the game, Caroline said, "Oh, please, call me Caroline. And I'd love to come to tea."

"I knew we would be friends." With a broad smile, Kimi became a little girl again. "I always just knew it."

Caroline had a powerful impulse to take the child into her arms and hug her. There was so much about Kimi that she knew without being told. She knew about the loneliness and uncertainty that was kept tucked away inside, out of sight.

Kimi had something Caroline had never had. She had a father, and she had a love from him that was strong and unconditional, and because of that she was a happy child. But in gaining a father, she had lost her mother, and with that, she had lost a part of herself that would always be shrouded in mystery.

"Sweetheart?" Duke called, coming up the staircase. "Are you up here? We have to go now." He came to a relieved halt. "Caroline, I was afraid I'd lost you."

"Kimi wanted to show me her room."

The little girl walked forward a few steps and slid in under Caroline's arm. With her hand on Kimi's shoulder, Caroline led her to the head of the staircase.

Duke let Kimi go by and caught Caroline's arm in his hand, guiding her shoulder against his chest.

"I'm sorry," he said with eyes that spoke his regret much more clearly than his words.

"For what?" Afraid that he regretted their kiss, Caroline tried not to show the aching panic that was rising in her.

"For the interruption." His voice was a caress and his lips were once again inches from hers. "I'd like to pick up again where we left off."

"Dad," Kimi called impatiently from the room below.

Caught between the real world and the magic that she felt when she was alone with Duke, Caroline couldn't answer.

"We'll talk later," Duke said, releasing her. "Do you want to go back to the office, or should I take you somewhere else?"

Leading the way down the next staircase, Caroline answered over her shoulder. "That's okay. I can take the trolley to Ariel's."

"No," Duke insisted, "I'll drive you."

Outside, he paused to lock the door and Caroline kept walking toward the gate.

"That's all right," she called. "I need the fresh air."

Kimi stood at the edge of the porch and waved. "Goodbye, Caroline."

At the gate, Caroline waved back. "Goodbye, Kimi. I'll see you again soon."

Closing the gate behind her, Caroline walked toward the trolley stop, gaining speed with each step that carried her away from the emotions she was afraid to feel and the hope she was afraid to believe in.

Chapter Six

She and Duke hadn't talked later. Caroline had need-lessly asked her grandmother to say she wasn't in if Duke called, and the next day at the office, she found that he had left town, called away suddenly on business.

That at least left her free to enjoy the Christmas party at Joey and Hilary Mason's. At least that's what Caroline told herself as she entered the elegant foyer of the Mason's large, modern home.

Joey greeted her at the door and handed her an eggnog. "Merry Christmas, ho, ho, ho! I'd take your coat, but you don't seem to have one."

"After Chicago's winters, I'm having trouble taking this weather seriously." Caroline took a sip of the eggnog. "This is really good. Did Hilary make it?"

"My wife is an excellent cook." Joey said, then pointed to the cup. "But that came out of a carton. I wonder if this is what Christmas is like in California. I almost hired a snow machine, just for a little atmosphere."

"Which way is the kitchen? I'm going to try to make myself useful."

Joey hooked a thumb over his shoulder. "Through there to the end of the house and hang a right. You can't miss it. It's big."

"What isn't in this house?" She looked around her again, still impressed that little Joey Mason had grown up to afford something like this.

He leaned closer and whispered as she departed, "The guest bedrooms are *tiny*."

After the cramped kitchen in her Chicago apartment and the ancient one in her grandmother's house, Caroline always felt a moment of shock when she walked into a kitchen like the one belonging to Joey and Hilary.

Big, bright and airy, the room had a breakfast bay at one end and a sun room at the other with a garden window in front of the triple-basined kitchen sink.

"Hi," Caroline said, trying not to feel overpowered. "I hope I'm not too late to help."

Hilary looked up from her efficient stuffing of mushroom caps. She was one of the many artists who had moved into the area over the years, drawn by the town's charm and beauty and by the lure of tourist dollars.

Small, dark and pretty, she was just the sort of woman who always made Caroline feel gawky and gauche with her own long legs and distinctly-colored hair.

"Why, Caroline, hello." Hilary's smile was warm and welcoming. "It's so sweet of you to offer. But I'd be scared to death you'd get something on that beautiful dress."

Caroline looked at the demure blue velvet dress that Hilary wore with only a lacy apron to protect it and had an irrational urge to slip out of her own high heels and tame her flowing mane into a discreet bun.

"Aprons are in the top drawer to the left of the refrigerator," Ariel said, pointing with the knife she was using to slice vegetables. "There's some cheese and a slicer there."

"Oh, but, Ariel," Hilary protested, "Caroline's a guest. I don't want her to have to work."

"Caroline's not happy unless you let her do something."

A glimmer of hope shone in Hilary's eyes when she looked at Caroline. "Is that true?"

"Sad but true," Caroline confirmed, remembering how, even as a child, she had come early to parties and gone straight to the kitchen. Mothers all over Eureka Springs had beamed with pleasure at the arrival of little Caroline Adams, and she had been a welcome and popular guest wherever she had gone.

"Well, grab an apron and dig in then," Hilary said with new enthusiasm. "I'm never going to get all of this done before people start arriving."

Relieved, Caroline joined in and amid cheerful chatter, they sliced and arranged and stuffed for the next twenty minutes until the doorbell sounded and Joey stuck his head in the kitchen doorway.

"They're he-e-re," he said in a singsong voice.

Her eyes wide with alarm, Hilary shoved a tray of canapés into his hands. "Well, give them a drink or something, honey, and keep them out of here. We're almost through."

In a few minutes, they had put the finishing touches on the remaining trays. With a crow of delight, Hilary brushed off her hands and took off her apron.

"Well, that's it, troops. Let's party." Picking up an open bottle of wine, she poured three glasses and passed them around. "I don't know what I'd have done without you two. I can't thank you enough."

"Oh, it was nothing," Caroline said.

"Sure, it was," Ariel contradicted. She looped her arm over Hilary's shoulder. "And all you have to do is show up early for my next party and work like a dog, and we'll be even. Speaking of parties, are you going to be able to help with that picnic a week from tomorrow?"

"For the famous Duke Hutchison? I'd do it just for the chance to meet him," Hilary answered.

"You haven't met him yet?" Ariel looked shocked. "But Joey's one of his best friends."

"No one's met him yet. The best I can tell, the man doesn't do anything but work. Speaking of which . . ." Hilary turned her intense, dark eyes on Caroline. "I heard you've got a job in his company. What's he really like?"

"Uh." Caroline glanced sideways at Ariel, asking for help. "He seems very nice."

Ariel shrugged and said, "You might as well know now, Hilary, because you're going to hear it sooner or later, anyway. Caroline and Duke have a past."

Caroline felt like dumping her glass over Ariel's head. That wasn't the kind of help she had been looking for. She cringed when she saw the speculation that entered Hilary's gaze.

"Oh, really?" Hilary asked.

"We dated some when we were kids, but that was a long time ago. I really don't know him anymore." Caroline glared at Ariel. "I don't even know why Ariel brought it up."

"Because after next Saturday, the whole town's going to be talking about it," Ariel said. "Once they see you two together at that picnic, that's going to be all anyone can talk about."

"Hey, we need a hostess in here," Joey called from the doorway. "What's taking so long, sweetheart?"

"Oh, phooey," Hilary moaned, looking from Joey to Caroline and Ariel. "Just when the conversation gets really juicy, I have to go play hostess."

Caroline touched Hilary's arm with a look of pleading. "Please don't repeat any of this."

Hilary patted her hand and gave her a smile of reassurance. "Don't worry. I wouldn't dream of discussing this with anyone else."

"Oh, thank you." Caroline felt an urge to hug her out of gratitude, but she restrained herself.

In parting, Hilary said, "But this really is fascinating, you know. Really fascinating."

Caroline watched Hilary until she was out of the room, then she turned to Ariel and whispered, "Oh, Ariel, you don't really think that's going to happen, do you?"

"What? People talking?"

"Yes."

Ariel shook her head sadly. "Caroline, you saw Hilary's reaction, and she doesn't know half of it. Everybody else still remembers how your grandfather snuck you out of town in the middle of the night. And how he spent the next year making Duke's life a living hell. And now, after more than a decade without either one of you stepping foot in this town, you and Duke are both back within a few months of your grandfather's death, and you expect people not to notice? They're gonna be on you like a duck on a June bug."

"But it's all just coincidence."

"Caroline, honey, that's even hard for me to believe." Ariel took Caroline's hand in hers. "Maybe it's just fate catching up with you and correcting something that should never have happened in the first place. But whatever it is, it is definitely more than a coincidence."

Before Caroline could argue, Tank's broad frame filled the doorway. "Are you two ever planning to join the party?"

Ariel looked at Caroline and shrugged. "I guess we should."

"I might as well try to enjoy one of my last nights of tranquility before all eyes are focused on me," Caroline said glumly.

"Caroline," Tank said, "I'm afraid your modesty outweighs your good sense. Any woman as beautiful as you always has all eyes on her."

He walked over to them and hooked his arm around Ariel's waist. "Just ask my baby here. She has to deal with it all the time. I hate to even let her go to the grocery store by herself anymore." He grinned at them and hugged Ariel against him. "Since all those articles came out about how the produce section is such a hot place to meet people, a concerned husband just can't be too careful."

"Or too silly, apparently," Ariel said, trying not to look pleased. "Let's adjourn to the living room."

Caroline followed them out of the kitchen, through a short, narrow hallway and into the dining room, where small groups milled around the food that was laid out over every available flat surface. The noise level in the room was a shock after the quiet of the kitchen and Caroline wondered if she was really in the mood for a night of festivity.

In spite of Tank's attempt to cheer her up with flattery, she still shuddered inside every time she thought of Ariel's prediction. After a childhood spent hiding from gossip and compensating for what she thought people were saying behind her back, she thought she had put all the old feelings of inadequacy and guilt behind her. Obviously, she hadn't, not if idle talk could upset her this much.

Still clutching her original glass of wine, Caroline resisted the urge to follow Ariel and Tank around all evening. Instead, she wandered from the family room with its huge stone fireplace and ceiling-high Christmas tree into the foyer. Here, guests had trickled halfway up the curving staircase, sitting in twos and threes on the carpeted stairs, laughing and talking, with paper plates balanced on their knees and glasses swaying in the air as they talked.

"Well, hello, beautiful. Hilary told me you were here somewhere."

At the sound of his voice, Caroline turned around and found herself gazing into the silvery gray eyes of a very relaxed Duke.

"You're back in town," she said, sounding as shocked as she felt. She had only come to the party because there was no chance of seeing him there.

"And it wasn't easy, either. But, to be honest, I didn't even know if you'd be here."

"Why wouldn't I be here?"

He shrugged. "I thought you might be trying to avoid me."

"I didn't have to. You were supposed to have been out of town," she reminded him.

"Then you *were* avoiding me."

"What gave you that idea?" Her voice sounded guilty and Caroline knew she was trapped. She didn't want to lie to him, but she didn't want to explain, either, because she really didn't understand herself all that well at the moment.

"I called your house Wednesday, before I left," Duke said quietly. He didn't seem angry, just very serious. "Your grandmother said you weren't home. She never was a very good liar. And she still isn't."

Caroline looked around. Their conversation was too personal to be carried on over the low roar around them. In the family room on one side and the living room on the other, the party continued enthusiastically. There seemed to be no quiet corner anywhere.

"We could go outside and talk," Duke said, as if he could read her mind. "At least there we could be alone."

"I don't think so." Ariel's prediction still nagged at Caroline. "Every time we're alone together things just seem to get more complicated. I'm not even sure it's a good idea for people to see us talking to each other."

With effort, she resisted the temptation to look over her shoulder to see who might be watching them.

"Don't you think that's carrying paranoia a little too far?"

"Duke, you're the one who told me how important it was for Kimi to be accepted in this town," Caroline argued.

"Do you really think it's going to help her any if the two of us become the hottest topic of conversation around?"

Duke stiffened and stepped closer. His voice was low and hard with anger. "I let rumor and innuendo run me out of this town once. It's not going to happen again."

"Maybe not, but this time, there's more than you and me to think of. There's a child involved here, and no matter how happy and well-adjusted Kimi may be, she's still vulnerable, Duke, and you know it."

"Nobody's going to hurt my child." His eyes were the threatening charcoal hue of thunderclouds.

"Then think about what you're doing. Just back off and think about it."

With that, Caroline turned and before Duke could stop her, she was gone. Her heels clicked across the flagstone floor of the foyer until she reached the carpeted family room. From there she sought out the first familiar face she saw, which was Hilary standing alone by the Christmas tree. "Well, the party certainly seems to be a success," she said, sounding only a little breathless.

"I just hope they eat all the food," Hilary answered. "I've been cooking for two days and it's very important to me that they eat the food."

When confronted by the playfully wild gleam of determination that lit Hilary's eyes, Caroline began to forget her own distress. "Well," she said with subdued but genuine laughter, "if you just look at them like that and tell them so, I don't think there'll be any problems."

"Good," Hilary answered, still glaring like a Kewpie doll possessed. "I've been practicing this look since noon."

"You're not encouraging my wife to do outrageous things, are you?" Joey asked, edging his way between them. He handed a fresh glass of wine to Hilary, whose expression smoothly changed from maniacal to wide-eyed innocence.

"Oh, no, sweetheart," she cooed. "Caroline would never do that."

Clearly charmed by his wife, Joey turned to Caroline with a proud grin. "She's such a goof. I never know what she's going to do next."

Hilary batted her eyelashes coquettishly and smiled, and Caroline knew that the irreverent Mason clan had found a kindred spirit in Hilary.

"Well," Caroline said, taking a reluctant step away, "I guess I'd better let you two get back to being host and hostess."

Joey shook his head and caught her arm, detaining her. "We only get serious about that if you have a house to buy or sell, and if you don't already have a Realtor."

"You mean the real reason for this party is to make business contacts?"

"Sure. You buy a big house so you can entertain prospective clients so you can make more sales so you can afford the payments on the big house you bought."

"Chilling, isn't it?" Hilary asked, still smiling as she waved to someone behind Caroline. "And Ariel did the decorating, so every time someone compliments me on the decor, I recommend her if they're looking for a decorator."

"Is that why Duke asked her to help him?"

Joey grinned. "Exactly. I love my little sister."

"And she really is a good decorator," Hilary said, growing serious. "Ariel really works to give you a home you enjoy living in."

"Well, I'm glad to hear that," Duke said, filling the void on the other side of Caroline as if it had been created for him.

"Hey, buddy." Joey reached across Caroline with enthusiasm and pumped Duke's hand. "Glad you could make it. How was your trip?"

"Mercifully brief. You're going to have to give me some pointers on party giving, Hilary. This one seems to be a smash."

Caroline tried to edge away and Duke's hand caught her elbow, discreetly holding her in place.

"Why, thank you," Hilary said. "Did you have any trouble finding Caroline earlier?"

"None at all. I'm just having trouble getting her to hold still once I find her."

Anger and embarrassment clashed inside Caroline and left her wanting to sink into the carpet and beat Duke over the head at the same time. She settled for glaring at him in silent fury.

"Some things never change, I guess," Joey said jovially.

Caroline turned her furious gaze to him, ignoring the avid curiosity on Hilary's face.

"Is there any place in this big, beautiful house where two people could go for a quiet conversation?" Duke asked, tightening his hold on Caroline while he looked from Joey to Hilary.

"Over my dead body," Caroline said between clenched teeth. She flashed Duke a look hot enough to melt the polar ice cap, jerked her arm free and whirled around.

Wasting no time in her getaway, she had made it halfway to the dining room when a man stepped into her path. Dressed in a conservative dark suit, he extended a freckled hand with broad, muscular fingers.

"Excuse me, but you're Caroline Adams, aren't you?" he asked in the kind of clear, lyrical voice that was made for the radio.

Caroline stared at the hand that grasped hers and tried to remember where she had heard that voice before. Curiosity overcoming her anger, she moved her gaze slowly up the long-limbed body in front of her to a friendly apple-cheeked face. It was topped by pale hair that was heavily streaked with the silver grey of time.

"I'm the Reverend O'Malley, Bill O'Malley to my friends."

His blue eyes twinkled with warmth and happiness, and Caroline felt herself instantly drawn to him. Putting some enthusiasm into her handshake, Caroline said, "Why, Reverend, hello. We were never introduced, but I remember you."

She knew now why she hadn't recognized him. He had conducted the service at her grandfather's funeral, and she remembered how moved she had been, not just by his words but by the deep sadness that he seemed to feel personally. Tonight, with a smile on his face, he almost looked like a different man.

"Well, I'm glad to hear that." The twinkle in his eyes dimmed slightly, as if he, too, was remembering their first acquaintance, and he dipped his head toward hers. "I really didn't come here to drum up business, but I've been looking forward to seeing you in church ever since I heard you had moved back. Maybe you'll be able to make it this Sunday. The children are going to entertain us with a special Christmas program they've been working very hard on."

"I'm afraid that I got out of the habit of church while I was living in Chicago. And I've just been so busy getting settled in again. But Gran's already told me I'll be there this Sunday no matter what."

The Reverend O'Malley gazed down at Caroline, and she could see the sadness again clearly, even through his bright smile.

"You have her eyes, don't you? I've always thought your grandmother had such beautiful eyes."

Caroline returned his smile, feeling complimented. She had never been comfortable when conversations touched on the way she looked. She had her grandmother's lavender eyes, her mother's pale cream complexion and the only blond hair anywhere in the family. The only thing she knew about her father was that he was almost surely a blonde.

"Are you enjoying yourself this evening?" she asked, changing the topic before the conversation could become uncomfortable.

"Very much, although I usually don't go to parties like this, and I never stay long when I do."

Intrigued, Caroline gazed into the blue eyes that seemed to reflect his every emotion. "Why not?"

"A man in my position has to be careful not to appear too human, and walking a tightrope in public can get very tiring. Besides, having me around makes other people nervous. They're afraid to have too much fun in front of me."

"That must be very lonely at times."

He tilted his head thoughtfully. "At times. But I have a wonderful wife to keep me company." Lifting his gaze, he searched the area. "She must still be in the dining room exchanging recipes."

"I was headed in that direction myself."

"Then perhaps we could go together."

Caroline smiled. "I'd like that."

As they walked side by side to the dining room, she found herself liking her companion more than their few minutes of conversation warranted. The longer she was around him, the more positive she was that, like herself, the good reverend had a secret pain buried deep within him. She wondered what this could be.

"Ah, there's my beautiful wife," he said with sudden feeling.

The words caught Caroline's wandering attention and she looked up to see a plump woman with salt-and-pepper hair wending her way toward them through the crowd. A bright smile lit the woman's face, and she stretched out her hands as she neared them.

"Bill."

The Reverend O'Malley reached out to take her hands and guide her under the mistletoe that hung from garlands overhead. He kissed her tenderly, then turned with a smile to Caroline, and through the smile, Caroline realized that even when he was happy, the sadness never really left him. Knowing that, she liked him even more.

"Patsy, my dear," he said proudly, "I have finally made the official acquaintance of Miss Caroline Adams. Caroline, I would like you to meet my wife, Patsy O'Malley."

Mrs. O'Malley's whole face seemed to glow as she looked from Caroline to her husband and back to Caroline. "Why, hello, dear, it's such a pleasure to meet you. I've heard so much about you over the years. Your grandfather certainly was proud of you, and I know your grandmother's just thrilled to have you back home."

"Well, thank you. And it's nice meeting you." She would have said more, but tears were welling inside her at the mention of her grandfather. This had been an evening of drastic ups and downs and her fragile emotions had taken a beating.

"I hope you'll come to dinner some time soon." Mrs. O'Malley glanced up at her husband and laid her hand on his arm. "Bill and I don't have any children of our own, and we like to have young people around. It keeps us from getting too set in our ways."

"Thank you," Caroline said in a voice that was openly unsteady. "I'd like that."

The kindness of the reverend and his wife only seemed to make her more emotional, and for one panic-stricken moment Caroline envisioned herself breaking down totally right in the middle of Hilary's carefully orchestrated party.

"Are you all right, dear?" Mrs. O'Malley asked. "Did I say something?"

Caroline shook her head yes then no. "I'm fine." She blinked back the tears she could feel wetting her lashes. "I think I probably need to check my makeup, though. Do you know where a powder room is?"

Mrs. O'Malley's hands touched Caroline's lightly and then retreated. "There's one between the kitchen and sun room. And I'm sorry, dear, I just wasn't thinking."

"It's nothing, really," Caroline said in a voice that was choked with unshed tears. "This happens at the darnedest times. It just comes up out of nowhere."

The Reverend O'Malley took his handkerchief out of his pocket and tucked it into Caroline's hand. "If you ever need anything, Caroline, even if it's just someone to talk to... I want you to think of me as a friend, because that's how I've come to think of you in just the short time I've known you."

Caroline felt the tears break free, and the emotions she had struggled to control came pouring out. "Thank you," she blurted, and ran for the bathroom.

Once there, she leaned her back against the door and sobbed heartbroken into the handkerchief, catching the tears at the corners of her eyes. She had never known her grandfather was proud of her. She had never known he talked about her to other people. She had never even been sure he really loved her.

He had been a hard man to live with and a hard man to love. But he was the only father she had ever known and without him, she felt lost and alone and sad, so incredibly sad for all the things that could have been different.

A hard knock on the other side of the door cut Caroline's heaving sobs to an uncertain hiccup.

"Caroline, are you in there?" Ariel called through the door.

Caroline turned the knob and stepped in front of the sink, opening the door enough for Ariel to enter.

"Thank goodness for waterproof mascara," Caroline said, turning her head from side to side to examine the damage of her brief emotional storm.

"Are you all right?" Ariel demanded.

"How did you know I was in here?"

"Duke told me. He was worried about you."

Defeated, Caroline sagged against the sink. "Oh, no." There was nothing she could do to get away from him.

"You two can play games if you want, but, Caroline, he still cares about you. And I know you still care about him."

"Please, Ariel, not now."

"When?"

"I don't know. I just know that right now I can't handle any more."

"Aw, gee, Caroline, I'm sorry." Ariel laid a consoling hand on Caroline's shoulder. "You're handling everything so well that sometimes I forget it's only been a few months."

Caroline shrugged. "Life goes on."

"Speaking of life, do you think you're ready to go back outside and face it? There were a couple of desperate-looking women waiting in the sun room when I came through."

"How do I look?" Worried, Caroline leaned toward the mirror, looking for smudges and not finding any. She stepped back and turned sideways, checking her dress.

"You look great. You always look great. Where'd you get that, anyway? It's gorgeous."

"Do you really think so?" Caroline looked at her reflection again, remembering how she had seen the dress in a store window and fallen in love with it. "I got it at that antique clothes store downtown."

The cream-colored material was a whisper-soft cotton covered with an overdress of ivory lace. The chemise bodice ended in a drop waist below the hip, and the skirt had a knee-length handkerchief hem. The square collar and long sleeves were lace.

"Really?" Ariel reached out and rubbed the cloth of the skirt between her fingers. "I wish I could look like that," she said wistfully. "But if I tried it, one of the kids would probably throw up on me."

Caroline laughed. "Ariel, you always make me feel better."

Ariel put her hand on the doorknob. "You ready?"

"Ready."

Her head high, Caroline smiled at the two ladies who were waiting just outside the door to the powder room.

"Did it cost much?" Ariel asked, exiting behind her.

"An arm and a leg."

"Oh, that's wonderful, Caroline," Ariel crowed with glee. "You always know how to make me feel better, too."

"That's what friends are for."

Caroline rounded the corner of the kitchen island and came to a halt in midlaugh. Leaning against the refrigerator with his arms crossed and a look of patient determination on his face was Duke.

Ariel kept going and Caroline reached out to grab her arm. "Wait," she whispered.

"Caroline, it's obvious that he wants to talk to you about something, and he's not going to give up." Ariel's voice was low and her back was to Duke. "Trying to avoid him is only going to make it worse. Just deal with him and get it over with." With that, Ariel turned on her heel and left.

Her heart pounding, Caroline put a hand on the kitchen island to steady herself and looked uncertainly at Duke.

He smiled. "The only private room they had to offer was their bedroom. I thought maybe I'd better reject it."

"Good thinking," she said quietly.

"This reminds me of old times."

Caroline glanced nervously at the door to the dining room. "This is going to look so obvious to anyone who comes through here."

"Ariel told me what she said to you. Is that why you're afraid to be in the same room with me now?" He frowned and shifted his weight, but didn't come any nearer. "There was a time when you weren't afraid of the gossip. What happened?"

Caroline didn't know what to say. That she had grown older? That pain had made her a coward? That everything she had said earlier was just so much bull and it wasn't really the gossip she was afraid of, it was him?

Without answering, Caroline shoved herself away from the island and bolted across the kitchen, heading for the breakfast nook and the French door that led to the patio. She didn't even know where she was going. She just needed to get away, to escape the hard knot of panic that was twisting tighter and tighter inside her.

In a few steps, Duke had caught up with her and swung her around to face him under the archway that separated the kitchen from the nook. His hands tightened on her arms, and he pulled her against him.

For an instant, Caroline saw only the desperate anger in his eyes. Then his lips slowly lowered to hers and his hands slid from her arms to her back. His mouth was warm and softly seeking. His arms gently drew her against him and there was no more fear.

Chapter Seven

"For tonight," Duke whispered when the kiss ended, "just for tonight, let's pretend we've never met before. I didn't know you when you were young. You don't work for me now."

Caroline looked into his dove-gray eyes that were so close to hers and contemplated the idea. She found it intriguing but flawed.

"I must be a terribly forward hussy," she said, tiptoeing cautiously into the mood, "to let you kiss me like this."

Duke shook his head and explained, "You've never been this way with any other man. You've never felt like this before. We saw each other across a crowded room and there were fireworks. You can't help yourself."

"But this is so unlike me. Won't people talk?"

"We're young. We're single." He adjusted his arms around her, pulling her still closer. "We don't worry about things like that."

Reality nudged her, but she chased it away. "Obviously, I don't have a grandmother."

"No, you don't," he agreed quickly. "You have an aunt. She's a very understanding person. She's been divorced herself, and she's dating again now."

Caroline almost laughed. She was beginning to think this might work. "And you? How about your life?"

"I'm an accountant. My parents live in a neighboring town. And I'm a little shy around women, but I think you might be able to bring me out of that."

"Hmm." She leaned back in his arms and gazed at him with speculation. "Duke's sort of an unexpected name for an accountant, isn't it?"

"It's just a childhood nickname, actually," he explained in all seriousness. "My real name's Daniel, or Dan. But I still like to use Duke because it gives me a certain distinction among the guys at the office."

Even fantasy had to have ground rules and Caroline decided it was time to establish hers.

"Well, now," she began carefully, "you do realize, Duke, that despite the powerful and undeniable attraction I feel for you, we're still going to have to take this kind of slow. Because I'm a nice girl from a good family, and I'm already a little shocked by the fact that I'm kissing a man I barely know in the breakfast nook of a friend's home."

Reluctantly, Duke loosened his hold and took a step back. "I believe some dancing has broken out on the deck off the family room. If we did a little of that, I could keep my arms around you without shocking you."

"I think that would be lovely."

He took her hand in his and led her out of the kitchen, through the dining room and into the family room. Walking beside him with their entwined hands held discreetly at their sides, Caroline felt as though she really was living a fantasy, although she was a little confused about which century it was set in.

The sad reality was that with Duke, she had always had to hide. Even now, she found it difficult to walk through a crowd with him, especially holding his hand. If he had had his arm around her waist, she didn't think she could have done it.

The French doors were open and he guided her through them and onto the deck. The night air cooled her flushed cheeks as Duke slid his arms around her and held her close for a slow dance.

"I can hear your heart beating," he said in her ear.

"I'm terrified."

"Then you must be slipping out of character, because there's nothing to be frightened of." His voice was a soothing caress. "It's just a dance. Everyone's doing it. Look around."

Caroline lifted her head from its hiding place on his shoulder and gazed cautiously behind her. There were at least a dozen couples scattered over the large deck, all clasped in each other's arms, swaying sensuously to the slow beat of a love song. No one seemed to be paying any attention to them.

"It's certainly a beautiful night, isn't it?" Duke asked.

She looked up at him, mildly surprised at the remark until she realized she was with Duke the accountant.

"Yes, it certainly is," she agreed, trying mightily to relax and enjoy their time together as an ordinary couple.

His hands slid over her back, pulling her gently nearer. One hand casually found its way down her side to her hip and the seam of her dropped waist. "I like this dress. It's so soft and kind of old-fashioned."

"It's an antique."

"Really?" He drew his head back and stared down at her. "Like a chair?"

Smiling, she said, "Well, I'm sure it's not really *that* old, but it is old. Somebody probably found it in a trunk when they were cleaning out their grandmother's attic."

She liked the romance of the idea. It felt comfortable and it helped to take her mind off of his hand, which still lingered possessively on her hip.

"Not anyone's grandmother we know, is it?"

"Not us." Caroline gave her head a quick, emphatic shake. "I personally don't have a grandmother. I have an aunt, though. You'd probably like her."

"Is she the understanding kind?"

"Oh, very."

"I'm sure I'd like her a lot." His wayward hand moved up to the middle of her back and held her just a little closer to him. "To get back to that dress, though, it has a sort of classic, romantic quality. Very beautiful. Just like the woman who's wearing it."

The compliment caught Caroline by surprise and she stopped dancing.

"Have I mentioned your hair?" He left one arm around her waist to hold her tightly against him while the fingers of his other hand slipped through her hair. "You have the most wonderful hair. It's so soft."

He lifted his hand, bringing her hair with it, letting the strands slowly sift through his fingers. "Look how it catches the moonlight, like holding stardust in my hand."

"Duke."

Caroline was having trouble standing still. The eyes that were gazing down at her were not the eyes of a new acquaintance. And what she saw in those eyes left her trembling with emotions that were too strong for the character she was supposed to be.

"You're the most beautiful thing I've ever seen in my life." Intensity vibrated in his voice.

"Duke," she pleaded, fighting to keep from backing away. She wanted to hear what he was saying, but she was afraid to. This wasn't the time. Not now, not in front of all these people.

"And your eyes." The passion in his voice had lessened. "They're the most amazing color." He leaned closer and peered intently into her eyes. "Are those contacts?"

Grateful for the relief, Caroline burst out laughing as the absurdity of their game struck home. "Oh, Duke," she said between laughs, "thank you."

He smiled sheepishly. "I was getting a little too serious there for a minute."

"No." She shook her head and calmed down to a chuckle. "We've just known each other too long and too well to pretend we haven't. There are too many undercurrents."

His arms tightened around her again. "I kind of like those undercurrents."

"Well," Caroline hedged, not willing to admit that she felt the same way. "They at least add spice. But they confuse the issue, too."

"And which issue is that, exactly?" The look in his eyes issued a challenge.

"Umm, well," she said, stalling, growing careful. One word too many and she could never take it back, and she wasn't ready for that to happen. "I think it's pretty obvious that there *is* an attraction...."

"Between us," Duke clarified when she appeared to be hesitating again.

"Yes. But I don't think we're either one sure if that attraction is real or just nostalgia."

"I think I'm pretty sure," he contradicted gently.

"Well, I don't know how you can be," she answered sharply and then caught herself.

She didn't want to argue. She didn't even want to have this discussion, but she couldn't afford to let him think she agreed with him, either. "It's been so many years since we first knew each other that we're practically strangers now."

"Caroline..." His voice held the unmistakable sound of patience wearing thin. "We couldn't think of each other as strangers if we wanted to."

"All I know," she said firmly, "is that whatever this is between us, it's moving too fast. And I don't like it."

"That's how it happened the first time, Caroline. That's how it is with us."

His voice was still gentle, but that didn't help. He made everything sound too easy, and it wasn't. If there was one thing Caroline was positive of, it was that nothing between the two of them was easy.

"I'm sorry. I just don't think I can do it. Not again." Her words were quiet, but the emotions inside her were anything but.

She pulled free of his restraining arms and started to walk away, but Duke recovered from his surprise before she could go two steps. Catching her just above the elbow, he swung her back around to face him.

"I waited thirteen years to find you again and I'm not letting you go that easily."

With a passion that made him reckless, he pulled her into his arms again. His fingers spread through her soft hair while his hand cupped the back of her head. His other arm tightening around her waist, he lifted her hard against him, and this time when his lips claimed hers, it was with the burning thirst of a desert wanderer.

Past and present fused, searing them both with the heat of a Sahara wind, and Caroline surrendered finally to the fire that had burned nonstop between them since the night they first met.

Overwhelmed by the desires he set loose in her, she clung to him. Reveling in the feel of his body hard against hers, she felt safe at last in the strong arms that held her.

Slowly, reluctantly, Duke drew his lips from hers and whispered, "Caroline, I'm sorry. But I just can't help the way I feel about you."

Still breathless from their long embrace, Caroline gazed up at him with her heart in her eyes. Adrift in the powerful currents that swirled between them, she was ready to concede. "Duke, I—"

The spontaneous applause that rose up around them startled her into silence. Caroline turned toward the sound and felt her shock become horror when she saw that the couples all around them were watching. Their faces wreathed in smiles, Ariel and Tank, Hilary and Joey, had joined an assortment of strangers and acquaintances on the deck to applaud the embrace Caroline and Duke had just shared.

Almost faint with dread at becoming the evening's prime entertainment, Caroline closed her eyes in self-defense. But instead of escape, she found the dark, rain-slick streets of her nightmares, filled with whispers and stares and pointing fingers. Frightened, she opened her eyes again only to encounter the same laughing onlookers, with their watchful eyes and clapping hands. To her, they all looked the same.

"Oh, God," she moaned in a voice so soft only Duke could hear her.

Desperate to get away, she twisted against his hold and almost broke free, but he tightened his grip and managed to stop her.

"Caroline," Duke whispered, trying urgently to calm her.

"No."

The word was nothing more than a cat hiss driven by fear, and the harder he struggled to pull Caroline back into his arms, the higher her terror built. Trying not to hurt her, Duke relented for an instant, and it was all the time she needed to twist away from him and escape down the steps that led into the dark yard and freedom.

Disoriented, Caroline ran straight ahead into the garden. Duke's heavy tread on the steps behind her only made her run faster down a path bordered by hay-strewn flower beds.

A graveled lane led from the back of the garden to a stand of tall pines, where pine needles covered the footpath and long shafts of moonlight shone through the darkness to illuminate the way. The needles quickly became slick underfoot, and the moonlight was too sparse for speed, forcing Caroline to slow her pace.

Eventually, the pounding rhythm of her heart began to ease, and in a calmer mood, she realized she shouldn't have run away. She had known it even when she was doing it, but the instinct had been too deep and she couldn't stop herself.

Instead, she should have smiled and laughed the whole thing off, but it was too late to change what had been done. She would have to find a way to face them all again, one by one, and ease the waking nightmare that she seemed to be caught in.

A cold, wet breeze led her to where the pines nestled the banks of a secluded cove. Moonlight glittered on the ruffled surface of the water, and Caroline smiled, unable to resist the memory of another night so much like this one when moonlight and its own special madness had led her into Duke's arms for the first time.

The steady lapping of the waves against the rocky shore had lent a sensual magic to that night, as well. She had been so sure of herself, so unafraid. All she had cared about was that she loved Duke. She had wanted him no matter what the price, and she had been paying that price ever since.

The snap of a twig and the rustle of leaves brought her out of her reverie. Knowing that it was Duke behind her, she turned and found him standing in the shadow of the pines.

"Are you all right?" he asked softly.

"Embarrassed, but all right."

He walked out of the shadows. "Do you hate me?"

"No," she said, surprised. "I did it to myself. I shouldn't have run. They were just kidding, and I..." She stuttered, hating to say it. "I made a big deal out of it. Now I have to live with it."

"Ariel feels terrible. She's afraid she caused it."

Caroline couldn't help laughing, just a little. "She probably did. It sounds just like her."

Duke shook his head, and Caroline wondered if she looked as hurt as he did.

"I caused it," he said solemnly. "I shouldn't have kissed you like that. Not there. Not in front of everybody."

"Don't apologize too profusely. It *was* nice, until I realized we had become the evening's entertainment."

He almost smiled. "I'm glad to hear you say that. But I did a lot of thinking while I was following you through the woods, and you're right. We're not kids anymore and there's a lot more at stake here than our own needs. So I'm going to do what you asked. I'm going to back off for a while to give us time to sort out our feelings. And to give the town a chance to find something else to talk about."

"Are you serious?" She had expected to be happy, but she wasn't. In fact, the thought scared her terribly.

"Yes." He looked sad but determined. "I'm just sorry it took me so long to get the message. I'm especially sorry for the pain I caused you tonight."

"Duke..."

"Umm, am I interrupting something?" Ariel asked, emerging from the pines. "I just couldn't stand it any longer. I had to see if Caroline was all right."

"I'm through." Duke looked from Caroline to Ariel. "I'll leave you two alone." With that, he disappeared into the shadows again.

Ariel looked at Caroline with a puzzled expression and together they listened in silence to the diminishing sounds of Duke's exit. Shock numbed the impact of his departure for Caroline, and she dreaded the moment when the shock wore off.

When there was nothing left to hear, Ariel asked just above a whisper, "What happened? Did I do that?"

"What happened is..." Caroline started to say, and then stopped while a thump of pain joined her heartbeat and an aching lump rose in her throat. "What happened is, I think I just got dumped."

Caroline stared at the food on her plate, her fork poised at the edge of a boiled potato, while her stomach churned with first happiness and then despair.

It was madness to be feeling the way she was feeling, but she couldn't stop it. Whenever she thought of the way Duke had held her while they danced and then of the kiss that had followed, a thrill of joy went through her and she wanted to hug those memories to her and forget everything else.

But then she would remember his parting words and she would feel like Scarlett O'Hara at the end of *Gone With the Wind.* Duke had finally given her what she said she wanted, and she was miserable. It wasn't what she wanted at all, and she didn't know what to do about it. She didn't even know if she *should* do anything about it.

Everything was happening too fast.

"Are you all right, dear?" Viola asked. "You're not eating."

The words pulled her back to reality and Caroline looked up from her plate to smile at her grandmother. "Oh, sure. I'm fine. I guess maybe I'm a little tired still."

"I guess that must have been quite a party last night. You know, Caroline, sometimes I wonder if I should have let you come back here. I didn't really stop to think how difficult it might be for you to make so many changes in your life all at once."

Caroline's eyes narrowed in suspicion. "It's a little too late to worry about that now, Gran."

Viola nodded. "I suppose."

"Why are you having second thoughts now?"

"Well, I didn't want to say anything, but I thought I heard you tossing in your sleep last night. I try not to worry, dear, but I've heard you tossing in your sleep several nights this week, and . . . Caroline, you're not . . ."

Caroline braced herself against the edge of the table. "Gran, I don't want to..."

"Are you having those nightmares again?" Viola asked.

"...talk about this," Caroline finished lamely.

"Oh, dear. You are, aren't you?"

"They're not bad. They'll go away once things settle down."

"It's that job." A bitter edge crept into Viola's voice. "Why do you insist on being around a man who gives you nightmares? He's already ruined your life once. Are you going to let him do it again?"

"Duke," Caroline said clearly as she neatly folded her napkin and put it on the table, "isn't the one who ruined my life. Duke isn't the one who sent me away. Besides, I'm only thirty. My life isn't exactly over yet."

"Well, it might interest you to know that I've been getting phone calls all morning long. You seem to have made yourself the talk of the town once again."

Her appetite gone and her morning damaged, if not ruined, Caroline shoved back her chair and rose to her feet. For a minute, she stood there next to the table with her fists clenched, staring down at her grandmother.

She wanted to storm from the room, to throw something, to shout. She wanted to do anything that would dispel the torrent of anger inside her. Instead, she just stood there, closed her eyes and took a deep breath.

"This is a very old argument," Caroline said finally. "We don't agree where Duke is concerned. We never have, and maybe we never will. But I am not a child anymore, and I'll make my own decisions."

"I didn't mean to make you angry." The righteous anger was gone from Viola's eyes and tears glittered in its place. Her voice warbled plaintively, making her sound very old. "We just did what we thought was best."

The band of anger around Caroline's chest tightened. "I know you did." For many years, she had secretly won-

dered if her grandparents had also done what they thought
was best when her mother had become pregnant.

She longed to ask if they had just been doing what they
thought was best when they sent her mother to stay with an
aunt in Denver until Caroline was born. Had her grandfather used the same threat with her mother that he had used
with Caroline, forcing her to choose between her own happiness and the freedom of the man she loved? Or had her
father gone away on his own?

Sadness slowly invaded Caroline's anger. The same sadness had been there all her life whenever she stopped to
wonder why she didn't have a father, and with the sadness
came guilt and shame. She had done something wrong, or
he would have been there. If she had been good enough, her
father wouldn't have gone away.

"We did the best we could," Viola said, sounding injured. "It wasn't easy without any help from your mother."

The logical side of Caroline took over. It was the side of
her that remembered what she had read in the psychology
books, the side that knew the child always feels guilty, the
side that refused to be manipulated any longer.

"I'm sure Mother had her reasons for the way she acted.
And I'm sure she has as many regrets as we do for the way
things were."

"Well, maybe you can ask her about it this weekend."

Caroline forgot everything else and stared at her grandmother with shock. "What do you mean?"

"She should be arriving anytime now," Viola said, as if
it were an everyday event.

"Mother's coming here? Why didn't you tell me?"

"As usual, Marion didn't bother to call until last night."

"You had all this morning." The very small ripple of
happiness that Caroline felt did nothing to lessen the rising
anxiety in her.

"Don't be cross, Caroline, please." Viola's tears threatened to return. "This weekend's going to be difficult
enough without you being cross with me."

"How long's she staying?"

"She didn't say."

Caroline took a deep breath and tried to steady her nerves. She had never understood why people took tranquilizers, but right now, she would have given anything for something to quiet the trembling that had started in her legs and was working its way up.

"Are you all right, dear?"

In disbelief Caroline stared at the genuine concern in her grandmother's eyes. "No," she said.

She didn't have the energy to lie, and if her grandmother didn't like the sound of the truth, that wasn't Caroline's problem, not today.

"Is there anything I could do?"

Caroline took another deep breath, focusing on nothing, and began to feel herself calm down. She exhaled slowly, still staring into space and said, "A one-way ticket back to Chicago is about the only thing I can think of that might take care of everything."

"Oh, no, Caroline, what would I do without you?"

She felt a twinge of satisfaction at the distress she heard in her grandmother's voice, and then instantly regretted her instinct for revenge. This was the Christmas season, the time for peace on Earth and good will toward men. It was the time to put aside old wrongs and find a way toward new beginnings.

"Relax, Gran. Leaving isn't the answer. It never has been. I think I'm going to go out on the front porch and get some fresh air before Mother gets here."

She left the room focusing on a better attitude. By the time she reached the hallway, she was almost looking forward to her mother's arrival. They had never been much of a family. Maybe this Christmas things could be different.

Caroline pulled open the front door and almost shoved the screen door through the petite brunette who stood outside with her hand raised to knock. Good will, hope and any semblance of cheer disappeared, replaced by doubt, uncertainty and a wild, aching loneliness.

"Caroline?"

"Mother."

The room was dark and the narrow canopied bed was strangely comforting. Caroline lay on her back with her arms folded under her head and stared at the barely visible pink-and-white checks overhead. The faint sound of singing was in the air, a simple, familiar Christmas carol piping from a radio somewhere in the neighborhood, through an open window and into the night.

Dinner had been an ordeal, and she had escaped to the peace of her room as soon as the plates were cleared from the table. Caroline didn't know who she felt sorrier for, her mother or her grandmother. They both so obviously wanted to reach out to the other, and yet they didn't seem to know how.

A timid knock at her door disturbed the quiet and Caroline raised up on one elbow. "Yes?"

"Hello, Caroline. Do you mind..." Her mother opened the door and stood framed in the backlight from the hallway. "Goodness, it's dark in here."

"There's a light by the door."

Marion flipped the light switch and smiled in relief when the light came on. "There, that's better."

Caroline sat up and swung her legs over the side of the bed. "What can I do for you?"

"Well, I was just wondering if you had seen my high school yearbooks. I can't find them in my room." Her mother took a step nearer, her gaze focused on the bed as Caroline stood. "I can't believe you still have that bed. I thought you would have redecorated as soon as you moved back."

"I think the same thing every time I walk in here. I guess I just haven't had time yet." An uneasy ripple of happiness went through her. She couldn't remember the last time she and her mother had exchanged casual conversation.

"That used to be mine, you know."

"The bed?" Caroline was only half listening. The rest of her mind was occupied with wondering why her mother had decided to visit so unexpectedly.

"Yes. It had a beautiful, white lace canopy and a quilt that Grandmother Adams made. I used to think I was the luckiest little girl in the world. Mother never told you it was mine?"

"No."

"Aunt Sylvia told me she had one just like it when she was a little girl, but Grandma Adams was gone by then and no one knew if it was the same bed or not."

"I had no idea. I was planning to get rid of it."

Her mother shrugged. "Well, you can if you want, but it's sort of a family heirloom." She frowned and tilted her head to the side, listening. "What in the world is that?"

Caroline turned and heard a clear and robust rendition of "Silent Night" that seemed to be coming from the street outside their house. With each line, the sound grew stronger until she could hear the tramping of many feet on the front porch. In unison, she and her mother looked at each other and began to smile. "Carolers?" she asked, charmed by the distraction.

"Oh, Caroline," Marion said gleefully, "have you ever gone wassailing?"

"I can't say that I have."

The carolers were inside now, and their voices filled the house, rising up the staircase to draw Caroline and her mother down to greet them.

At the head of the staircase, Marion took Caroline's hand. "Let's go," her mother urged, looking like a schoolgirl all aglow with excitement. "We'll have fun. I promise we will."

Not knowing how to react to this new incarnation of her mother, Caroline hung back. "They haven't asked us."

"They will. The bigger the group the better when you're caroling. Anyone's welcome."

Still holding her hand, Marion drew Caroline down the stairs behind her. At the foot of the staircase, Viola was passing out hot cider to the happy group of singers.

"Caroline," Ariel called out, "we've come to get you."

"See?" Marion whispered in Caroline's ear.

Kimi Hutchison separated from the crowd and moved to the staircase, where Caroline stood poised on the bottom step.

"Hello, Caroline," the little girl said with a hesitant smile. "You'll go with us, won't you? It's a lot of fun."

"Hello, Kimi." Caroline left the staircase and leaned forward, automatically returning the smile. She touched the little girl's pink cheek and felt the coolness of her skin. "Is it very cold outside?"

"No," Kimi answered, shaking her head emphatically. "Daddy made me wear a scarf and gloves and all that stuff, but I had to take them off because I was getting too hot."

"So now Daddy's having to carry them."

Startled by Duke's voice at her shoulder, Caroline gasped and snapped upright.

"Didn't mean to scare you," Duke said.

A slow grin curved across his face as he stood just inches away, staring down at her. The wind had ruffled his dark hair and left strands dangling across his forehead. His gray eyes twinkled with humor.

"You didn't." Caroline felt her heart pounding harder the longer she gazed up at him.

"Just nervous today, huh?"

As if it answered everything, she asked, "You've never met my mother, have you?"

His brow quirked just slightly, and speculation intermingled with the fun that sparkled in his eyes. "No, I haven't."

Caroline turned slightly to include her mother who stood behind her on the staircase. "My mother, Marion Michaels. Mother, this is Daniel Hutchison, better known as Duke to his friends.''

"Mrs. Michaels." Duke extended his hand without hesitation. "A pleasure to meet you."

"Mr. Hutchison," Marion said, taking his hand cautiously.

"Call me Duke, please."

"Why thank you." She smiled and seemed to blossom. "I'd like it very much if you'd call me Marion."

"Marion it will be, then."

With growing discomfort, Caroline watched her mother change again from the daughter and mother she had been all day to a woman who was not yet fifty and who still had the charm and beauty to attract a much younger man.

The transformation was startling, but even more startling was the jealous resentment Caroline discovered in herself while she watched the mutual interest that sparked so clearly between Duke and her mother.

Impulsively needing to insert a wedge in that interest, she slipped her arm around Kimi's shoulders. "And this is Kimi Hutchison," Caroline said, including Kimi in their intimate circle. "Duke's daughter."

Just as Caroline had done earlier, Marion stepped down and leaned toward the little girl, reaching out to take her hand. "Hello, Kimi. It's nice to meet you. And how old are you, sweetheart?"

"I'll be eleven in two months," Kimi said proudly.

Marion's smile widened, and she leaned even closer. "I have a little girl who's twelve," she told her, speaking just to Kimi. "I'll bet you two would like each other. Maybe I can bring her with me sometime when I come to visit."

Caroline closed her eyes and set her jaw, fighting back the angry, hurtful monster her jealousy became at her mother's thoughtless words. With billowing pain, she slowly reopened her eyes and looked at the stranger who stood beside her, the stranger who was a loving wife and mother to her family in Kansas City, the stranger Caroline barely knew.

A hand touched her waist, penetrating the haze that had enveloped her and Caroline turned her head to find Ariel standing next to her. Her soulful brown eyes gazed into Caroline's lavender ones and projected a silent understanding and a sharing of pain that went beyond friendship.

Through all the lonely years of Caroline's childhood with a mother who was never there and grandparents whose protection was smothering, Ariel had been her friend, sister and family. She had been the lifeline in an empty sea, and she seemed to have an unerring instinct for when Caroline needed her most.

Thank you, Caroline mouthed silently. In answer, Ariel's hand gently patted her back.

"Hello, Mrs. Michaels," Ariel said. "I'm Ariel, Caroline's friend. I don't know if you remember me."

Abandoning her conversation with Kimi, Marion straightened and stared blankly at Ariel before she broke into a grin of recognition. "Of course, I do. You're the little redhead Caroline met in kindergarten. I remember the day she brought you home with her. You two were so cute together with all your whispering and giggling."

Caroline batted her eyes against the sudden sting of tears. As quickly as it had come, the angry jealousy was gone and a baffling need to cry had taken its place all because her mother had remembered a scene from her childhood that Caroline had forgotten.

Blinking to hold back the tears that wouldn't go away, Caroline raised her head and found Duke watching her with a frown of concern. She shrugged and tried to smile, aware that she must seem like an emotional basket case. Her life had changed so drastically since her grandfather's death and so many things had happened so fast that she had never taken the time to truly grieve.

Now her suppressed emotions seemed to be rising to the surface at the slightest provocation. Raw, uncontrollable and out of proportion to the cause, her pain had become an emotional firestorm with triggers that reached all the way back to her birth.

Again, the touch of a hand drew her back from her thoughts and Caroline looked down to see Kimi tucking her small hand into Caroline's.

"We're ready to go now." Her wide, innocent eyes were darker than brown and stared up at Caroline with gentle pleading. "Please say you'll go with us. It would be so much more fun with you."

Caroline looked into Kimi's eyes and saw her own motherless childhood looking back at her. She recognized the quiet, deep hunger for something that was missing, for the gentle, perfumed love that was a mother.

"Of course, sweetheart." She brushed Kimi's soft, pink cheek with her hand and, once again, found herself trying not to cry. "I'll go just for you."

"It's getting cold," Marion said. "I'm going to go on in."

Caroline nodded and lingered beside the car. On the back seat, bundled in a blanket, Kimi slept the sleep of childhood. The spot on Caroline's lap where Kimi's head had rested all the way home felt cold.

"She'll be all right," Duke said quietly, leaning near to keep his voice from carrying to the sleeping child. "When we get home, I'll carry her inside and she'll never know she's been moved."

"She's such a wonderful little girl, Duke. You've done such a good job with her."

"She's been my life. Everything I've done has been for her."

"She really seemed to have fun tonight."

"So did you."

Caroline laughed, remembering the hours spent walking and singing, the hot chocolate and cider to soothe the tired throats, the joking and laughter.

"Yes, I did," she agreed. "I had a lot of fun."

She looked at Duke, standing beside her and smiling down at her in the moonlight. Moonlight always seemed to become magical when she was with him, and tonight was no exception.

"Look, I've been thinking..." Duke said hesitantly. "About what I said last night—"

Caroline held up her hand to stop him. "Before you say anything else, maybe I should tell you. My grandmother was getting phone calls all morning about last night."

"Damn." He glared at the sky and balled his hand into a fist for emphasis. "Damn."

She knew how he felt. Anger, frustration and the interference of others had haunted them since the day they had met. "Life isn't always very fair, is it?" she asked quietly.

"No, it's not."

Almost involuntarily, Caroline glanced at the sleeping child in the car, the little girl who was Duke's life. Following her gaze, he slipped his hand into Caroline's.

"Come on," he said, stroking the back of her hand with his thumb, "I'll walk you to your door."

They walked slowly, hand in hand, cherishing the quiet of the night and the darkness that gave them respite from the watchful eyes of the world.

On the porch, he took her other hand in his and stood looking down at her with great reluctance. "I've got to go. If she wakes up and I'm not there, she'll be scared."

Caroline nodded her understanding, so close to tears, she was almost afraid to talk. Even more than she had the night before, she felt that tonight was really goodbye. She'd see him at the office, but it wouldn't be the same. For them, Cupid's arrow always seemed to miss.

His hands slid to her wrists, then up her arms, and he slowly drew her toward him. "Just one last time," he whispered. "For old times' sake."

Gathering her against him gently, Duke lowered his lips to hers for a lingering, sadly tender kiss that was filled with deep, slow-burning passion and a love that was stronger than heartbreak.

"Someday, sweetheart," he said as he lifted his head and stepped away, "there'll be a time for us."

With that, he left, wasting no time in his exit. Caroline stood on the porch and watched his swiftly retreating back, held ramrod straight all the way to the car. If he looked back before he drove away, she didn't see it, and if he knew she was crying, he didn't show it.

Chapter Eight

"It was scandalous," Viola said angrily as soon as she and Caroline entered the back door to find Marion in the kitchen. "Absolutely scandalous, Marion. I don't know what's gotten into you."

Caroline had been aware of her grandmother's silent fury all the way home from church. What had started as displeasure earlier in the morning had grown to outrage, and she winced in sympathy for her mother, who abruptly turned and would have marched from the kitchen if Viola hadn't blocked her path.

"Well?" Viola demanded. "I want an explanation."

"For what?" Marion asked. Without raising her voice, she stood her ground.

Caroline could feel the anger quivering between the two women, one resentful and rebellious, the other righteous and indignant. Without any effort, she envisioned the battles that must have once been waged.

"For what?" Viola spat out. "For embarrassing this entire family, that's for what. Don't think people didn't notice, and don't think they won't talk. And what am I going to tell them? That somewhere along the line, I just failed with you? That no matter what I do, you somehow find a way to disgrace this family."

"I know this is a small town, Mother, but surely people have better things to talk about than whether or not I was in church this morning," Marion said, her voice barely more than an icy hiss.

Her indignation unabated, Viola answered bitterly, "I begged you to come with us, but no, you're too good for that. Ever since you snubbed the minister at your father's funeral and then ignored everyone else, people have been talking, and I don't know what to tell them. The least you could have done was just show up and pretend that we're a family. It's Christmas Eve, Marion. Can't you ever think of anybody but yourself?"

Marion's whole body went stiff with fury. "All I ever wanted to do was to get out of this town," she said with her voice finally rising as her reserve broke. "I don't know why I even bothered to come back." In tears, she pushed past her mother and stalked out of the room.

"I didn't raise you in a barn, Marion," Viola shouted after her. "The least you could do is act like you have some manners. And I've got the minister coming over here this afternoon to talk to you!"

On the last word, her voice broke, and Viola, too, turned in tears and fled toward her downstairs bedroom. Shaken, Caroline stood in the kitchen and waited for the angry echoes to leave the air. She had been looking forward to lunch when they left the church, but now her appetite was gone.

She didn't know whether to go to her own room or leave the house for a while, until her mother and grandmother had a chance to calm down and forget their bitter words. She had seen enough of their arguments in the past to know that in an hour's time, she would be the only one who was still upset by what had happened.

The chiming of the doorbell settled her quandary, and Caroline left the kitchen to answer the bell. When she opened the front door to find the Reverend O'Malley standing there, she couldn't help thinking that for a Christmas Eve, the day wasn't showing much promise of peace on Earth, at least on this corner of the earth.

"Reverend O'Malley," she said, sounding more despairing than welcoming.

"Hello, Caroline. Your grandmother had asked me to stop by."

He smiled and stood waiting on the porch for an invitation inside.

"Oh, yes." Echoes of her grandmother's raised-in-a-barn remark rang in Caroline's ears while she hastened to unlock the screen and hold it open for him to enter. "Come in. Please."

"I hope this isn't an intrusion," he said softly, once inside the foyer. "But I couldn't help noticing that your grandmother seemed a little upset after church. I'm not really sure that your mother will even want to talk to me, but I thought it was best that I at least stop by and see how everyone is doing."

He paused and looked at Caroline as if waiting for an answer. She looked back at him, not quite certain what to say.

Sensing her uncertainty, he asked, "Have I come at a bad time?" He peered around. "It seems quiet enough. Maybe too quiet?"

Caroline sighed and decided that in his line of work, he must have seen more than one domestic battle. "They've gone to their respective corners."

"Ah." He nodded with understanding. "I suspected as much. Well..." He paused and frowned in thought, then finally said, "Well, a promise is a promise. Do you think your mother would see me?"

"I have no idea." She hated the thought of involving herself in the affair. So far, the battle had been between her mother and her grandmother, and Caroline had no desire to find herself in the middle.

"Do you think you could ask her?"

The question was gentle and filled with understanding, and it left her with no way out. "Of course," she said, giving in with a smile. "Would you like to wait in the parlor?"

Returning her smile, he shook his head. "I might as well stay where I am. I don't think I'll be here too much longer."

Grateful for the sense of humor he brought to a difficult situation, Caroline excused herself and climbed the staircase to the second floor. On the landing, she turned and found her mother standing at the other end of the hall, her hand on the balustrade at the back of the open stairwell.

When Caroline opened her mouth in surprise, Marion quickly lifted a silencing finger to her lips, then motioned Caroline toward her. Advancing slowly, Caroline mulled over the realization that her mother had been eavesdropping on the conversation below. As she reached her mother, Marion took her hand, pulled her into the guest room and shut the door.

"Who is that?" Marion asked in a loud whisper.

"The minister."

"My God, she was serious. Did he ask for me?"

Caroline looked closely and didn't see the anger she had expected. Instead, her mother seemed lively, almost flattered.

"He wants to talk to you, if you'll talk to him."

"Ooh, I don't know." Marion stepped back, her eyes narrowed in speculation, a half smile on her lips. Then she shook her head. "No. No, I can't." Her gaze was serious and determined when she touched Caroline's arm and said, "Tell him I'm sorry, but I just can't."

Marion turned and walked to the window. She stood there with her back to the room, staring out. She didn't say anything else, and eventually Caroline realized the conversation was over and left.

She had never understood her mother. Years ago, she had given up trying. "Flighty" was the description her grandmother used, but the word she had always thought of in connection with her mother was *dramatic* and her actions today certainly strengthened that view.

The reverend was waiting where Caroline had left him, just in front of the door. He raised his eyebrows in question as she neared, and she shook her head.

"I'm sorry. She said no."

He looked more disappointed than she had thought he would. "That's it? Just no?"

"Well, actually, she said to tell you she was sorry, but she just can't." The message seemed to satisfy him, though he looked sadder than he had a moment earlier, and Caroline found herself adding, "For just a minute, I thought she was going to agree. She looked like she really wanted to but was almost afraid to."

He nodded slowly and then smiled. "Well, we did our best. I guess your mother and grandmother are capable of working out their problems without our help."

"In all honesty, I don't understand half the arguments they have." Hesitating, she didn't know how to go on. Confiding wasn't something she'd had much practice in, but she found this man so easy to talk to, she found herself wanting to open up to him. "Things between the two of them are pretty...well...difficult." At a loss for words, she hesitated before going on. "I'm not sure how much you know about our family background."

He looked a little embarrassed. "Quite a bit, Caroline. Ministers hear a great deal over the years."

"Oh." His admission stunned her, and for all her desire to unburden herself, Caroline now found that she just couldn't.

Dealing with her own illegitimacy was difficult enough. Even worse was the knowledge that her mother's transgressions and Caroline's very existence had brought a shame to the family that couldn't be erased, but to know that everyone still talked about it after so many years was an unending humiliation she found hard to bear.

"I'm sorry, Caroline," Reverend O'Malley said gently. "I didn't mean to upset you. You, of all people, have no guilt. Whatever shame exists certainly doesn't belong to you."

"I'm afraid that's where you're wrong, Reverend," Caroline answered in a matter-of-fact voice that held no self-pity. "It *is* mine and there's nothing I can do about it."

He shook his head. "I can't accept that, but I won't try to convince you now. Tell me, is your mother going to be here long?"

"I don't know," she said. "I don't think so."

"I'm not surprised." For a second, he seemed lost in thought. Then he returned, focusing all his attention on her. "Caroline, when I told you that I wanted to be your friend, I was serious. You have a lot of pain that you're keeping hidden."

When she started to protest, he held up his hand to stop her and went on. "You hide it very well, but it's there and I can feel it." The blue eyes that seemed far too sad and knowing for a gentle country minister were trained on her. "I want us to talk about it sometime. Do you think we could do that?"

He seemed so sincere, and again Caroline felt the tug on her heart that this man so unreasonably aroused. In her whole life, she had never discussed her birth with anyone. That wasn't good, and she knew it. But knowing what she should do and being able to do it were two different things.

She would like to try, though, and if she was ever going to talk to anyone, she thought it might be this man, who saw so much so clearly, this man with the sorrowful eyes and the generous heart.

"I think we could do that," she agreed, feeling bold beyond measure for even considering it.

"Good," he said with a nod. "And, Caroline?"

"Yes?"

He grinned. "Call me Bill."

"Bill," she repeated, and smiled as she spoke.

Moving toward the door, he said, "Well, I'll be going now. I just wanted to make sure you were all right before I left."

Caroline held the door for him. As dismayed as she was at his arrival, she was even sorrier to see him go. "I wasn't when you got here, but I feel better now. Thank you."

"My pleasure." He ducked his head modestly. "Too often, children are trampled accidently in the arguments of adults. I know your grandmother and mother fight. And I don't want to see you trampled."

Mystified, Caroline laughed. "How do you know all this?"

He touched her hand lightly in parting. "I take the time to listen. And I care."

"Well, Bill, I think you're in the right profession." Moved by his concern, she felt tears forming, and for once, they weren't tears of sadness.

"Merry Christmas, Caroline."

"Merry Christmas, and thank you again."

She closed the door behind him and turned around, feeling much less alone. A small pang of hunger growled in the pit of her stomach and she wondered how long it would be before the others left their rooms.

"Caroline."

At the sound of the voice overhead, Caroline looked up to see her mother leaning over the upstairs railing.

"Is he gone?" Marion asked just loudly enough to be heard.

"Yes."

"Come up and talk to me." She motioned Caroline forward with her hand and then disappeared from view.

Torn between a desire to be alone and curiosity, Caroline climbed the stairs and went to her mother's room where

Marion stood staring at the street in front of the house through the chiffon window curtain.

Open on the bed were the old high school yearbooks Marion had been asking about. Caroline had retrieved them from her own room before church that morning.

"I knew him in high school," an animated Marion said, turning from the window. "He was a year ahead of me."

"Who?"

"Bill O'Malley. Did he say anything about me?"

Her mother's excitement was puzzling. Caroline tried not to frown as she answered. "Not really."

"Surely he said something." Drawing aside the curtain, Marion stared once more out the window while Caroline spoke to her back.

"He wanted to know if you would be here much longer, and I said I didn't think so."

Her mother turned around, looking disappointed. "That's all?"

"He wasn't here for very long."

"Hmm." As quickly as it had appeared, Marion's disappointment was gone, and she sat on the bed with the four yearbooks in a semicircle around her, the picture of thoughtfulness.

It was obvious to Caroline that there was a lot going on below the surface she didn't know anything about. Until this moment, it hadn't occurred to her that her mother might have been trying to avoid someone when she refused to go to church that morning.

Her curiosity piqued, she thought back over the events of the morning and the peculiar excitement that the minister's visit had stirred. Caroline emerged from her reverie with the uncomfortable suspicion that it had been Reverend O'Malley her mother had been avoiding that morning and that he knew it. Her thoughts once again on his visit to their home, she said, "He did seem rather disappointed that you wouldn't talk to him, but he never actually said it."

"Hmm," Marion said again, a little sadder this time.

Reaching a dead end in the other conversation, Caroline turned her attention to the yearbooks that were spread open, not to her mother's class, but to the class that had been a year ahead.

Her endless curiosity stirring again, Caroline leaned nearer, scanning the pages until her mother's slender fingers closed each of the books and ended Caroline's study.

"Why did you have these?" The softness of Marion's voice didn't disguise the accusation behind it.

"I used to look at them," Caroline said, trying not to sound as defensive as she suddenly felt. The endless hours she had spent pouring over the yearbooks, looking for clues to her father's identity and spinning fairy tales about who he might be, was her secret, and it wasn't one she was ready to share.

"Why?" her mother asked even more softly and with much less accusation.

There was a spot at the end of the bed, just big enough to sit on, that wasn't covered with yearbooks. "To see what you looked like." Caroline edged herself into the spot and offered a truth she was willing to share. "To see what your life was like when you were young. I never knew you were homecoming queen until I saw it in here." She touched the book nearest her.

Marion smiled indulgently and opened the yearbook from her junior year to the picture of the homecoming court. As she stared at the page, her smile grew wistful with the happiness of memory and the sadness of loss.

When her mother's hand unconsciously left the yearbook to touch her stomach, Caroline could read her thoughts. It was in the spring of her junior year that Marion had become pregnant with Caroline.

When the minister had said that the guilt wasn't hers, it had made Caroline feel better. But how could she really believe that, Caroline wondered, when it was her birth that had cast such a huge shadow over so many lives.

Every time her mother or her grandparents had looked at her, they had seen the shame her existence had brought to the family. Every time Caroline had walked down the street, she had imagined the fingers that were pointing and heard the whispers that followed her.

Right or wrong, guilt had been with her her whole life, and whether it should have been hers or not, she still felt it keenly.

Looking to see where her mother's thoughts had gone, Caroline noticed the page of black-and-white snapshots Marion was absorbed in. Her finger rested at the edge of one picture.

Intrigued, Caroline leaned nearer to see a young man stretched out on the grass under a tree. In the corner of the picture, a girl sat on the ground next to the boy. Only her skirt was visible with her legs tucked under at her side. One of her hands was spread on the ground at the boy's shoulder.

"Did you know him?" Caroline asked softly, and motioned to the picture.

"Only a little," her mother answered with a gentle shake of her head. "And yet, it seemed like so much more."

Caroline pointed to the skirted girl. "Is that you?" Something in her mother's attitude made her sure of the answer before she even asked.

"Yes," Marion said, not disappointing her.

"What was he like?"

"Just a boy. A lot of people called him a hoodlum. But he wasn't. He was a poet."

Marion smiled and sighed and moved deeper into her memories. "He had the most beautiful voice and the most wonderful way of talking. Maybe his poems weren't really all that great, but when he recited them, I thought he was brilliant. He was so romantic, but not many other people saw him that way."

"What happened to him?"

"He was a year ahead of me in school. He left right after graduation and he never came back, at least as long as I was here. I can't blame him, really. This town didn't hold much for him then."

From the look of loss on her mother's face, Caroline wondered if there might not be more to the story. Her heart skipped to a faster beat when she thought that this romantic rebel might even be her father. But it wasn't likely.

She forced her imagination to slow down and be reasonable. Her mother had never said one word about Caroline's father, and if this were the man, she wouldn't be talking about him now.

The silence that surrounded Caroline's birth was strict and unbroken. The last time she had asked her mother about her father, Marion had flown into a rage and Caroline hadn't heard from her for a year. No one knew his identity, not even Caroline's grandmother.

"Sweetheart?"

Caroline looked up and found her mother staring at her. Marion held her gaze for a long time, then finally said, "I love you."

Caroline gladly relinquished the metal spoon she was using to serve baked beans and slipped away from the park shelter where the serving tables were set up. Under a nearby tree, she slumped to the ground and wondered if she could close her eyes without falling asleep.

Dawn had come late, slowed by dark, heavy clouds that threatened to make their picnic in December as impossible as it sounded. But by eleven, the clouds had blown away and the sun had come out, and from noon until almost five she had been standing in a serving line at a lakeside park, helping to feed a steady stream of sweatsuit-clad people.

Ariel and Tank were in charge of the games. Horseshoes, volleyball, three-legged races, you name it, people were playing it. Duke was chief chef, overseeing the grills where burgers and hot dogs were being churned out in staggering numbers.

Martha had been in charge of the cooking and serving of the baked beans, potato salad and fresh rolls that had kept the hungry game players returning for helping after helping throughout the afternoon.

And as the guests grew tired, rented school buses had pulled into the parking lot every hour, shuttling eager new faces from town and carrying away the ones who were ready to call it a day. Longingly, Caroline watched another set of buses pull away. She could almost hear the sighs of the people on board.

"Tired?"

At the sound of Duke's voice, a little of Caroline's exhaustion lifted. She turned her head until she found dirt-stained jeans with patched holes at the knees and hightop basketball shoes that looked as though they might once have been white.

Dragging her gaze slowly upward, she came to where a flannel shirt was tied just below his waist. Its tail flapped in the breeze behind him, and the white T-shirt he had stripped down to was streaked with grease from the grill and clung to his chest and stomach in damp circles.

"You're a mess," she said without sympathy. She steadfastly ignored the effect he was having on her heartbeat.

Duke sat on the ground next to her, pulled loose the tail of his T-shirt and wiped his forehead. His tanned face was flushed, and dark tendrils of hair clung to his forehead.

"Thanks," he said. "I'd return the compliment, but except for that smudge on the side of your nose, you don't look too bad. Are you sure you've been working hard enough?"

"Very funny," Caroline said. As tired as she was, she *did* feel like laughing as she lifted a hand to her nose to search for the smudge.

"The other side."

She transferred her search to the other side of her nose and scrubbed diligently. "Is it still there?"

"Let me see." He turned her head and peered at her face. With his thumb, he gently brushed at the slope of her nose while his hand cupped her cheek.

"How big was that smudge?" Caroline asked, growing suspicious.

"Not very big." With his legs crossed, he sat almost touching her and leaned forward at the waist. "Do you think anyone would notice if I kissed you?"

Her heartbeat kicked into overdrive, and Caroline looked around cautiously. All around them were people from the office, people from the town and people she'd never even seen before.

"Are you out of your mind?" she whispered.

"I guess so." He sighed and sat back again. "Did you get to have any fun today, or did Martha work you too hard?"

Caroline groaned and rolled her eyes in an automatic gesture of fatigue while she tried to think of something nice to say about Martha.

"I guess that pretty much answers my question," Duke said.

"Oh, no." Afraid he had misread her, Caroline leaned toward him and put her hand on Duke's arm. "She's great. The picnic wouldn't have been nearly as good without her."

Duke patted her hand. "You don't have to tell me Martha's virtues or her drawbacks. It's my fault for not seeing to it that you got more time to enjoy yourself."

Caroline shook her head. "I was just doing my job. After all, this was my idea, and Ariel's."

"Well, I was going to tell you this officially next week, but I guess it wouldn't hurt to say it now, unofficially. This was a great idea. It's worked beyond all my expectations."

She gave him a reproving look. "You expected it to not work at all," she reminded him.

"I thought it was a pretty dumb idea, yes," he agreed. "And at about ten o'clock this morning, I was ready to wring your neck."

Remembering the anxiety she had endured that morning, she smiled all over again in relief. "I've never been so glad to see the sun in my whole life."

"You should have been. The high school gymnasium was not a great backup plan."

"It's a small town. There's not a lot here."

"You're not going to interrupt me like this when I thank you officially, are you?"

Caroline looked remorseful. "No, sir. I'm sorry, sir."

Duke frowned like a man who was too tired to have much of a sense of humor when the jab was directed at him, and she quickly changed the subject. "It's going to be dark pretty soon."

He relaxed slightly and stared at the sky, calculating the time they had left. "I know. I guess we need to start herding these people out of here."

Caroline glanced over at the shelter and saw that the remaining food was being packed away. "Looks like Martha's closing up." In the parking lot, she saw two empty buses arriving. A crowd of people already waited to board, and more seemed to be moving in that direction. "It *was* a success, wasn't it?"

Duke's hand closed over hers. "A very large success, and one I'm very grateful for. You do an excellent job, Miss Adams."

"Why, thank you, Mr. Hutchison." The time for joking was over and she felt a little shy in the face of his praise.

"What time should I pick you up tonight?"

She turned her head toward him in a slow take. "I beg your pardon?"

"The dance? What time should I pick you up?"

"I was just going to drive myself," she answered, hoping to convey without actually saying it that she had things to do and didn't need the distraction—or the temptation. "I have to be there early."

"So do I. We might as well go together," he answered not taking the hint.

"But won't that look—"

"At the risk of being blunt," he interrupted, "I don't care how it looks. Will seven be okay? I know that doesn't leave you much time to get ready."

Caroline tried not to roll her eyes in exasperation, but it wasn't easy. They had discussed this into the ground already. "I thought you said—"

"I know what I said," he interrupted again. "And I might have been a little hasty."

She stared at the ground while she waited for her topsy-turvy emotions to end their roller-coaster ride.

"Oh, Duke." Her heart was in her throat and she couldn't say anything else even if she knew what she wanted to say.

Her mother had left Christmas Day and Duke had been out of the office most of the week, leaving Caroline with a lot of time alone and a lot of time to think, and she had missed him in spite of what they had decided. As hard as she had tried not to, she had really, really missed him.

"Okay," she said finally.

"Okay?"

"I'll be ready at seven."

"Caroline."

Almost reluctantly, she looked up at him, but he seemed as speechless as she had been.

"Do you have a way home?" he asked after a long, difficult silence.

"I drove."

His hands hung at his sides, clenching and unclenching, and Caroline knew, the same way she knew the night she first met him, that things were different and would never be the same way again.

* * *

Caroline sat at her vanity and held a strand of pearls at the base of her throat. She turned her head first one way and then the other, checking the contrast of the pearls against the paleness of her skin and the white, fifties-style, off-the-shoulder dress that she wore.

The pearls were the right kind of jewelry for the dress, but the color wasn't right. Putting the strand back into a drawer of her jewelry case, she pulled out another drawer and then another, not satisfied with anything she saw.

"Caroline, dear, I have something I thought . . ."

With a cry of fright, Caroline whirled around and pressed her hand against her pounding heart.

"Did I scare you, dear?" her grandmother asked.

Caroline took a deep breath and began to calm down. "You just startled me a little."

It had been years since her grandmother had climbed the stairs. Arthritis and a fear of tripping had long since confined her to the downstairs, and Caroline couldn't imagine what had prompted her to make the treacherous climb this evening.

"I'm sorry." A mischievous look crept into Viola's eyes and she chuckled. "I guess you didn't expect to see me up here, did you?"

"No."

Amused by the look of triumph on her grandmother's face, Caroline felt a smile tug at the corners of her mouth. For days, she had sensed that her grandmother wanted to say something. Caroline only hoped it was something that could be said quickly, because Duke would be here soon and she wasn't ready yet.

"I brought you something."

Viola reached into her pocket and withdrew a ribbon with a pendant on it.

"I didn't know if you had a necklace to wear tonight. But I thought this would be lovely with that dress. And with your hair." She walked toward Caroline, holding the pendant out to her. "Let's just see how it looks."

Caroline turned to face the mirror and lifted her hair while Viola unclasped the narrow black velvet ribbon and slipped it around Caroline's neck. The pendant, a large, bloodred garnet, nestled in the hollow of her throat.

"Oh Gran." Caroline's fingertips touched the delicate band of gold filigree that surrounded the stone. "It's beautiful."

"It was my mother's. I always meant to give it to you someday."

Frightened suddenly, Caroline let her hair fall back around her shoulders and turned to search her grandmother's face.

"Gran?"

"Oh, child, don't look at me like that." Flustered, Viola waved her hand in the air between them. "I don't have to be sick to be nice to you. We've certainly come to a pretty pass, haven't we?"

Caroline rose to her feet and held out her arms to the frail woman she still loved with all her heart, no matter what came between them. "Oh, Gran, I'm sorry."

Viola put her arms around her granddaughter's waist and gave her a quick but heartfelt hug. Then she stepped back and said, "I'm the one who has to apologize. I hold on too tight. I did it to your mother and I ended up driving her away. I did it to you and I ended up sending you away. There's hard feelings between your mother and me that I don't think will ever end. I don't want that between us, Caroline. You're the light of my life and the one joy I have left. Sit back down there." She pointed to the vanity. "There's something I have to say."

Caroline obeyed, and her grandmother pulled a chair to the edge of the dressing table and sat down.

"Having your mother home," Viola continued, "got me to thinking about a lot of things I've done wrong. Maybe, thirteen years ago, I had cause to keep you from that Hutchison boy. But I've got no cause to do that anymore, no cause at all. You're a grown woman, and he's a respected, successful man. And that little daughter of his is just as cute as a bug."

Stunned, Caroline was almost afraid to breathe. "What are you saying?" she asked, just above a whisper.

"I'm saying that I won't stand in your way. I love you, and I want you to be happy. And if that Hutchison boy is what you want, well, then, I won't say another word against him."

Caroline almost laughed, she was having so much trouble believing what she was hearing.

"You're serious? This isn't just some kind of reverse psychology you learned from Granddad?"

"I just ask that you conduct yourself like the decent young lady that you are." Viola lowered her voice confidentially. "And, just to save everybody a lot of trouble, you might want to do as much as you can in private, considering how some people in this town love to call me and report every little thing they see."

"Gran, I love you." Caroline caught her grandmother's hands in her own and kissed the older woman's soft, powdered cheek. "I don't know what I'm going to do. I don't even know what I want. But you sure have made it a lot easier for me."

"Then that makes me happy." Viola clapped her hands on her knees and stood. "Are you ready?"

"I just have a few more things to do."

"Then I'll get back downstairs and open the door when he gets here."

Her head still swimming with surprise, Caroline watched her grandmother go out the door. Then she turned back to the mirror for a few last-minute touches.

"Wow." It was all she could think of to say.

"I have just two questions," Duke said as he held her hand down the front walk. "Who was that woman? And what has she done with your grandmother?"

Caroline almost giggled. "Was she nice to you?"

"Yes."

"She came up to my room and she gave me this pendant." Caroline slid the back of her hand under the pendant and held it toward the streetlight next to where Duke's car was parked. "And she said... Well, I can't tell you everything she said, but..." She paused again and shrugged. "I think she's decided to like you."

Duke came to a halt at the white picket gate leading from the yard to the sidewalk that ran in front of the house. He stared down at her with genuine surprise.

"Good grief. You mean she no longer opposes the match?"

Caroline knew him well enough to recognize the anger that bubbled just beneath the surface.

"Basically," she said, beginning to wish she had never mentioned the subject.

In a quiet, deceptively gentle voice, he asked, "Tell me, does this newfound acceptance have anything to do with the fact that I own my own company and no longer have grease under my fingernails?"

She had barely won approval in one sector when she lost it in another. Caroline could feel her shoulders sag with the weight of defeat.

"I shouldn't have said anything."

Duke took a deep breath and released it slowly. "No. No, you should have."

He slipped his arm around her waist and pulled her against him, hip to hip. With his finger, he tilted her head up until he could look into her eyes.

"I'm sorry. I took a nice moment and almost ruined it. I...I still have a lot of anger. I'm not proud of it, and I keep hoping it will go away. But so far, it hasn't."

"Maybe this can be a first step for all of us."

"Maybe."

He smiled a lopsided little smile that was tough and tender at the same time. It was a smile Caroline remembered well. It had always made her stomach do somersaults, and tonight was no exception.

"That would be nice, wouldn't it?" he asked. "By the way, have I mentioned yet how beautiful you are tonight?"

"No, but it's very nice to hear."

He led her to his car and opened the door for her. With their hands side by side on the door frame and the door between them, Caroline said, "I think it's only right to tell you. You look very nice yourself in that tuxedo."

"Well, thank you." His smile was the slow, lazy one that always made her feel like warm butter inside. "That's very nice to hear."

His hand left the door and slid under her hair and around the back of her neck. Holding her head still, Duke kissed her gently and delicately. The only things that touched her were his hand and his lips.

He drew away long enough to tilt his head to the other side, and then he kissed her again.

"I guess we should go now," he said when the second, more thorough kiss ended.

With shaking hands, Caroline tried to tuck her full skirt around her. "I guess," she agreed.

Her knees trembled as she bent toward the passenger seat. Duke's strong hands caught her just before she fell.

"You need some help there?" he asked, bending over her.

"If you help me any more, I think I may pass out."

Duke laughed and guided her into her seat. Caroline smoothed her skirt down around her knees, which was as far as it went, then drew the rest of her long, stockinged legs in after her.

Under the streetlight, her bare shoulders against the white of her bodice gleamed like pearl on pearl. He took her hand in his, lifted it to his lips and kissed the inside of her wrist.

"I'm glad you're with me tonight," he said when he released her hand. "I'm very glad."

Chapter Nine

After taking a chance on good weather for the picnic, Caroline and Ariel had played it safe on the dance and rented the ballroom of one of the larger motels at the edge of town. For anyone who had too much to drink, rooms were available, and the couches grouped throughout the lobby were a haven for tired feet.

"Well," Ariel said, propping her own tired feet on the coffee table in front of the sofa, "it's not the most romantic setting in the world, but it certainly is functional."

Caroline couldn't quite bring herself to put her feet on the table, but she did slip out of her shoes. "Ahhh," she breathed, wiggling her toes in relief.

"I'll take that as a sign of agreement," Ariel said. She rested her head on the back of the couch and sagged into the cushions.

"We're not ever going to do this again, are we?" Caroline asked. "Where did we get the idea of having a dance after a picnic that lasted all day?"

"I think it was one of those things that sounded like a good idea at the time." Ariel sat a little straighter. "Why are you complaining? You've been dancing all night."

Before Caroline could answer, a soft hand touched her shoulder and a little voice whispered in her ear. "Hi."

She turned to look over her shoulder and found Kimi leaning against the back of the couch, smiling. She wore a velveteen dress of powder blue. Her hair was pulled back in a French braid, with a blue ribbon interwoven.

"Well, sweetheart," Caroline said in surprise. She took Kimi's hand and led her around the end of the sofa to sit beside her. "What are you doing down here at this time of night?"

"Martha let me get dressed and come down to watch. We've been sitting over there." She pointed to an alcove where Martha's sleeping figure was slumped in a chair. "She fell asleep, so I thought I would come over and say hi."

Caroline laughed and put her arm around the little girl's shoulder, hugging her nearer. "Have you been having fun?"

"Oh, yes. I just love parties. And I've been watching you." Kimi's hand touched the white taffeta of Caroline's skirt with reverence. "You're always so pretty, and you always smell so nice."

"Oh, Kimi, thank you. That's a lovely compliment." The adoring brown eyes that stared up at her caught at Caroline's heart.

"My mother had long hair like yours. It was all the way down to her waist."

On the last word, the little girl delicately stifled a yawn, and Caroline felt the tug on her heart strengthen. "I know," she said gently. "I saw her picture."

"You did?" Kimi's sleepy eyes widened with surprise.

Caroline nodded and smiled as she smoothed a stray hair back from the little girl's face. "Your father showed me your picture, and hers was next to it. She was very beautiful. Just like you are."

Kimi's head slumped back against Caroline's arm, and Kimi struggled to keep her eyes open. "I imagine sometimes that she's tucking me into bed at night. Her hands are soft, and when she kisses me good-night, her hair falls over her shoulder and brushes my arm. And she smells good, just like you do."

Cradling Kimi in her arms, Caroline brushed the little girl's soft, dark hair with her cheek. "You know, Kimi," she said in the quiet voice of bedtime stories, "I never had a father when I was growing up. I never even had a picture. But I used to pretend, just like you do. My father would sit on the edge of my bed at night, in the dark, and we'd talk. Whenever I was lonely or afraid, he'd always be there."

"Wow," Kimi whispered in a voice groggy with sleep.

Caroline smiled to herself and listened to the gradual change in Kimi's breathing as the girl drifted off to sleep. It felt good to have someone to talk to, someone who would understand, even if it was only a little girl.

"I wasn't supposed to hear that, was I?" Ariel asked quietly.

Caroline lifted her cheek from the top of Kimi's head and turned her head slowly to Ariel, sitting on the other side of her.

"No, you weren't."

She had forgotten Ariel was there. For those few minutes, she and Kimi had been alone, sisters in the world of semi-orphans.

"I can't believe that the whole time we were growing up I never knew you felt like that," Ariel said. "You *never* mentioned your father."

Keeping her voice soft so that she wouldn't disturb Kimi, Caroline answered, "Children can be great actors. I'll bet Duke has no idea how much Kimi misses her mother."

"She seems like such a happy little girl, but then, so did you."

"I think Kimi *is* a happy little girl. She just wants to have a mother."

Ariel laughed suddenly. "And to think, I always wanted to be just like you."

"What?" Caroline had trouble keeping the disbelief in her voice at a low volume.

"Well, your grandparents may have been strict, but they obviously adored you. And your mother was more like a big sister, and I always thought that would be so neat. And then you were so popular in school."

"I was not," Caroline said indignantly.

"Caroline." Ariel looked at her as though she were crazy. "In the first grade, half the little boys in school took one look at you and fell in love. And I don't think most of them ever got over it."

"You're out of your mind."

"Look, I was your best friend. I was the one who got ignored while everybody fell all over *you,*" Ariel said firmly. "I ought to know."

"Ariel." Caroline was beginning to get upset. "What are you talking about? I never had any boyfriends. Nobody *ever* asked me out."

"Well, of course not. Between your shyness and your grandparents' overprotection, nobody could get near you, but that didn't mean they didn't want to. Why, I know Joey was devastated when Duke came in and walked away with you before anyone else had a chance to make a move."

"Are you serious?" Ariel was so certain of herself that Caroline almost felt she should believe her. But the idea was so ridiculous she couldn't take it seriously. She didn't want to take it seriously.

"Of course, I'm serious," Ariel said. "You can ask anybody. Here comes Duke. Ask him."

"No."

"Oh, Caroline, look at yourself," Ariel scolded. "You're still doing it. Pull your head out of the sand and take a real look at life before it passes you by."

Confused, frightened and very uncomfortable, Caroline begged, "Please, Ariel, don't say anything to Duke. This isn't the time."

"Okay, but we're going to talk about this later," Ariel warned.

"Fine," Caroline whispered hurriedly. Duke was almost to them. "I promise. Just not now."

Duke stopped next to the coffee table in front of Caroline and smiled down at her with the sleeping Kimi in her arms. "How did this happen?"

Caroline turned her head and nodded toward Martha, then turned back to face him. "Kimi lulled her to sleep and then came and found me, the best I can tell." Her heart was still pounding from her conversation with Ariel, and she was working hard to seem relaxed.

"I guess I should take her up to bed."

He leaned down and took Kimi gently into his arms without waking her. As he straightened, Caroline slipped her shoes back on and stood.

"Could I go with you?"

Her arms felt cold and empty without Kimi snuggled against her. She wasn't ready to break the bond she felt with the sleeping child, and she definitely wasn't ready to be alone with Ariel.

"Sure." Duke looked surprised but pleased. "I'd like that."

Leaning over to say goodbye, Caroline touched Ariel's arm. "Thank you," she said, more with her eyes than with her words.

Ariel laughed, unable to stay serious for long. "Have fun." She waved them both away. "You don't have to hurry back. I'll take care of things here."

Caroline walked beside Duke to the elevators, being careful not to bump into Kimi's dangling legs. Tall for her

age, the preteen was showing signs of growing into a colt-
ish young lady.

"That was kind of her," Duke whispered. He nodded his
head in Ariel's direction. "Do you think she was trying to
give us a hint?"

"Knowing Ariel? Yes," Caroline answered, trying not to
sound as stingingly sarcastic as she felt.

The elevator doors opened and they entered.

"Which floor?" she asked, poised to punch the button.

"Four. Did I interrupt something when I walked up? You
two seemed deep in conversation, and then you just
stopped."

"It was nothing I wasn't ready to get away from."

"Ah, one of Ariel's lectures." He nodded with understanding, and when the elevator doors opened, led the way
to his door. "The key's in my shirt pocket. Can you get it?"

He leaned toward her, and Caroline caught the lapel of
his tuxedo between her thumb and forefinger and pulled it
far enough out for her to reach her other hand inside.
Feeling her way into his shirt pocket, she was acutely conscious of the muscular chest under her searching fingertips.

"Thanks," he whispered again when she withdrew the
key and stepped back from him to unlock the door.

"Think nothing of it," she said coolly, and walked ahead
of him to hide her burning cheeks that were almost surely
too pink to be overlooked.

Inside was a living room and kitchenette. Doors opened
off the living room on either side. Duke headed for the one
to the right, and Caroline followed him into a bedroom
with two double beds that were already turned down and
waiting.

Caroline glanced around the room looking for some hint
as to whether Kimi shared her room with Duke or with
Martha, but the room was spotless, with the sterility of
hotel rooms everywhere. She finally gave up and joined
Duke beside the bed.

After he had spread a sheet over Kimi and kissed her good-night, Caroline leaned over the sleeping little girl. She let her hair fall forward as she kissed Kimi's cheek.

"Good night, sweetheart," she whispered.

For an instant, Kimi stirred. Her small hand brushed Caroline's arm. Her fingers curled through Caroline's hair and she smiled. Then she was asleep again.

Once they were in the living room again, Caroline said, "Duke, she's still dressed."

He nodded. "Martha can get her undressed and into a gown without waking her. I'll leave it to her." He walked to a cabinet and opened the doors, lifting a decanter. "Do you want a drink? I hate to leave her alone before Martha gets here, and I forgot to have someone wake her."

Caroline looked at the door and then around the empty room with just the two of them in it. Her heart still pounded from her intimate rummage through his shirt pocket. "Maybe I should go get Martha," she offered.

He gestured to the sofa. "Why don't you sit down? We have so little time to be alone together."

She started to argue. After all, there was a party going on downstairs that he was hosting and for which was she co-hostess along with Ariel. With them both gone, Ariel was on her own, and that really wasn't fair.

"What can I get you?" Duke asked.

"A wine spritzer," she replied without hesitation.

Duke was right. They never spent any time alone together, and there was no reason why they shouldn't. After all, Ariel had given her permission.

Caroline settled into the corner of the couch and tried to relax. Duke brought her drink and instead of sitting with her, walked on to the windows that overlooked a tree-covered valley by day. By night, there was very little to see.

"How was your mother's visit?" He turned around to look at Caroline but didn't leave the window.

"It was okay," Caroline said, thinking that uncomfortable conversation topics seemed to be the theme for the evening.

"You know, I was barely aware that you had a mother. She seemed very nice, but I got the feeling that the two of you aren't particularly close. But, of course, you might have just had a fight."

"No." Caroline took a drink of her spritzer and cast a glance in the direction of the hall door. She couldn't think of a better time for Martha to come bustling in and free her from what was beginning to feel like an inquisition.

"Then, you two are like that all the time?" Duke asked.

"Like what?" She could feel herself getting more tense by the minute. She loved her mother, and when the two of them were alone, they got along fine. But when other people were around, things changed.

"Like strangers," he said, apparently intent on getting an answer to whatever question was bothering him.

Caroline set her drink down and met his gaze across the room. If he was determined to badger her, she might as well let him know how well she liked it.

"Duke, in the years that you knew me, how often did you see my mother?"

He shook his head. "Like I said, I wasn't even sure you had one. The best I could tell, your grandparents were raising you."

"So that ought to tell you how much she was around. Why are you asking me all this?"

"Because," he said, growing as stern as she was, "after I met your mother last weekend, I began to realize how much I didn't know about you."

"And so now you want to sit here and ask me questions until you think you know it all?" she demanded.

"Well, I guess not." He was almost shouting before he remembered where he was and lowered his voice. "I didn't realize it would upset you so much."

"Okay." Caroline took a drink of the wine and set it back down. Then she stood and began to pace behind the couch. "You want to know about my mother? I'll tell you about my mother."

She stopped pacing and stood still, her hands on her hips. "She was too young when she had me, and she didn't want the responsibility of raising me. So she left me with my grandparents while she went away to work and to get married and raise another family. I have a half sister and two half brothers, and she's *their* mother."

Caroline took a deep breath and began to pace again. "To me, she was just a name on a present twice a year. And now that my grandfather's dead, all of a sudden for some reason, she wants to be my mother."

When she stopped again and stood glaring at him in silence, Duke asked quietly, "What about your father? Where's he been all this time?"

Caroline shook her head and took a step backward. She was too tired to be angry anymore. None of this was Duke's fault. He was just asking questions. He had finally noticed all the gaps in her life and he wanted answers, but they were answers she wasn't prepared to give.

She couldn't explain the way she felt, and she couldn't stay in this room with him any longer.

"I'll tell Martha you need her."

Caroline hadn't even made it to the door before he stopped her. His hands caught her elbows and he turned her around to face him.

"Do you know what's unbelievable?" His tone was gentle and filled with understanding. "I always thought I knew you so well, and I never knew you at all. Even then, you were holding all this inside, and I never bothered to ask."

Unwilling to let down her guard, she held herself stiffly away from him. "Now that you've asked, do you really know that much more?"

"I know that I was wrong to blame your grandparents for everything that happened. I know that whatever secret you're protecting now, they were trying to protect then."

"What secret?" she demanded, afraid to learn which one of the many he was talking about.

Her life was a patchwork of secrets, some small, some large and some very dark. She felt trapped, wishing that she'd told him herself long ago about all of them.

"I don't know," he answered, and let his hands fall from her shoulders. "And I won't ask anymore. I'll just let you tell me when you're ready."

"Really?" She was still tense, still waiting.

"Really."

"Just like that?"

"Just like that. Want to dance?"

Caroline let out the breath she had been holding and relaxed, allowing herself an exasperated smile.

"Come on," Duke urged. Taking her hand, he led her into the center of the room. He pulled her closer, sliding his arms around her waist, and they began to sway.

"There's no music," Caroline murmured in his ear, though it really didn't matter. With her cheek against his, she could almost hear the band playing. She could almost feel the cool night breeze flowing around them.

"I'll hum," he offered.

"Oh, Duke."

Laughing, she threw her head back and looked up at him. Her words were hardly spoken when he kissed her, a light, quick kiss that was barely a nibble.

"Caroline," he whispered, then kissed her again, a second light kiss, so quick it blurred into the third.

Lingering, his lips searched hers, gently at first, then deepening, seeking answers he couldn't find anywhere else. For Caroline, he had only to touch her and she was alive with desire. The passion that Duke aroused in her was instant. At the first brush of his lips, she was his.

His arms tightened around her, crushing her against him while his kiss grew urgent, and then as suddenly as it had begun, it ended. One minute passionate, and the next minute withdrawn, Duke lifted his head and looked down at her.

Caroline could feel his chest heaving against hers. In the grimace that twisted his face, she could see the effort it took for him to stop. She could feel his tensed muscles as he struggled for self-control, and from the hard pounding of her own heart, she knew she could be no help to him.

If he were to sling her over his shoulder and carry her off to his room, she wouldn't offer a whimper of protest. Whenever she was alone with him, her fickle resolve crumbled and she was helpless to do anything about it.

He had only to take her in his arms and look down at her with the fiercely controlled flame of passion that was burning in his eyes at this moment and she would be his until the end of time.

He only had to ask.

"I can't help myself," he whispered fiercely. "I'm in love with you and there's nothing I can do to stop it."

"Duke." She breathed his name with the longing that he alone aroused and time left untouched.

Gritting his teeth against the feelings he was powerless to control, Duke said, "I know this isn't the time or the place, but I want you so badly."

A glimmer of sanity fought its way through the fire that burned in her. There was a child sleeping one room away and a housekeeper who could walk in on them at any moment, and yet, Caroline would risk it all if he asked. She had no shame, no dignity, only a raw burning need that no one but Duke had ever awakened.

"I know." Her voice was breathless with desire, and she didn't know how to stop the feelings that were overtaking her. "I'm no good at this. I don't know what to do."

"Caroline, sweetheart. I'm no help." Duke held her closer and brushed his lips against her hair. "Believe it or not, you're the only woman I've ever wanted this way, and you just drive me right out of my mind."

"Then I guess it's hopeless."

A calm descended over him and Duke gave up the struggle. "I guess it is."

Without another word, he slipped his hand under her knees and lifted Caroline into his arms. He turned and carried her toward the second bedroom.

"Oh, Duke," she protested without really meaning it, "we can't."

He nudged the door closed and carried her to the bed. "I can't stop," he said in a voice thick with desire as he lay down beside her and slid his fingers through her hair. "Not now." His face lowered toward hers. "It's too late."

He kissed her, and the faint voice of reason in the back of her mind whimpered into silence. Her whole body throbbed with the need that he alone aroused and time left undimmed.

"Oh, Duke," she said again, really meaning it this time.

His hand slipped under her arm to the zipper at the side of her dress, and Caroline moaned as a chill of expectation went through her. She rolled to the side and raised her arm and in seconds, Duke guided her to her feet and steadied her as she stepped out of the dress.

She stood there caught in a broad wedge of light that shone through the half-open bathroom door, torn between the heat of passion and the cowardice of modesty. The sheer fabric and lace of her strapless demibra left little to the imagination, and the matching bikini panties weren't much better.

"Caroline," Duke said, smiling as he studied every inch of her, "do you have any idea what a garter belt and stockings do to a man when they're on a pair of legs like yours?"

Trying hard not to squirm or, even worse, hunch forward with her arms crossed in front of her, Caroline said, "No."

He reached out and laid his fingers flat against her wrist, then smoothed his hand slowly up her arm to her shoulder.

"Let me show you," he crooned, and gathered her into his arms for a deep, lingering exploration of her mouth by his, while his hands slid down her nearly bare back and over her almost bare hips.

Caroline moaned again, softly, with pleasure, from deep in her throat. She felt her knees growing weaker, while her heart beat faster and harder with each breath until there seemed to be no room left for it inside her.

"I love you, Caroline," Duke whispered, reluctantly ending their kiss. "I love you so much." He touched her shoulder again, caressing it. "Your skin glows like pearls."

His fingertip slid across her collarbone and down to the hollow between her breasts. Caroline caught her breath and held it as his hands cupped her breasts from underneath and lifted while he leaned to kiss each swelling mound above her bra.

His hands moved on to the fastening in the middle of her bra, releasing it as Caroline let her breath out in a shivering sigh. Then he dipped his head again to draw the tender tip of her breast into his mouth.

Caroline gasped and clutched his shoulders to steady herself. Her fingers slid over the smooth fabric, the shoulder pads, the collar at his neck.

"Duke?" she said in a warbling voice that didn't sound like hers.

He raised his head and kissed her firmly, deeply, in a kiss that left her branded as his. "Yes?"

"You're still wearing your tux."

He looked down and chuckled. "You're right. I guess we'd better slow this freight train down."

He moved to the head of the bed and folded back the bedspread and arranged the pillows. Guiding Caroline to the smooth sheets, he had her sit on the edge of the bed while he knelt in front of her and removed her high heels.

Wordlessly, he spread her legs wider, holding them apart with a hand on each thigh. Caroline's shallow breath caught in her throat as she watched him lower his head and, with slow, deliberate sensuality, kiss the tender flesh on the inside of each thigh just above the tops of her stockings.

Still quaking inside, she drew a deeper breath when he straightened and unfastened her hose from her garter belt, then slid her stockings slowly down her legs and dropped them next to her shoes.

He kissed her tenderly on the lips as he stood. "Why don't you stretch out? I'll be back in a minute."

Caroline slid contentedly into the nest of pillows as Duke went into the bathroom and closed the door. She drew the sheet over her and had barely had time to ask herself what in the world she was doing when the bathroom door opened and the light went out.

Seconds later, the sheet was tugged out of her hands and Duke pulled her to his side of the bed and into his arms. Chest to chest, stomach to stomach, long legs entwined, Caroline sighed with happiness as they nestled together in the quiet, dark bedroom.

"One more thing," Duke said softly.

His hand slid over the hollow of Caroline's stomach, sending the desires that had almost quieted into a riot again. She gasped and curled away and then back toward him. Following the movements of her body, his hand slid lower, inside the lace trim of her panties.

His other hand moved down and caught the other side. With one, swift tug, he had the panties down to the top of her thighs.

"Oh," Caroline said as realization dawned. She slipped her legs out while he held the underwear, and in seconds, the pile of lingerie on the floor was complete.

"Now, where were we?" Duke asked with a smile in his voice. He pulled her back into his arms. "You smell wonderful. Like lilacs. If you only knew how I've longed to have my bed smell of lilacs."

"Oh, Duke." Melting inside from the emotion that filled her heart, Caroline smoothed her hand over the rounded muscles of his chest. "I'm—"

Duke rolled her away from him and onto her back as he rose up on one elbow. The sudden tension in him startled her. "What's wrong?" she asked in a whisper.

"Wait." He touched her lips with his finger and then sat up, leaning forward as he listened.

The sound of the door opening in the next room was like ice water poured down Caroline's back. A shaft of light from the living room suddenly shone under their door like an intruder into their bedroom. She held her breath, and her heart began to pound, this time with the panic of the guilty.

Duke pulled the sheet over her and slipped on a robe as a light knock sounded on the bedroom door.

"Yes, just a minute," he called in a hoarse whisper and hurried to open the door just a crack.

"I'm so sorry, Mr. Hutchison, sir. I just wanted to see if you were here and to apologize. I don't know what came over me, sir. I'm just mortified."

"There was no harm done, Martha. I should apologize for not waking you before I brought Kimi upstairs, but I didn't think of it. And then I didn't want to leave her alone while I went back down."

"Of course, sir. No, the fault was entirely mine. I just didn't see any harm in letting her watch the party for a little while, but I don't know how I fell asleep like that, sir. I'm just mortified."

"It was perfectly natural, Martha. There's nothing to apologize for. Don't give it another thought."

"If you're sure, sir . . ." she said uncertainly.

"I'm sure, Martha. You just go on to bed and don't worry about it."

When she heard the door close again, Caroline pulled the sheet down from over her eyes and began to look around the dark room for her clothes. Her dress was a white blob over the back of a chair. The rest of her clothes were invisible somewhere between there and the bed.

Climbing back into the bed, Duke slid his arm around her waist and pulled her against him.

"Now," he whispered in her ear, "where were we *this* time?"

"My purse is on the couch," Caroline whispered back.

"Do you need it?"

"She'll see it."

"That's okay."

"No, it's not. She'll know I'm here." Caroline poked a stiffened finger into the mattress for emphasis. "She'll know I'm *here*."

"Sweetheart, Martha's not going to say anything. If she were a gossip, I wouldn't have kept her with me all these years."

"I'm not worried about *that*." She threw the sheet back and climbed out of the bed in one motion. "I must have been out of my mind."

"Hold it," Duke protested, and followed her out of the bed. "What are you doing?"

"I'm getting dressed."

"Now?"

"I'm sorry, but I can't stay here. Your daughter is sleeping one room away. What if she wakes up and comes looking for you?"

"Oh, Caroline." Duke caught her to him and cradled her in his arms. "I know you're right. I should never have asked you to stay, but it's going to take all my strength to let you walk out of here right now."

The touch of his body against hers, warm and strong, flesh on flesh, reminded Caroline painfully of what she was giving up.

"It's going to take all my strength to go," she said with feeling, "but I can't stay here now. It isn't right. If Martha or Kimi knew, it would make me ashamed, and that's not how I want to feel with you."

"I'll get dressed and take you home."

"You don't have to. Ariel and Tank are probably still downstairs." All she wanted now was to get out as quickly and painlessly as possible. When she thought of the shame she would have felt if they had been caught, it gave her cold chills.

"I don't think so. But it doesn't matter. You came with me and I'm taking you home," Duke said with determination.

"Thank you."

He kissed her softly on the lips, and his arms tightened around her in one last, sensuous embrace.

"Thank *you*," he said, and released her. "Here." He handed her his robe. "You can put this on until we get your clothes gathered up."

She had one sleeve on and was searching for the other when he turned on the table lamp beside the bed. Caroline froze, forgetting that she was still half naked, and took a long, lingering look at what she was walking away from.

He stood unashamed in the pool of light, his long legs spread slightly for balance, his arms loose at his sides. Dark curls covered his broad, muscular chest, narrowing at the top of his ribs into a single line of hair down the center of his flat stomach to a tight mat of curls at his groin. From this sprang ample evidence that he was not yet ready for the night to end.

Caroline gasped and turned away, but the image lingered and she felt the flames inside her that never quite died. This was going to be a hard night to forget.

"I know how you feel," Duke said from close behind her. He lifted the shoulder of the robe and guided her arm into the sleeve that had eluded her. "It's going to be a long night."

He arranged her hair over the collar of the robe and kissed her gently on the cheek. Then he leaned down and retrieved her bra and panties and handed them to her.

Still flustered and trying to avoid getting another good look at him, Caroline knelt and gathered up her stockings and garter belt. When she rose, Duke handed her her dress, holding it in front of him discreetly.

"I'll dress out here, if you want to take the bathroom. If you need any help with zippers or anything, just whistle. You do know how to whistle, don't you?"

Caroline puckered up and blew. The only sound that came out was the whishing of air.

"Oh, well," he said with a shrug and a slow grin, "it works in the movies. Maybe you can just whisper instead."

"Let's hope I won't need to."

Inside the bathroom, she slipped into her underwear and tried to steady her trembling hands. Every time she thought of Duke, she felt like crying. In spite of what she had told him, in the deepest part of her heart, she wished Martha hadn't come back when she did.

She knew what she had said was right, but what she really wanted right now was to be lying in bed with her head on Duke's shoulder, lost in the memories of their lovemaking. Instead she was struggling to close the side zipper of her dress without causing permanent damage to the skin along her ribs.

Tomorrow, she might look back on this night with embarrassment and disappointment, but right now, she was just glad she still had the drive home to be with Duke.

When she finally finished, she rolled her stockings and garter belt into a ball and held it in her fist. Breathing a sigh of relief, she stepped out of the bathroom and found Duke sitting on the foot of the bed, looking as irresistibly handsome as he had when he picked her up that evening.

With his rumpled black hair and brooding gray eyes, he looked like an advertisement for something sinfully sensuous. All he needed was a cigarette dangling from his full lips and he could be a poster boy for dangerous sex appeal, or so it seemed to her at the moment.

"You ready?" he asked, standing.

"I just need to get my purse."

"Stand by the door. I'll turn out the light."

Caroline did as she was told, waiting at the door until Duke found his way to her through the darkness. Then he opened the door and entered the darkened living room first, leading her by the hand to the outside door.

He opened the door to the hall and looked out.

"The coast is clear. You wait here, and I'll get your purse," he whispered.

Using the light from the hall, he found her purse and they left the suite. At the elevator, Caroline whispered, "The coast is clear?"

"I've always wanted to say that."

"At least you got *something* you wanted tonight."

He tilted her head back and kissed her.

"I got a lot that I wanted tonight. You don't have to get everything to be satisfied. I'm happy just to be with you."

Touching him was enough to make her tingle all the way down to her toes. When his whispery growl told her the things she needed to hear, she felt herself turning to soft taffy inside.

"I wish things had been different. I wish—"

The elevator pinged, cutting off her sentence as the doors opened and a couple stepped out. Duke guided her inside and pushed the Down button.

"Don't these people ever go to bed?" he grumbled, seeming as upset as she was that something always interrupted them every time they got a minute alone together.

The trip down and through the lobby was uneventful. Getting into Duke's car, Caroline realized she still held her stockings and garter belt clutched in one hand and her purse in the other. While Duke started the car, she opened her small evening bag and stuffed the embarrassing contents of her other hand inside the bag.

"Are you going to be all right?" Duke asked quietly, once they were on their way.

"What do you mean?"

"I just don't want you to feel, well, uncomfortable tomorrow."

"I think a little embarrassment might be natural."

He lifted her hand and kissed it. "Not between us, Caroline. I don't ever want you to feel that way."

He laid her hand on his thigh and held it there, his fingers interlaced with hers, until he had to move his hand to shift.

At her house, he walked her to the door. The moon was bright, not quite full. The stars were out, and the air was clear, crisp and cool. Under a yellow porch light, Caroline felt past her stockings to find her key.

Duke laughed and looked around. "I feel like I'm back in high school. I wonder how many people are going to be watching if I try to kiss you good-night."

Caroline found her key and closed her evening bag. "I guess we'll know in a day or two."

"Yeah, I guess we will."

He gathered her gently into his arms. With the memory of their last embrace burning between them, his kiss was laced with regret for what had almost been. At the same time, it held a promise of passion that was ripe and waiting for a day that would come.

When his kiss had said all there was to say, Duke took the key from her and unlocked the door. He took her hand in his and closed her fingers over the key.

"Sweet dreams," he said, and turned and walked away.

Caroline watched him until his car was out of sight. She knew it was too late for caution. She was in love, purely and simply. Nothing had changed. When she was with him, there was magic in the air.

A pain went through the small of her back like the stab of a knife. She screamed and tried to run away, but she couldn't move. Another searing, jagged pain sliced through her stomach and down the inside of her leg. Her cry became a moan.

The mist that surrounded her deepened to a gray fog, and she could feel herself sinking down into a bottomless pit of darkness. She tried to reach out, but her heavy arms flailed uselessly.

The darkness began to spin, sucking her deeper into the pain. The only sounds now were the rapid pounding of her heart and her moaning gasps for breath.

"Caroline! Caroline, wake up."

The frightened voice was in her ear and rough hands shook her. The blackness began to part, and Caroline bolted upright in panic.

"What..." She reached blindly toward her grandmother, who caught her hands and held them.

"Oh, Caroline, you scared me to death."

Viola sagged onto the side of the bed. Caroline reached up to brush a lock of hair away from her face and found that her hair and her forehead were both wet with sweat.

Even now, her heart pounded at a frantic pace and she was short of breath. Terror clung to her.

"Are you going to be all right?"

Her grandmother's worried face peered close.

Already, the nightmare was fading. Caroline tried to remember what had scared her so, but all she could remember was pain and darkness.

"Did something happen last night, Caroline? I've only seen you like this one other time."

Caroline shook her head. She couldn't talk about it yet.

"Let's get you into some fresh clothes, and then I'll make a pot of coffee and we can talk." Viola felt Caroline's face with the back of her hand. "You don't seem to have a fever. Can you walk all right?"

Caroline pushed back the covers and stood up. She felt as weak as if she'd been sick for days.

"I'll be all right. You go make the coffee. I'll be down in a minute."

Painfully, she dragged herself into the bathroom. Her muscles ached and her head throbbed. She felt sick, but she knew she wasn't. She was scared. Some nameless, faceless dread had wrapped itself around her and wouldn't let her go.

By the time she climbed out of the shower, all clean and scrubbed and fresh again, she felt almost strong enough to sit up through breakfast. Not quite ready to face the day, she pulled on a pair of lounging pajamas and a robe and went to join her grandmother in the kitchen.

"Just sit down, dear. Muffins will be ready in a minute, and there's fresh orange juice on the table. I'll bring your coffee."

Caroline sat at the table and watched her grandmother bustle around the kitchen with more energy than she had displayed in months. It reminded her of childhood days she had almost forgotten and of nurturing she had once taken for granted.

"Here's your coffee, sweetheart," Viola said, setting a steaming cup in front of Caroline. "And here's your orange juice." She poured a glass and set it beside the coffee. She felt Caroline's forehead once more and nodded with approval. "You seem to be doing just fine. How are you feeling now?"

"Like I've been run over by a truck." Caroline took a drink of the orange juice and shook her head in disgust. "It's just a dream. I don't know why it affects me like this."

Viola put the muffins on the table and sat down beside Caroline. "You wouldn't ask that if you'd heard the scream you let out. And your bed looks like there was a battle fought on it."

Her grandmother's soft hand cupped her cheek, and Caroline looked up from her study of the tablecloth.

"You looked so happy when you left last night. I thought maybe if I stopped fighting you, it would help somehow. Now I don't know what else to do and I just can't stand to see you hurting like this, Caroline."

Lavender eyes filled with caring stared into hers, and Caroline wished she had an answer. But she didn't. Nothing she had tried had worked.

"I think it's just too much, too suddenly. I'm not really over Granddad yet. And being back home again stirs up so many memories. Now, seeing Duke again, with so many things that were never resolved . . . if I just had a little more time. If everything wasn't all happening at once."

Her face full of regret, Viola shook her head. "I've worried over the years that you'd never gotten over him. Sometimes, you have to make the same mistake more than once before you learn better, and I'm afraid that's what we did with you. When your mother had you, it was a different time and to have a child out of wedlock could ruin a girl's life forever. But how can it have been that bad when it gave us you?"

Viola's hand closed over her granddaughter's and squeezed. "We shouldn't have tried to protect you so much," she continued. "We should have let you live your life without so much fear. Mistakes aren't always so bad. Some wonderful things can come out of them."

"Are you trying to tell me that nightmares or no nightmares, I should try to finish what Duke and I started all those years ago?"

Viola smiled and shrugged. "I guess that's what I'm trying to tell you."

"Oh, Gran, I just don't know." Caroline shook her head. She was too tired to even try to think of the possibility.

"Then tell me this, Caroline." Viola patted Caroline's hand again to make sure she had her attention. "You've spent a lot of time with Duke over the last few weeks. Judging from this morning, I'd say something significant must have happened with him last night. Are you in love with him?"

Regardless of what she decided, one thing Caroline could never deny was that she loved him. "Yes," she said, looking her grandmother in the eye.

"Does it bother you that he has a child?"

"No." She remembered the feel of Kimi's small hand on her hair the night before. "I think she's wonderful."

"Then what's the problem?"

Caroline thought for a moment, and then said with a shrug, "The nightmares? I guess there's nothing left now but the nightmares."

"I'm sorry, child." Viola put her hand on Caroline's arm. "I'm really sorry. I wish there was something I could do."

"So do I, Gran." She stood. "I think I'll go for a drive and then try taking a nap."

"Do you want me to take a message if someone calls?"

Without thinking, Caroline said, "No. No, I don't think I want to talk to anyone. Why don't you just tell everyone I'm gone for a few days?"

Viola looked concerned. "But, dear, it's New Year's Eve. Don't you have plans? What should I tell Ariel?"

"I don't know. I just know I have two days before I have to go back to work and I don't want to talk to anyone. That includes Ariel. And that especially includes Duke."

"If you say so, dear." Viola still frowned with unspoken worry.

Caroline kissed her on the cheek and hugged her gently. "I'm just tired, Gran. I just need to get some sleep. And to have some time to think. Everything will be all right." She patted her grandmother on the arm, reassuring herself as much as the older woman. "You'll see."

Chapter Ten

The door to Caroline's office opened and Duke walked in looking haggard in spite of the well-cut suit he wore. He closed the door and leaned against it.

"At least talk to me."

"I . . ." She looked up at him and knew the pain he felt, because she felt it, too. "I can't think of anything to say."

"Tell me what a bastard I am for trying to pull something like that."

Caroline looked down at her hands, spread open over the papers she hadn't been able to concentrate on. "No. I was as much to blame as you were. That's what makes it so bad."

"Look, what we did—or almost did—may have been bad timing, but that's all it was. I'm in love with you, Caroline, and I know you love me, too. Can't we just stop all this foolishness and do something about the way we feel?"

She didn't know what to say. He was right, but it didn't make any difference. The more she tried to follow her heart, the worse the nightmares became, until finally, she was afraid even to sleep.

Everything seemed so hopeless. She wanted him so much, and there was nothing she could do. Just being near him had become a torture, and she didn't know how much longer she could bear it.

"Caroline." Duke whispered her name as he knelt beside her and lifted her chin until he could look into her eyes. "Sweetheart what is it? I know you're keeping something from me and it's tearing you apart. Please, trust me. Whatever the problem is, I'll understand."

Nearly in tears, Caroline took a deep breath. It wouldn't be easy, but she had to at least try to explain to him. Maybe then, he would see why she couldn't give him what he wanted, why she might never be able to.

Forcing the words out, she said, "I have dreams. Bad ones."

"Nightmares?" Duke frowned, trying to understand more than she was saying.

"Yes."

He pulled a chair around the end of the desk and sat facing her. "How long have you had them?" he asked, taking her hand in his.

"Always. At least, it seems like that long." She stared at their hands, unable to look him in the face. "They started when I was seven or eight, about the time my mother left, I guess. And the older I got, the worse they got, until I met you."

"And then?" he prompted.

She looked at him for the first time since he had sat down with her. "And then they got really bad." Amazingly, as she spoke, she felt the hard knot of desperation in her chest begin to ease. "The more I saw you and the closer we got, the worse my nightmares were."

"And you never told me?"

"No." She shook her head. "I never told anyone."

"And now they're back again." Duke frowned, and the soft edge of his voice grew sharper. "You didn't have them the whole time we were apart?"

"Except for when I was married." She began to relax, relieved to have the confession over with and at least one of her secrets finally out in the open. Surely now he would understand why there could never be anything else between them.

"You had the nightmares when you were married?" he asked quietly. His hand tightened on hers, and he moved closer. "Then it's not just me? It's any man?"

"What?" Caroline looked at him in surprise. She had expected him to give up, but instead, he was pressing her for more answers. "What do you mean?"

"I mean you had these same nightmares when you were married to a man you said you didn't love." Growing intent, he leaned forward in his chair, nearer to her. When she tried to draw away, he caught her arms and held her still. "You told me your marriage was annulled because you had a problem, not him. Did you make love to him, Caroline? *Could* you make love to him?"

She stared at Duke, wide-eyed, trapped in her chair and desperate to get away from the questions he kept pounding her with. "I don't know what you mean."

Speaking slowly and pinning her with his soft, gray gaze that was more powerful than a truth serum, Duke asked, "What I mean is, did you consummate your marriage, Caroline? Did you ever, in all the time you knew him, make love to the man you married?"

Defiance blazing from her eyes, Caroline set her jaw with grim determination. "No."

Duke released a huge sigh of relief, let go of her arms and sat back in his chair with a smile. "Well, that's wonderful." His smile widened. "Hot damn, that's great!"

"I don't know what's so great about it."

"Because you made love to me, sweetheart," he said tenderly. "Nightmares and all, you made love to me thirteen years ago, and you were ready to make love to me again last weekend. And that gives me hope.''

Caroline wished she could feel the same way. Duke made it sound so easy, and she'd give anything if it could be.

''Duke, it's not a question of my loving you,'' she said sadly, while tears began to burn in her eyes and tear at her heart. ''Because I do. It's a question of my living with that love, and I just don't know if I can do that.''

''We'll find a way,'' he promised, leaning near again to take her hand in his.

''You haven't been inside my head.'' She pulled her hand away reluctantly and he let her go. ''You don't know what it's like.'' She pushed her chair away from the desk and stood up. ''I'm sorry, but I have to go now. I don't think I can work anymore today.''

Duke stood, his whole body stiff as he fought his impulse to stop her. ''Caroline.''

''I'll be back tomorrow.'' She opened the door and turned to look at him one last time. ''But please, please, leave me alone. I don't think I can take much more.''

''If that's the way you want it, I'll try.'' He stood straight, his head held high, still fighting himself to remain where he was while she walked out the door.

''That's the way I want it,'' she said in a voice that made a lie of her words. ''I'm really sorry. I wish it could be different.''

''I'm sorry, too, Caroline. I love you.''

The tears she could see glistening in his eyes were what hurt her the most. For thirteen years, she had wondered what it would be like to be with Duke again, and now she had her answer.

Maybe someday, somehow, there would be a time for them, but that time wasn't today, and tomorrow might as well be a million years away.

The weeks that followed went slowly. A blast of winter blew through, layering the terraced town in white. The littlé tourist paradise slipped into its silent season, the private winter months when no outsiders visited and Eureka belonged to its residents alone.

Caroline moved into the guest room, and in their spare time she and Ariel began refinishing the canopy bed that was to be Caroline's special gift to Kimi. In the attic, she found the lacy canopy that her mother had remembered, and from a trunk of old quilts, Caroline selected an appliqué quilt of a shepherdess and her flock that was just the right size for the twin bed.

Ariel had begun work on Hurley House. The first room she furnished was the sitting room off the master bedroom. It was done as an office for Duke, and he began to put in long hours in the privacy of his new home.

Caroline had barely seen him for weeks, except for church on Sunday, and even then, he kept his distance. But between Ariel and Kimi, she knew practically every move Duke made, and she had a feeling he knew as much about her.

Whether she wanted to think about him or not, it was almost impossible to keep others from mentioning him when so many areas of their lives touched. And since her nightmares had stopped again, she had even begun to wonder if she hadn't been wrong to banish him from her life in the first place.

By the first week of February, the last lingering traces of snow and ice had melted and the sun glowed over the stark, brown landscape. Evergreens edged lawns, while amaryllis bloomed in windowsills. The first, false blush of spring fooled man and nature alike.

Caroline descended the staircase of her grandmother's house feeling revitalized. Ariel had been there, and they had worked all morning at rubbing down the bare wood of the canopy bed, coaxing out the patina that had been bruised but not destroyed by the coat of white paint that had been carefully removed over the past month.

After Ariel left, Caroline had showered and dressed in clothes suitable for a spin through the foothills in her newly repaired car.

"Hi, Gran. Did they deliver it?" she called, quickly scanning the table by the entryway for her car keys.

Viola came into the hall from the kitchen at the back of the house. "They called and were very apologetic." She wiped her hands on the dish towel she had with her.

"Oh, no." After three days without her car and a morning spent in diligent labor, Caroline was ready to get out of the house, even if she had to go on foot. "What did they say?"

"It won't be ready until this evening. Because they promised it to you for Monday, they're going to stay tonight until they finish it and drop it off on their way home."

Torn between gratitude and disappointment, Caroline sagged against the front door and crossed her arms. "Phooey."

"I told them you were very grateful," her grandmother said sternly.

"I am, but it's such a beautiful day. I wanted to go for a drive this afternoon. Wouldn't you like to go for a drive, Gran?"

"When you've never driven, dear, you just don't think about things like that. Would you like some lunch?"

"Have you got any pizza? I was kind of in a mood for pizza."

Viola harrumphed in disgust and went back into the kitchen.

"Rats." Caroline walked into the parlor and looked around without much enthusiasm. A half-formed idea of changing shoes and taking a walk downtown had begun to take shape when something with a loud engine pulled up outside and stopped.

Curious, she walked to the window and pulled the lace curtain aside. In the street at the end of the walk sat a big, black motorcycle. Entering the gate was a vision out of the past.

Duke, dressed in blue jeans, motorcycle boots and a black leather jacket, left the gate to the white picket fence ajar and started up the walk with a purposeful stride. The jacket blew open to reveal a white T-shirt underneath, and Caroline felt her knees weaken.

Common sense, caution and every negative feeling she'd ever had about him drained right out of her and she reached the front door before his firm knock had a chance to sound more than twice.

"Hi." She sounded winded but inviting.

Duke frowned down at her for a second and then said, "You seem friendlier than I expected."

"It kind of surprises me, too. Do you want to come in?"

"Are we alone?" He peered into the darker hallway behind her.

"Gran's in the kitchen."

"What the hell," he said with a shrug and came inside.

Caroline stepped backward toward the parlor door and gestured. "Want to sit down?"

Duke walked into the parlor and looked around. He seemed restless and eager to be moving again.

"Aren't you going to ask me why I'm here?" he asked, turning from his inspection of the parlor to look at her.

"Well, to be truthful, it hadn't occurred to me. I was sort of at loose ends, and just as I was wondering what I was going to do next, you drove up."

"Then you don't have any plans?"

"None. My car's in the shop and I'm stranded."

"Would you like to get out of the house for a while?"

"Yes." She couldn't hide the enthusiasm in her voice. If anyone short of an ax murderer had made the same offer, she'd probably have said yes, but not quite as happily.

For the first time since his arrival, Duke smiled. "You were bored, weren't you?" His eyes held a familiar warmth as he looked at her.

Caroline laughed. "Yes."

"Good. Let's go."

"Gran?" She turned toward the dining room and waited for an answer.

In a moment, the swinging door to the kitchen opened and Viola appeared in the doorway. "Did you call me?"

"I'm going out for a while," Caroline said.

"Well, have a good time." Viola stared at Duke as if she were seeing a ghost, but otherwise, she did an admirable job of keeping her curiosity under control. "It's nice to see you again, Duke."

"Thank you, ma'am. It's nice to see *you*. How are you doing today?"

"Better all the time, thank you. Well, you two be careful."

"Don't you worry, Mrs. Adams, I'll take good care of her. And I'm not quite sure where we're going, so we may be gone for a while."

"Well, thank you for telling me. I won't wait supper."

With a smile and a wave from her grandmother, Caroline and Duke turned and left.

"That was almost scary," Caroline said as they walked toward the bike.

"I know. When I was younger, I would have given anything to have had her treat me like that."

"If you'd owned your own company then, she probably would have."

"I guess there's a lot to be said for the passage of time."

She smiled up at him. "Yeah, I guess there is. Where are we going?"

"I'm not sure yet."

He swung his leg over the motorcycle and straightened it. Then he held out his arm for her and guided her on behind him.

When the engine roared to life, Caroline wrapped her arms around his waist and pressed herself tightly against his back. "You know," she said, raising her voice over the noise, "I'm really not dressed for this."

"Just hold on tight. I'll take care of you."

The words were hardly out of his mouth before the motorcycle shot forward and they were off. Like something out of her memories, they circled down through the town and back up the curving residential streets. Only this time, their ride wasn't under the cover of darkness. This time, they were together in the daylight for all to see.

Caroline knew without being told that this wasn't just a pleasure ride. There was a reason behind the motorcycle, what he was wearing, even the ride itself. But only Duke knew why he was recreating the past this way, and so far, he wasn't telling.

Eventually, their tour of the town took them to the overlook that had served as a lover's lane as far back as anyone could remember. A lonely place in the daytime, it had been Caroline's haunt since childhood. It was also the first place Duke had ever kissed her, and it held a very special place in her heart.

He cut the engine and the cycle rolled to a halt well back from the rim. "This bring back any memories?" he asked quietly.

"Of course it does," she said, smiling as she eased her grip on his waist and began to flex the blood back into her stiff fingers. "This was where you took me the first time we were ever alone together. I didn't tell you that day, but I used to ride my bicycle up here a lot when I was a kid."

Dismounting, he held out his hand for her. "Why?"

She shook her head. "It doesn't matter. Just daydreaming." She took his hand and eased herself off the cycle.

The sun was warm and the day was pleasant, and while she had been riding, Duke's body had shielded her. But the wind was strong here, halfway up the mountainside, and even with the heavy sweater she wore, Caroline felt herself growing chilled.

Duke slipped his hand in hers and led her toward the stone wall that edged the overlook. "So far, this is a lot easier than I thought it was going to be."

He sounded perplexed, and Caroline laughed softly, enjoying his company again after being away from him for so long. "When are you going to tell me what this is all about?"

He turned and leaned his hip against the top of the wall, still holding her hand. "That part's simple. I just can't accept the fact that it's over between us. We never even gave it a fair shot, and I know we can find a way to make it work if we just keep trying."

Caroline looked at him, squinting one eye slightly in the bright afternoon sun. "Two weeks ago, I would have argued with you."

"Two weeks ago, I didn't have the guts to confront you. Does that mean you're willing?"

Caroline pulled her hand from his and walked a few feet away. Her fingertips braced on the top of the wall, she looked at the valley below. Houses climbed the sides of the hills. From above, the colored rooftops seemed to be nestled among the trees.

On another hilltop miles away, the Christ of the Ozarks statue, with arms outstretched, stood sentinel over the valley.

"You know," Caroline said in a voice softened by faraway memories, "my mother ran from this town. She hated it here. I used to think I felt the same way."

"It gets into your blood, doesn't it?"

She looked at him, surprised by his understanding. "Yes, it does." She smiled. "I never thought I'd say it, but it's really good to be home."

"I know how you feel. A lot of people think I came back here because of you, and maybe that was part of it." He turned and looked out over the valley. "But I could never get this place out of my mind. There's a peacefulness about it that I missed once I was gone from here."

"You know, it amazes me how much alike we are in some ways."

He grinned. "Did you miss it, too?"

"I tried not to, but I did."

Gently steering her back to his question, he asked, "So, are you going to give me an answer? Should I repeat the question?" He paused, and when he heard only silence, he went on. "Would you be willing to give it another try? To give *us* another try?"

"What if I say yes?" she asked cautiously, not ready to give him an answer.

"Then we go someplace where we can be alone and we really talk."

Caroline took a deep breath. Before they went any further, she had to get something out in the open. If she really loved him, and she did, then she could tell him the one thing she had never talked about with anyone else.

Over the past month, her nightmares had gradually disappeared, but she knew it couldn't last. The private terrors that haunted her in the night would return again and again until she had finally confronted all the fears she kept hidden.

Staring out over the valley, Caroline took another deep breath and confronted the darkest of her secrets. "Duke, did you know that I'm illegitimate?"

"No," he said with hardly a pause. "But I suspected something like it."

Finally daring to look at him, she raised her eyes and peered out at him through her lashes. "You did? Why?"

"You were reared by your grandparents. You had their name, not your father's. And the way they guarded you," he said with a shake of his head, "wasn't normal. But you never mentioned it, so I never asked. I knew whatever secret you were hiding wouldn't affect the way I felt about you."

"How could you know that?"

"Sweetheart." He put his hand over hers on the stone ledge and looked into her eyes with all the feeling he had for her. "I loved you. There was nothing that could have changed the way I felt about you."

Almost weak with relief, Caroline wanted to laugh and cry at the same time. It had taken her almost thirty-one years to say the words aloud, and now that she had, they seemed so much less important.

"That wasn't easy for you to say, was it?" Duke turned her to face him, guiding her into his arms at the same time. "You're shaking like a leaf. Here, put your arms inside my jacket."

She slid her arms around his waist and snuggled against his chest, feeling safe and warm, the way she always felt when she was with him.

"Where do we go from here?" she asked, gazing up at him. He had brought her this far. She was content to let him take her the rest of the way.

Duke kissed her gently, giving her the love she needed and withholding the passion that would come later.

"The sky's the limit," he promised, holding her close against him until her trembling finally subsided.

The tree-shadowed dirt road opened without warning into a flat, grassy clearing, several acres wide. The perimeter was rimmed by forest, and in the corner farthest from the road was an old building, its red paint faded to barely more than a stain.

Duke turned the bike soon after they entered the clearing and headed toward something that looked like a footbridge crossing what looked like . . .

"Is that a creek?" Caroline shouted in Duke's ear.

"Yeah," he shouted back to her.

Across the creek, a path led from the footbridge to a ramshackle cabin that seemed to be clinging to the side of the mountain with nothing more than stubbornness to hold it there.

"What is *that* thing?" she shouted, holding on to Duke with her left arm while she raised her right to point toward the cabin.

Pulling to a halt a comfortable distance from the creek bank, Duke cut the motorcycle's engine and turned his head to look at Caroline.

"What?"

In the sudden quiet, she could hear the rushing of the creek and the rustle of the wind through the dry leaves that still clung to the trees. It took a minute to refocus her attention.

"What's that?" she said, pointing again to the cabin.

"It belongs to a friend of mine."

"You mean someone lives there?" Caroline couldn't quite keep the shock out of her voice.

Duke chuckled and climbed off the cycle. He held out his hand to her. "It'll surprise you when you see it up close."

"I was afraid you had something like that in mind." She slipped her hand in his and let him steady her until she got her land legs back under her. "And that?" She pointed to the red building.

"An old mill. See the waterwheel out back? They still use it sometimes."

"For what?" Incredulous, Caroline watched while the waterwheel churned away, carrying a steady flow of water from the creek behind it, across the top of the wheel, and dumping it in a narrow waterfall back into the creek in front. It was very pretty to watch and it made a lovely sound, peaceful and exciting at the same time.

"Stone-ground flour and cornmeal," Duke said. "This used to be a full-time working mill. It's locked up today, but I'll get the key sometime and show you around inside."

Turning slowly around to study him, she said, "You're just full of surprises, aren't you?"

His black hair was windblown, but he had the kind of hair that never really looked bad. Wet or dry, combed or uncombed, it had the kind of texture and cut that managed to look flattering no matter what.

His gray eyes were cautious. "What do you mean?"

"Well, if all you ever did was ride around on motorcycles and work on car engines," she said, realizing for the first time that she knew as little about his background as he did about hers and that she wasn't the only one who had never talked about herself.

"Then," she continued, "where did you learn about cabinetmaking, and how do you know so much about a place like this?" She held out her hands, indicating the rustic retreat he had brought them to.

"Well," he said, smiling, "I guess that's what we're here to find out, isn't it?" He slipped his hand into hers and led her toward the footbridge. "You ever cross one of these?"

She frowned at the rope-and-wood-plank contraption as they neared it. "No."

"Well, it's kind of like walking on a trampoline, and you'll probably feel better going across it by yourself. I'll wait here until you're across."

Caroline came to a dead halt, pulled her hand free of his and shook her head. "Absolutely not."

"It's easy. You just hold on to the rope handrail and be careful to put your feet on the wood planks. It'll bounce a little, but that's okay. And don't worry if it sways. It won't do it too much."

She looked at him. "You're serious, aren't you?"

"I'd walk with you if it would help, but it won't. It would make it worse. And if I tried to carry you, we'd probably both fall right over the side into the creek."

"But, Duke," she reasoned in a last-ditch effort to talk him out of it, "what could possibly be over there that I would care that much about?"

"Sweetheart." He cupped her face in his hands and looked down at her with such love and tenderness, Caroline knew she had lost the battle even before he kissed her.

His lips on hers were warm and firm. Their taste was sweet. His tongue gently touched her lower lip, tickling, tantalizing and then retreating. His hands on her face pulled her closer while his mouth pressed harder, opening to her, drawing her in.

Caroline slipped her hands inside his jacket and around his slim waist, pulling him into her arms. His hands moved to her shoulders, pressing her against him, and his mouth slipped away from hers.

"Oh, baby." He laid his cheek on hers while he gasped in air. "What were we talking about?"

"You were telling me why I had to walk across that thing." She pulled an arm out from his jacket to point to the swinging bridge.

"Because that—" he pointed to the cabin that looked as if the weight of a bird could topple it "—is where we're spending the night."

"Oh, Duke," Caroline moaned, "couldn't we just pitch a tent?"

"Trust me." He led her by the hand to the bridge and guided her onto the first plank. "Now go," he said, releasing her shoulders.

Unwilling to look like more of a coward than she already did, Caroline took a deep breath, held on to the rope railings and cautiously worked her way, plank by plank, across the bridge. When she reached the middle, the up-and-down bounce and side-to-side sway were at their worst, and the hip-high handholds didn't offer much reassurance.

After a momentary paralysis and a fleeting mental picture of the whole apparatus tipping upside down and leaving her dangling from the handrails while the creek rushed by below, Caroline managed to get moving again and safely crossed to the other side.

Duke followed her over with disgusting ease.

"It gets better the more you do it," he said. He put his arm around her and kissed her comfortingly on the temple.

"The second half wasn't so bad," she admitted, happy just to have it over with.

He kept his arm around her while he led her up the dirt path to the cabin, which did look better up close, Caroline was relieved to notice. More of it was tucked back into the hillside than she had been able to see from across the creek. And the wide front porch that jutted out into the air was well braced from below.

The comfortable porch swing and chairs looked inviting, and the weathered gray exterior was actually stained cedar in fairly good condition. "This isn't so bad," she said as she stood on the porch waiting for Duke to unlock the door.

From here, the creek and the old mill with its waterwheel, even the swinging bridge, made a cozy picture. She could almost imagine this place in the summer. It must seem like a little piece of heaven.

"You're starting to like it, aren't you?"

She turned around to find Duke smiling down at her. He glanced out at the view she had been studying.

"This place has a lot of memories," he said quietly. "Some good, some bad. But it's always been very special to me. I'm glad you like it."

"I guess I should try trusting you more often."

"That's what I'm hoping for. And now..." He scooped her into his arms.

"What are you doing?" Caroline gasped.

"Carrying you across the threshold," he said. Tucking her tightly against him, he started toward the open door.

"We're not *married*."

"Don't quibble." With a flourish, he swept through the doorway and into the cabin.

"I don't think that's a quibble," Caroline said.

From the vantage of his arms, she gazed around the room. The furniture, what little there was of it, was simple, but the woodwork and built-ins were obviously hand-crafted with talented and loving care.

"Who lives here?" she asked as he left the living room with her still in his arms and started toward the back of the cabin.

"We'll get to that later."

The stone fireplace that separated the living room from the dining room was open on both sides. The kitchen was roomy and the cabinetwork was beautiful.

"Did you remodel this place?" she asked as he carried her down the hallway, not even slowing down at the first door they passed.

"No."

The bathroom door was open, and in the flying glimpse she caught, it looked as good as the kitchen. The hallway ended abruptly and Caroline found herself still in Duke's arms in a room that was as dark and silent as a cave. Her arms tightened around Duke's neck.

"Where are we?" she whispered.

He twisted slightly and flipped a switch on the wall. A brass floor lamp with a rose-colored tiffany shade came on across the room, lighting the darkness with a soft, pink-tinged glow. A few yards from the floor lamp, in the center of the room against the back wall, was a four-poster bed.

The wood was dark, almost black. The back of the bed was high and solid looking. The posters were tall, round and massive. It was a bed Henry VIII would have been at home in. It was a bed built to last.

Duke carried her across the room, straight to the impressive bed, and deposited her on the white cotton comforter that covered it. He leaned over her prone body, his arms supporting his weight on either side of her, and said, "I love you. With all my heart. And I want you more than I have ever wanted anything in my life."

Caroline raised her arms to encircle his neck. "I'm yours," she said softly. "I've never been anyone else's but yours."

He leaned nearer and kissed her, gently, to seal the unspoken pledge they had just made to each other. Then he walked to the lamp, switched it off and back on to a lower wattage, an intimate, rosy hue that was closer to candlelight.

"I'm going to lock the front door," he said with a nod in that direction. "There's a robe on the bathroom door if you'd be more comfortable."

Caroline sat up and dangled her feet off the side of the high bed. She was a little nervous and a little scared, but she was mostly happy. She looked at Duke, standing by the lamp and looking back at her, and she saw yesterday and today blending into one.

He looked so much like he had the last time she had felt like this, the last time, the only time, she had known they were going to make love, known she was going to be truly and totally his.

The memories made her impatient, and she could see he was feeling the same way. She straightened her knee, extending her leg toward him and wiggling her booted foot. "Could you help me with these before you go?" she asked in a voice that was husky with invitation.

Duke shrugged off his jacket and laid it across a chair. Then, almost as an afterthought, he pulled his T-shirt over his head and tossed it on top of his jacket. "Sure."

She watched him come toward her, his eyes locked on hers, and felt the tension build inside her until she was weak. He took her boot by the heel and tugged it free with one pull, then reached for the other one and did the same while Caroline leaned back with her arms braced behind her.

"Anything else I can do for you, ma'am?" Duke asked. He slid his hands under the edge of her sweater and encircled her bare waist.

"Oh, yes," Caroline whispered as she wrapped her arms around his shoulders, "much, much more."

Wasting no motions, he took the tail of her sweater and peeled it upward over her head and down her arms. Leaving it wrong side out, he laid the sweater on the bed and reached behind her to unhook the sheer black bra she had chosen on a whim that morning.

Then he stepped back and took a long look at her sitting on the side of the bed, bare breasted in stretch pants and cotton socks. "I'd better go lock that door while I can still move," he said in a husky rasp.

Dropping back onto the bed with a groan as Duke left the room, Caroline stared at the ceiling and tried to catch her breath. Inside her, a fire burned that left her reckless and unafraid and impatient.

She rolled onto her side, grabbed the comforter at the head of the bed and pulled it toward her as she stood. Hurriedly slipping out of the rest of her clothes, she dropped them next to her boots, then swept her sweater onto the pile on the floor.

When she straightened, she saw Duke leave the bathroom and reenter the bedroom, his eyes on her. His jeans were unbuttoned and unzipped. Riding low on his hips, they left a wide vee exposed down the front of his flat stomach. A dark line of hair led her eyes to the base of the zipper where his jeans stretched taut over an outline that took her breath away.

"I carried the image of you in my mind for thirteen years," he said, stopping just in front of her, "and I told myself that no one could be as beautiful as I remember you were."

Before Caroline's trembling legs gave way, Duke lifted her and laid her in a soft tumble of pillows, sheets and comforter. The cool fabric felt good against the rising heat of her skin as she watched him slide his jeans down over his hips. He left them on the floor by her clothes and slipped into the cozy nest beside her.

His mouth covered hers, plundering her softness, draining her, filling her, loving her with his lips, while his body slid over hers, flesh on flesh, abrasive and tender, soft and hard, needing and yielding.

Breathless, he finally pulled his mouth from hers and moved his body to the side, still touching her lightly. His lips left a trail of light kisses across her jaw and down her neck while his palm cupped the base of her breast. His thigh brushed over hers. His thumb stroked the outer edge of her nipple, then moved slowly toward the aroused tip. His mouth followed, soothing and tantalizing at once.

Alive to his every touch, Caroline twisted under him. Her mind longed for the feelings he aroused to go on forever, but her body cried out for the release only he could give her.

"I don't want to rush you," he whispered, raising his head from her breast.

His breath burned over her, sending the fire inside her higher. She could hear her heart pounding, her blood racing through her temples. She tried to answer, but she couldn't speak.

His hand slid over her stomach and moved lower. His fingers spread, weaving their way through the silken curls of pale gold at the juncture of her thighs.

Caroline moaned softly and trembled as his hand moved deeper, urging her legs apart. Again, he followed the path of his hand with kisses. He wound a bright curl around the tip of his finger and sighed.

"I've always remembered your silver-and-gold hair," he said softly. "*All* of your silver and gold hair." He kissed the tender flesh at the top of her thigh. His hand flattened on her, the pressure driving her wild with pleasure while his fingers combed through the hair over her mound again. "I remember the moonlight shining down on you, turning the golden strands to a shimmering white, like jewels sparkling in a nest of silk. I remember how I felt that night, seeing all of you for the first time, touching you where I'd never touched you before...."

His voice died away, and his hand spread her legs wider. As he lowered his head to kiss the shining mass of curls, Caroline caught her breath in a shuddering gasp and then released it in a moan of unbearable pleasure when the tip of his tongue found the bare flesh that was hidden beneath and slipped deep within the crevice that awaited him.

When he raised himself on strong arms and slid his legs between hers, she was almost too weak with desire to move. When she felt the pressure of him against her, she lifted instinctively to meet him, and when she felt the length of him slowly fill her, a joy that had no name swelled inside her, as well.

It wasn't the first time, and yet it was. She had been with him before, and yet this was fuller and sweeter. This time, she was a woman and he was a man. This time, there was no one who could send her away when the morning came.

Her blood roared inside her head. Her body throbbed with every move he made. They were alone together, locked in each other's arms, teetering at the top of the world. A hot, dry wind raged over them, its howl filling the air with every thrust of their bodies. Joined in immortal combat, each strained toward the other's finish, intent on the other's pleasure. And when the end finally came, they both cried out in victory and collapsed in each other's arms.

Drowsy, drained, light-headed with happiness, Caroline lay with her head on Duke's shoulder. His arm encircled her, holding her close to his side. "Shouldn't I go home now?" she asked, hoping he would have a reason why she shouldn't.

"There's plenty of time." He patted her arm. "We'll sleep for a while, and I'll take you home when the alarm goes off. You'll be back in plenty of time to wake up in your own bed tomorrow."

"I don't really want to go." She snuggled closer. She could gladly stay here for the rest of her life, in their little nest in the trees, with the world safely locked outside. "Whose place is this, anyway?"

"It was my father's. I guess it's mine now."

Caroline turned her head to look up at him, almost awake at his unexpected statement. "Your father? I thought there was just your mother and your sisters. I didn't know you had a father."

"He didn't live with our family." Duke brushed her hair away from her face with his hand and kissed her lightly on the forehead. "I guess I might as well tell you, since you've told me so much. My dad was an alcoholic. Mom ran him off when I was just a kid, but I used to come visit him up here a lot. He did all the work on this place. He taught me everything I know about cabinetmaking."

"Where is he now?"

"He died a few years back. He was pretty old by then, and he'd gotten pretty bad toward the end. But he was still my dad, and I loved him. I guess I'll always keep this place, to remember him by, if nothing else."

"Oh, Duke." Caroline put her hand on his chest. "I'm sorry. I can't believe I knew so little about you."

"We were young. Our minds were on other things." He smiled, and they laughed together.

"Yeah, I guess you're right," she agreed, still smiling.

He hugged her to him. "Let's go to sleep. We've got the rest of our lives to talk about the past."

"I love you." She kissed his chest and turned more of her body toward his.

"I love you, too, sweetheart," he whispered in her ear. "We're finally together, and that's all that matters."

"Sweetheart." His breath was a caress against her cheek. "Wake up, honey."

His arms were wrapped around her, and Caroline opened her eyes slowly, reluctant to leave the warmth of his embrace and the sweetest, most peaceful sleep she could remember.

Lifting her head from his shoulder, she looked at him and smiled. The lamp, not much brighter than moonlight, still bathed the room in its rosy glow. The comforter shut out the chill of the air. "What time is it?" she asked, wanting to laugh from the sheer pleasure of awakening with Duke still beside her.

"You don't want to know." His voice sounded gravelly with sleep, but happy. "If we hurry, you can be asleep in your bed at home before the sun comes up."

"But I'll be alone." Her arm tightened around him. "I hate to leave."

"I know, sweetheart." His hand slid through her hair, and he kissed her gently. "This night has been like a dream come true, but it's only the first of many. I promise you that. I don't want to frighten your grandmother, though. And she'd be scared if she woke up and you weren't home yet."

"Oh," Caroline groaned and tried to straighten up. "Reality." She pushed back the comforter and was halfway out of the bed before she remembered that she wasn't wearing anything. She stopped abruptly and pulled the sheet up to her shoulders.

"Not a bad idea, actually," Duke said from behind her, "if we're going to get out of here any time soon. If you could hand me my jeans, I'll go into the bathroom to dress and give you some privacy."

"It seems like a silly time to be modest," Caroline said softly, pulling the sheet with her as she leaned down to lift his jeans from the pile of clothing on the floor.

Duke moved nearer, and his hand closed over hers when she turned to hand him the pants. His chest brushed her shoulder while he kissed her, slowly, deeply and tenderly. When the kiss ended, he looked into her eyes and asked, "Do you still feel shy?"

"No," she answered, flushed and breathless. The sheet had slipped from her hands and she had no desire to retrieve it.

He kissed her again lightly and slid away toward his side of the bed. Then he stood and stepped into his jeans while she watched with unabashed interest. "Someday," he said, smiling as he fastened the top button, "you won't remember what it's like to be shy with me. Now get some clothes on, pretty lady, before I forget all my good intentions."

Duke started toward the bathroom without looking back, and Caroline began to gather up her clothes. She hated to go, but she knew he was right. It was Sunday morning, and they both had family waiting at home. This might be the first night they'd shared together, but it wouldn't be the last. They had the rest of their lives, and it would only get better.

"Sweetheart?"

Her clothes bundled in her arms, she straightened and looked at him, standing in the doorway. She smiled and felt herself turn soft inside. "Yes?"

"You mind if I call you later this morning? Just to make sure you're up in time for church?"

Her smile broadened. "I'd love it. I'll be waiting."

Chapter Eleven

Gasping for breath, Caroline bolted upright in bed. Her heart was pounding, and when she wiped her hair from her face, tears streaked her hand.

Like a cobweb, fragments of the dream still clung to her. She was alone, cast out. The streets were dark, wet and empty, and she was a child grotesquely swollen by the child she carried within her.

She shivered and climbed from her bed to shower and change, but even then, the fear and despair of the dream wouldn't let go. It didn't seem fair to have been so happy when she fell asleep only to awaken to the aftermath of yet another nightmare.

Outside, the pale blush of dawn promised another mild and sunny day. Inside, the house was dark and bleak. Caroline grabbed a jacket from the hall tree by the front door and left.

Guided by instinct, she took the long, curving road that led to the overlook where Duke had taken her. She hadn't told Duke the day before, but this same road had served as a lovers' lane when her mother was a girl. Like a ritual, Caroline had ridden her bike to the high, secluded spot to sit for hours staring at the sky and the town below.

She had imagined that this was where her mother and father had gone to meet and in her child's mind, she had hoped that by some magic, her father would be drawn back to the spot. She had been sure that someday, she would find him here and that they would know each other instantly when they met.

Those were childhood dreams. On this morning, she only hoped that she could find some answer to her despair in this secret place. If she could only find some way to put the past behind her, then maybe she could have a future with the man she loved.

After last night, she couldn't give Duke up. No matter how many days began with fear and cold sweats, she couldn't stop loving him, and she wouldn't try to live without him.

To her surprise, the flat parking area of the overlook wasn't empty when she turned into it. A car was parked at the back and a man dressed in jeans and a sweatshirt stood at the stone wall, staring out over the valley. His back was toward her, and a ball cap covered his head.

Jarred by the presence of another person so early in the morning, Caroline left her car as quietly as possible and walked to the rim of the lookout some distance away from him. Hoping that her arrival had gone unnoticed, she tried to regain the sense of solitude that she always found here, but her despair fought against her.

She wanted to cry. She wanted to shout. She wanted to be alone. Why, this morning of all mornings, did there have to be someone else using her private retreat?

"Would I be intruding if I said good morning?" a quiet voice asked.

She might not have answered if the voice hadn't been so familiar. Caroline slowly turned her head toward the man and when she saw the expressive blue eyes and the apple-cheeked face of the Reverend O'Malley, she couldn't help smiling just a little, in spite of her surprise.

"Good morning, Rev—Bill," she corrected, remembering his request.

"Very good." He grinned broadly at her use of his first name.

"I'm still having trouble with that." She found herself warming to his company quickly.

"Just keep practicing. It'll seem more natural eventually."

"I haven't seen you up here before."

"I come often, especially on Sunday mornings. This is my time to be alone."

"Oops, sorry." It hadn't occurred to her to think of herself as an intruder.

"No, I didn't mean it like that. Is that why you're standing so far away?"

"Sort of."

"And sort of because you came here to be alone, too?" Caroline smiled again. "Sort of."

"Would it help to talk?"

"I don't know."

"Why don't you come a little closer and we can try?"

As Caroline moved closer, she saw that in spite of his jovial smile, his blue eyes were as sad as ever. Shorn of his dark suit, he seemed younger and more human. He seemed more like a Bill and less like a Reverend O'Malley.

The closer she came to him, the more she realized that his distress was almost as acute as her own. She knew enough about pain to know that his was an old wound and one that he kept close to his heart, but she couldn't help wondering what secret could weigh so heavily on a man like him.

"You've been crying," he said.

Caroline shook her head, automatically rejecting his sympathy. "Only a little." She couldn't afford to feel sorry for herself, not if she was going to find a solution to her dilemma.

"Well, I know your grandmother's doing better, so this is either simple grief or something else has happened with Duke."

Shocked, Caroline stared at him. "What do you mean, something else?"

"To be perfectly honest, Kimi had told me you two weren't speaking. She was very concerned. In some ways, you know, she's a very lonely little girl."

"Damn," Caroline said, feeling tears sting her eyes. She had forgotten that every sway in her relationship with Duke left other people hanging in the balance, as well.

"And your grandmother has talked to me some."

"About what?" She was beginning to feel trapped.

"About her guilt, mainly. And some about the dreams you had when you were young—and are still having, it seems. If what she says is true, these nightmares seem to have become the main stumbling block. And then, of course, there's Martha."

"Martha?"

"Duke is not worth shooting lately, apparently."

A small part of Caroline wanted to laugh, but a larger part wanted to cry. "I don't know what to do," she said helplessly. "I really don't."

"Do you love him?"

Her heart swelled with feeling. Memories and emotions flooded her. Love was such a small word to describe so much. "Oh, yes."

"I have to tell you, I've already talked to Duke about this."

Again, she was shocked. "When?"

"Friday evening. He was very troubled, and he's not a man who tolerates such things easily."

"What did he tell you?"

"That he was ready to do almost anything to get you back."

"Do you know about last night?"

"Well, I know what he wanted."

"Oh."

"Caroline, I can only tell you that when two people truly love each other, there is nothing more precious on Earth. Don't squander the chance that you two have for happiness."

"I don't want to." Tears of despair welled up inside of her. "I really don't want to, but I don't know what to do. I'm so afraid."

"What are you afraid of?" he asked gently.

"Of being alone." It hurt unbearably to put names to the fears that haunted her. "Of being pregnant."

"Is that what your dreams are about?"

"Yes." She refused to break down and cry, but it took all her strength to keep from it.

"But Duke wouldn't do that to you. He loves you."

Her voice was so low she almost whispered. "My father did it."

There were tears in her eyes in spite of her efforts, and when he put his arm around her shoulder to comfort her, she was surprised to see that there were tears in his eyes, as well.

"Oh, Caroline, Caroline. I'm so sorry. If you could only know how sorry I am."

"I know it doesn't make sense, but that doesn't matter. I can't make the feelings go away."

"I'd like to tell you a story. It may not help, but it's something I've wanted to tell you about since I saw you at your grandfather's funeral."

He took her hand and led her to a bench tucked under overhanging trees at the side of the overlook.

"This is a very personal story," he began slowly. "I guess everyone has a first love that they never forget. Most of us never get a second chance at it. In a way, that makes you a very lucky person."

"I know. I spent thirteen years dreaming that someday I'd meet Duke again and that this time we'd be together forever."

His hand tightened on hers. "There's still a chance. Don't give it up without a fight."

"Tell me your story."

He put his arm around her shoulder and stared at the vista that spread out to the side of them. "I came from a very poor family. In school, my friends were all pretty rough, and the only girls I dated were the ones who were called 'easy' back in those days."

He looked at Caroline and smiled. "Doesn't sound like a minister, does it?"

"No."

"Well, it was the farthest thing from my mind in those days, I'll tell you that. Anyway, the nice girls in school wouldn't come near me. One date with me and a good girl's reputation would be shot."

"You were that bad?"

"It didn't take much to be bad in those days. Not that there wasn't plenty of sinning going on in the fifties. You just didn't dare get caught."

"Yeah, I know about that," Caroline said with a nod.

She understood that sort of thing very well. This was the same generation her mother had grown up in, the same generation that had no mercy on unwed mothers or their children.

"But there was this whole other side of me that nobody knew anything about. Things were so black-and-white then. If you went all the way with girls, drank beer and smoked cigarettes, you were a hoodlum. If you wrote poetry, you were a sissy. And if you did all of it, you kept it hidden."

"You wrote poetry?"

"It wasn't great poetry, but it meant a lot to me at the time. And there was one girl, a beautiful girl. Really classy, popular at school, family had money. The kind of girl I couldn't touch with my little finger, and she liked me. She liked the dreamer who wrote poetry. Liked him enough to fall in love with him. She even liked him enough to defy her parents for a while."

"Just for a while?"

"Just for a while. It was hard, but I tried to understand. I was a senior and she still had a year to go. She was too young to get married, and I didn't have anything to offer her. But understanding didn't make it any easier. After we broke up, I didn't even wait around to graduate. I got out of this town like I was on fire, joined the navy, got my diploma and eventually went on to college."

The parallel was all too clear. "And you went on to be somebody, just like Duke did." She wondered how much farther the comparison went. "And the girl? What happened to her?"

"Too much." He shook his head sadly. "Much too much, but it was years before I found out. I met Patsy while I was in the navy. She loved me when there wasn't much there to love, and she'll have my heart till the day I die. The only disappointment in our lives is that we've never been able to have children."

"You may have lost your first love, but your story still had a happy ending. Unless..." She paused, almost afraid to say it. "You're not still in love with that girl, are you?"

"Oh, no. No, I love my Patsy." He shook his head emphatically. "No, it's what I found out later that tears my heart out to this day."

"What?"

"There was a child, a child I never knew about. And when I found out, my heart broke with joy. I wanted that child, but she wasn't mine to have. There were too many other lives at stake, too many innocent people who would be hurt."

"People like Patsy?"

He shook his head. "I told her, eventually, and she felt the same way I did. We would have adopted the girl if we could have, but there's no proof that I'm the father. Logically, I know that I am. In my heart, I know that I am. But other than me, only the mother knows for sure, and she's never said. I don't know that she ever will.''

"Oh, my God. That's terrible.'' Trembling from emotion, Caroline caught her breath and felt a tear slip from her eye. That girl could have been her.

She would have given anything to have a father, even one who didn't care. And this man's heart was breaking for a daughter who might never know the way he felt.

"Even if you can't prove it, go to her,'' she urged. "Tell her. Believe me, she wants to know.''

He wiped the tear that trickled down her cheek. "Do you really think so?''

"When I was a little girl, I prayed every night for a father. Any father. It didn't matter. I just wanted to know who I was and where I came from. I just wanted somebody to belong to.''

"Would you settle for an Irishman?'' he asked quietly. "One who's a little wayward and a whole lot late?''

"What?"

"I have no proof, Caroline. But your mother, Marion, was the girl in my story. And you *do* seem to have my hair. You wouldn't know it now, but my hair was once a light blond, like yours is.''

Caroline stared at him, numb with shock, while her heart throbbed in her ears. She couldn't believe it. Not after so long. It couldn't be this easy.

"Say something, child, please. I love you so much and I've waited so long to call you my daughter.''

"I—I—'' So many thoughts, so many emotions were battling to be first in line that she was left paralyzed by indecision.

He caught her hands in his and looked deep into her eyes with his heart laid bare in his. "At least, tell me if you're happy.''

"Yes,'' she said at last. It was all she could say, but she said it with feeling. "Yes.''

"Thank God." He smiled with relief, and a single tear escaped his brimming eyes. "You have no idea how frightened I was. I was afraid I would tell you and you'd hate me and it would ruin your life." He shook his head, laughing. "I imagined all kinds of things."

"Oh, Daddy." Caroline drew in a long, ragged breath. She had waited her whole life to say that word to someone. Hesitantly, she reached out to trace his features with her fingertips. "I've dreamed of this for so long, and I never really thought it would happen."

"I should have done something a long time ago. If I'd had any idea of what you were going through, I wouldn't have let anything stop me. Can you forgive me?"

"There's nothing to forgive," she said softly with a glow of happiness that lit her face and made words unnecessary.

"I love you, Caroline. I've loved you since the first day I knew you were alive, and when I finally met you and saw what a beautiful person you were, inside and out, I've been so proud I could hardly stand myself."

"Oh, Daddy." Her words were a sigh of love as she slipped her arms around his waist and laid her head against his shoulder. "I've waited my whole life to hear you say that."

Her father wrapped his arms around her and held her tight. "Caroline, my daughter, my child," he murmured while his hand smoothed her hair, "we have so much time to make up for."

Caroline nestled against him, absorbing the comfort of his embrace. Her whole life, she had thought she was a mistake, an unwanted, unloved mistake. And all that time, she had been wrong.

"We have the rest of our lives," she said, raising her head to give him another smile filled with all the love in her heart.

He looked down at her and touched her cheek with his hand. "My darling child."

The harsh roar of a motorcycle startled them both, and they turned to look in unison. In a spray of gravel, Duke slid the massive black cycle to a halt behind Caroline's car, blocking her in.

Cutting the engine abruptly, he left the bike standing not a foot from Caroline's back bumper and stalked toward them. His angry steps chewed up the distance while his blazing eyes warned that he was in no mood for small talk.

"Goodness," Bill said, taking a judicious step away from Caroline. "Did you two have a fight?"

"No." She tore her gaze from Duke and looked at her father with a worried frown. She hated to end their reunion so abruptly, and she was torn between the instinct that warned her she should be alone with Duke, at least until she found out why he was so upset, and the instinct that told her to cling to the father who had been lost to her for so long.

"I think I should be going and leave you two alone to talk," Bill said, making the decision for her. He leaned toward her and gave her a quick kiss on the cheek. "We'll finish our catching up later."

Caroline caught his hand in hers as he began to back away. "Don't go." She felt like her heart was breaking.

"I love you, sweetheart," he whispered. "I'll talk to you this afternoon." He slipped his hand from hers and turned to find himself facing Duke. "Good morning, Duke." He nodded cordially. "I was just leaving."

Duke glared and watched him walk away. Then he turned his furious gaze on Caroline. "What the hell was that about? And why didn't you take my calls?"

"Your calls?" Confused, she looked from him to the retreating back of her father and then back to blazing anger on Duke's face.

"Yes, my calls. After last night, I thought everything was great between us." A stricken glimpse of pain flashed through the anger. "Then I called this morning and got the same old song and dance from your grandmother. What does it take for you to be in when I call?"

"I'm sorry, Duke. I wasn't home. I forgot you were calling."

"You forgot? Yeah, I guess I can see that." Gritted white teeth added to the grim set of his mouth. "And that brings us back to my first question."

Caroline could feel her own anger rising, and she hoped he wasn't about to say what she thought he was about to say. "Your first question?" she asked with a quietness that hid her pounding heart.

"Yeah," he said and jerked his thumb over his shoulder in the direction of Bill O'Malley's retreating car. "What the hell was that about?"

"Duke," Caroline said in a last attempt to be reasonable, "you can't possibly think there was anything going on."

"Why would I think that? Last night, we made love like we were the only two people in the world. And this morning, you were gone again, just like last night never happened."

"I had a dream..."

"I'm sick and tired of hearing about your dreams, Caroline. Every time I get near you, you have another nightmare. Is this how you deal with your nightmares? You go up to lover's lane and snuggle up to a married minister? Making love to him doesn't give you nightmares?"

Instantly furious, Caroline fired back, "How dare you?"

"How dare I? I'll tell you how I dare. I've given it everything I've got to give, Caroline. I've tried everything I can think of and nothing works. I might as well be that same twenty-one-year-old garage mechanic with grease under my fingernails who's standing on the outside looking in and wishing there was some way I could get near you. Because your family is still standing between us and you're still running away every time I get too close."

Moved by the passion beneath his anger, Caroline found her own temper replaced by tenderness. "Duke." She reached out to him.

He caught her by the shoulders and pulled her into his arms. "What kind of fool do you think I am, Caroline? You think I couldn't see the look on your face when I drove up? You think I didn't see his arms around you?"

"But you don't understand—"

"Sure I do." His gaze turned hard. His mouth twisted with contempt and he released her suddenly and stepped away. "I thought I knew you. But I just found out that I don't know you at all. Maybe you changed in the thirteen years we were apart, or maybe you were never what I thought you were in the first place."

"What is that supposed to mean?" Caroline demanded, instantly furious at the insult in his words.

"I thought you loved me," he said in an icy hiss. "I thought last night meant as much to you as it did to me. But I guess I'm just another fool, just like the good reverend there. Sounds like he thinks you're in love with him, too."

He moved nearer, touching her with his body but not with his arms as he glared down at her. "Well, what about it, Caroline? Which is it? Do you love him? Or do you love me? Or do you even know what love is?"

"Do I know what love is? Yes, I do. Do you? Do you care about anything I have to say? Do you care about how I feel? At least Bill listens to me. At least he cares. Do I love him? Yes." She stood straighter, and her words rang with defiance. "Yes, I love him. I love him very much. What do you have to say about that?"

"I hope you're both very happy." His words were soft, quiet and cold. He turned and stalked back toward his motorcycle, his swift, sure steps taking him quickly away.

"Duke!" she called after him in a strangled whisper. Too stunned to go after him, Caroline watched him leave. Something inside her felt cold and frightened as she listened to the heels of his boots crunching heavily in the gravel.

She hadn't meant to say the things she had said. She couldn't even remember everything she had said, and the thought frightened her.

He rode away without looking back, in another spray of flying gravel, and she watched with the last of her happiness draining from her heart. She had come to the mountaintop seeking a solution, and she had only found more questions.

She loved Duke, and at the thought of losing him, her nightmares seemed insignificant. She should have explained who Bill O'Malley really was and why they had been embracing. But Duke had been so angry, she hadn't had a chance to begin, and now it was too late.

Vainly, she tried to recapture the joy she had felt at finally finding her father, but when her thoughts returned to Duke, her battered nerves vibrated like glass chimes in a high wind. Something had changed on the mountaintop that morning. When she remembered the way Duke had looked at her just before he left, it sent cold chills down her back and she didn't know what to do about it.

Caroline gently rubbed over the handcarved rosettes in the front of the old vanity. Traces of faded blue paint still stained the crevices, and she was careful not to remove all of it. In no mood for the reflective quiet of church when she had returned home that morning, she had let her grandmother ride with a neighbor and had stayed home to work off some of her despair.

She wanted to call Duke, but she was afraid to. She had never seen him so angry, and some instinct told her to stay away until he had a chance to think things through. All she could do was try to keep busy and occupy her mind with something else.

The bed she and Ariel had been refinishing for Kimi was almost completed, and Ariel had brought over her latest find, the delicate vanity, as another piece to be redone for Kimi. Tank had already put a new mirror in the top's centerpiece that lifted up to reveal a makeup tray. Caroline's contribution was to clean and polish the vanity, leaving a faintly blued patina on the bare wood. And this morning, the harder she polished, the better she felt.

Working silently, she heard the stairs creak and the hallway groan as footsteps made their way toward her old bedroom. She turned just in time to see her father appear in the doorway.

"Hi," Caroline said, breaking into a smile, "uh..." She glanced behind him, unsure what to call him within earshot of others. "Bill?"

"Hi. Your grandmother's downstairs. I gave her a ride home and thought I'd see how you were doing." He came into the room and pushed the door partially closed behind him. "Duke wasn't in church, either. I was kind of hoping you two would be together."

"No such luck." Caroline left her kneeling position by the vanity and took a seat in one of two raggedy armless upholstered chairs that were destined to be repoufed, recovered and freshly flounced for addition to Kimi's room. She motioned for him to sit in the other.

"Did he tell you why he was so upset?"

Caroline groaned softly. "I hate to even tell you."

"If it's too personal." He lifted his hands to stop her if she didn't want to go any further.

"It's too embarrassing, but I guess you should know. He was mainly upset because he had seen us together and misinterpreted."

"Oh, dear." Bill frowned. "I hadn't even thought of that, but I guess it makes sense."

"It does *not*," Caroline said indignantly. "How could he think such a thing?"

"Does he know—" he slowed down, searching for words, "—about your birth?"

"I told him last night."

"And that you didn't know who your father was?"
She nodded.

"Did you try to explain this morning?"

"No. He was too upset, and then he made me angry."

"So now he thinks I was making a pass at you?"

"Not exactly."

"What *does* he think?"

"He thinks I'm in love with you and that we're having an affair," she said almost under her breath.

Shocked, her father drew back. "Why would he think that?"

Caroline had trouble looking at him. "I told him."

"Caroline!"

For an instant, she wanted to smile, thinking that Bill sounded just like a parent. Then she remembered the seriousness of her situation. "Well, he made me angry," she said defensively, "and so I admitted that I loved you. But he came up with the affair part all on his own." Just thinking about it, she got upset all over again. If Duke had only let her explain, none of this would have happened.

"Well, I guess he might be justified. It was a pretty emotional scene he was watching. I suppose if Patsy didn't know the truth and had driven up on us this morning, she might have been tempted to jump to the same conclusion."

"But you're not that kind of person, and neither am I. And if somebody really knows us, he should realize that," Caroline argued.

"Logically, yes," Bill agreed with the wisdom and understanding gained from years of counseling troubled souls. "But love has the power to override logic, especially when that love is twisted by jealousy. Would you like for me to talk to Duke for you?"

"I don't know if he'd listen." Her dejection was apparent in her tone. She had already had her miracle today, and she was afraid to hope for another one.

"I don't know, either, but it's worth a try."

Before Caroline could answer, there was a light knock at the partially open door, and Kimi poked her head inside.

"Did I hear my daddy's name?" she demanded without preamble.

Bill smiled. "The ears of children," he said in an undertone to Caroline.

"Have you been listening at keyholes?" Caroline demanded in return.

"Didn't have to," Kimi said, advancing into the room with a buoyant, untroubled step. "The door was open. Anyway, Dad's gone."

"Gone?" Caroline echoed. She could feel the hollowness of great sorrow beginning in the pit of her stomach. What had she done?

"Boy, was he mad. He said he wasn't, but he was."

"Where was he going?" Caroline asked, trying to sound as if her future happiness wasn't in the balance. "Did he say?"

"Business," Kimi said with a shrug. "He just said 'business.'"

"That usually means the old plant, doesn't it?"

Kimi nodded. "Sometimes." She glanced toward the minister still seated across from Caroline as if she just remembered he was there. "Uh, Ariel sent me after you."

Taking the cue, Bill rose. "Well, I guess I should be going now."

Torn between wanting to pump Kimi for every ounce of information she contained and wanting to keep her father around a little longer, Caroline stood with him. "Are you sure?"

He patted her hand. "If you need me, call."

Caroline walked with him into the hallway while Kimi wandered deeper into the bedroom. "I still can't believe it," Caroline said in an undertone. "I'm actually discussing my problems with my father and asking his advice. I'm almost afraid to go to sleep for fear I'll wake up and find out it's all been a dream."

"No fear of that." He kissed her cheek lightly.

"So, Dad," she whispered, "what am I going to do? Now I can't even explain it to him. He's gone." She tried not to show the despair she was feeling, or the guilt.

"It'll work out." Bill slipped his arm around her and held her close. "I know that doesn't sound very reassuring right now, but it *will* work out. And quit feeling guilty. The argument was as much Duke's fault as it was yours."

"I just keep thinking of all the things I could have said differently."

"I'm sure, once Duke calms down, he'll feel the same way. And once he finds out the truth, he'll feel even worse." With a final hug, he released her. "So for now, quit worrying about it and go out and have some fun."

Caroline smiled. "Yes, sir."

"Come over for supper tonight, if you can. Patsy's dying to see you. And we have to figure out how we're going to start breaking this news to the world."

"Oh, Dad, I love you. I don't know what I'd do without you right now." Caroline gave him a quick hug and stepped back. "I'll be over tonight, if I can."

Back in the bedroom, Kimi turned to greet her when Caroline returned. "Did you do that?" The little girl nodded toward the refinished bed in the corner. "It sure looks different."

"It gives me something to do," Caroline said, slipping her arm around Kimi's shoulder and turning her toward the door before she noticed too much. She would never have left Kimi alone in the room if she'd been thinking straight.

"Hey, you two," Ariel's voice called from below, followed by the sound of her footsteps racing up the stairs. "Get a move on."

"Oops," Kimi said, grimacing. "We're supposed to go pick out furniture with her."

"I guess we'd better go, then." Caroline hugged the little girl closer and smiled at her. "I've got nothing *else* to do today."

Chapter Twelve

Caroline walked into the suite behind the bellboy, who wasn't doing a very good job of hiding his smirk.

"Which room should I put your bags in, ma'am?"

"Whichever room is not Mr. Hutchison's."

She had had about enough of third-party messages and was more than eager to face Duke in person.

"Uh, I think this might be for you, ma'am."

The bellboy pulled a note off the bedroom door and handed it to her. He went into the room to set down her luggage while she opened the envelope and pulled out a handwritten note.

Caroline,

Charge anything you need to the room. I've arranged for a car to pick you up in the morning and take you to the plant. Someone there will show you around and answer any questions you might have. I'll

be away for a few days, so you have the suite to yourself.

Duke

Caroline crumpled the note into a ball and threw it across
the room. After two weeks of messages shuttled through his
secretary, Duke had finally summoned her, with no notice,
to the Rhode Island plant, only to have her booked into a
suite he was already occupying, and then he didn't even
have the decency to be on hand so she could tell him off in
person.

"Have a good night, ma'am," the bellboy said on his
way out.

Have a good night, indeed. She looked around the ster-
ile room in frustration. She was alone in a strange town
with no transportation and nothing to do. Of all the high-
handed, inconsiderate tricks anyone had ever pulled on her,
this had to be the worst, and if Duke Hutchison thought he
wasn't going to hear about it, he had another think coming.

Four days later, Caroline looked up in answer to a rap-
ping on the wall outside her makeshift office at the old
plant. Duke stood in the doorway.

"How's it going?" he asked, giving her a smile that was
too smooth to be sincere.

"It's a mess."

Still smiling, he nodded. "Yeah. The person who used to
have this job left about a month ago and we couldn't re-
hire since all the duties are going to be transferred to you in
Eureka. No matter how much you plan, transitions always
seem to get messy before they're over."

"I'm not sure I'll have this under control by tomorrow," she said, hoping he would take the hint and tell her
how long she was expected to stay.

"Fine. Take your time."

Obviously, a hint wasn't going to work. "Do you have any idea how long I should plan to be here?"

"As long as it takes. I don't want to pressure you. Is the suite comfortable enough?"

"Well, now that you're here, I've been wanting to talk to you about that." What she really wanted to do was shake him until the real Duke came out of hiding, the one who was supposed to be angry with her. This man was as mellow as vanilla pudding, and that definitely wasn't like Duke.

"Is there a problem?"

"I just think it would be better if I had a room of my own."

"Oh, well, if my clothes are in the way, I can get them out because the suite is yours. I won't be staying there."

"Well, no, they're not in my way."

"Good, then that's settled." He glanced at his watch. "I have to be going now. Just leave a message with Sharon if you need anything."

And with that, he was gone, leaving Caroline to fume in silent frustration.

Tuesday of the following week, she left work late and drove to the hotel in a rental car. Tired, but finally making headway with the backlog of work, she slipped into a robe and curled up on the couch to relax while she made a phone call home.

"Gran, hi, how are things?"

"When are you coming home, dear?"

Caroline slid down into the corner of the couch and crossed her ankles on top of the coffee table.

"Soon, I think. The end of this week, if I can bring some of this work back with me. And I don't see why I can't."

"That's nice, dear. I just don't like sleeping in this big, old house by myself. Oh, by the way, the Reverend O'Malley was asking about you on Sunday."

"Oh, really? You have this number, don't you? It would be all right if he wanted to call me here."

"Caroline, dear, don't be silly. Why would he call you? I'm sure he was just being polite. But he did ask me to pass along the message, and so I did."

"Well, thank you very much, Gran. I guess I'd better go now. I have a lot to do this evening."

"Okay, dear. You take care of yourself, now. I worry about you up there in the North all by yourself."

"Gran, I lived in Chicago by myself for a lot of years. Besides, this place is almost as quiet as Eureka."

"Is it really, Caroline? You're not just saying that to make me feel better?"

"It's very rural here. And the countryside is beautiful."

"Well, then, I guess I'll try not to worry about you so much. You sound like you're doing just fine."

Caroline hung up and looked around the room. If going out of her mind with boredom was doing just fine, then she was doing just fine.

She leaned over far enough to grab her purse strap at the other end of the couch and dragged the purse over to her. Rummaging through the contents, she located her address book and dialed the number for Bill O'Malley.

"You have reached the O'Malley residence," the answering machine said. "I'm sorry that no one is home right now, but if you will leave..."

Caroline waited for the beep and left her name and number and the message that she wasn't calling about anything important. She was just bored and lonely for a friendly voice. When she hung up, she was more bored and lonely than ever.

With nothing else to do, she went to bed, only to toss and turn for hours wondering where Duke could be and when she would see him again. It had been almost a week since she had looked up to find him standing in the doorway of the cubbyhole she was working out of. It had been a week of long, difficult days and longer, lonely nights.

He was finally giving her what she had once asked for now that she no longer wanted it. He was treating her as a co-worker and nothing more. He was giving her time and space without pressure, and she had never been more miserable in her life.

When she finally fell asleep, it was with memories of their last night together, memories that drove her wild with longing and left her desperately unhappy.

Caroline opened the door to her suite two days later and knew instantly that something had changed. The air smelled fresher. The hollow emptiness that always greeted her was gone. A vase of flowers sat in the center of the coffee table.

Trying to suppress her quickened heartbeat, she walked cautiously into the room and set her briefcase on the breakfast bar separating the kitchen from the living room. A hum like that of a giant, irritated bumblebee came from behind the closed door of Duke's room, but Caroline was still afraid to hope.

She went into her room and hung up her suit jacket. Underneath it she wore the high-necked blouse trimmed with antique lace and the dusty-rose corduroy skirt that she had worn to her interview. She slipped out of the cream-colored flats she had worn to the office and into the mauve high heels that she had packed on a whim.

Removing the combs that held her hair neatly away from her face, she leaned over and shook her hair loose. Then she straightened from the waist and flipped her head back, watching in the mirror as her hair settled into a wild, untamed mane around her face and down past her shoulders.

Caroline leaned close to the mirror and dabbed fresh gloss on her lips, then sprayed cologne behind her ears and over her hair. Halfway angry that any man could make her this desperate to attract him, she walked back into the living room, ready to make Duke want her again if it was the last thing she did.

But when she saw him leaning against the door frame of his room wearing nothing but jeans and a towel around his neck, her vaguely formed plan fell apart.

"Hi," he said, not moving from the doorway. "I hope you don't mind the intrusion. I just stopped by to grab a few things."

"Oh." Her spirits sank to her toes. "Then you're not staying?"

He lifted one end of the towel and rubbed the back of his neck. "Well, I thought if you hadn't eaten, maybe we could have dinner together. But I realize you probably have plans already."

Her spirits took wing. "No. None at all."

"Great." He turned and disappeared into his room. "Is there anyplace special you'd like to eat?"

"I really haven't been out very much. I usually just eat up here."

Duke reappeared, buttoning his shirt. "How depressing. I hadn't meant for you to be quite so neglected. But I like to be home for the weekends, so I flew back to Eureka last week and just got back here today."

"Oh?"

Caroline tried to smile, but she could feel her face stiffening with anger. While she had been sitting here alone, depressed and overworked, he had been at home with his family.

"Yeah." He was studying his cuff, concentrating on getting a button through a buttonhole that had been starched closed. Without looking up, he turned and went back into his room.

"How's work coming?" he called over the sound of drawers opening and closing.

"I'm close to getting caught up. If you don't mind my taking the last of it back with me, I think I'll be through by the end of this week."

"Oh, really?" He walked back into the room wearing a dark green sweater over his white shirt. He was still barefoot. "That's amazing. I never thought you'd get through it that fast."

"There's not much else to do here."

"Yeah." He smiled at her and ran a hand through his rumpled hair. "I guess you're right. Well, just let me find my shoes and I'll be ready. I know a great place near here. Do you mind if we walk?"

He wandered back into his bedroom without waiting for a response or even really looking at her.

By the time they finished eating and began the slippery trek back to the hotel, Caroline was fuming. She might as well have been an empty chair for all the attention she had gotten over dinner. He had talked about business, and every time she had turned the conversation to anything remotely personal, he said, "Oh, yeah?" or "Really?" or "I guess you're right," and then changed the subject again.

She had never spent such a frustrating evening in her life. She was beginning to think that the only thing worse than not seeing Duke was seeing him. He'd not only turned into a bore, he'd turned into an insensitive bore, and what was even worse than that was she still wanted him in spite of it.

Caroline stepped onto the curb and felt her foot slide sideways. "Ah!" Her flailing hand found Duke's arm and clung.

"Are you all right?" He reached across with his free hand and grasped her elbow.

"Dandy." With one foot still in the street and pain shooting up the side of her leg, she glowered up at him in the lemony glow of the streetlight.

"Those high heels aren't very practical for walking in weather like this." He helped her onto the curb and steadied her across the ice.

Through gritted teeth, Caroline answered, "It didn't seem this bad earlier."

What had been a thin layer of slush when they had left for dinner had frozen into a glaze of ice patches. But the real problem was that she had been angry and thinking about everything but where she was walking. She wouldn't have been wearing those stupid heels, anyway, if she hadn't been trying to impress him.

"You're limping. Did you hurt your ankle?"

"I'll be just fine."

Still angry, she tried to limp on ahead of him, but his longer legs and two good ankles made it impossible. By the time they reached the suite, the shooting pains were subsiding and had been replaced by a throbbing tenderness around her right ankle that showed signs of improvement with care.

Caroline sank gratefully into the corner of the couch. Duke followed her. Slipping her shoes from her feet, he lifted her legs onto the couch and examined her injured ankle.

She watched him resentfully, wincing as he ran his fingertips over the tender flesh. All evening, he had treated her like furniture. Now, when she was in too much pain to be romantic, he couldn't be more attentive.

"Ow," she said, jerking her foot away when he ceased his probing and began to twist her foot from side to side.

"Well, it doesn't seem to be broken," he announced.

"I could have told you that." She was really beginning to resent all the attention her ankle was getting while the rest of her was still being ignored. "I walked a block on it."

He retrieved a pillow from the other couch and slipped it under her ankle, then stood back to analyze the effect.

"It's not even very swollen. I think I have aspirin in my bathroom. You just stay there."

Caroline thought briefly of a sarcastic retort and decided it wasn't worth the effort. "Thank you," she said meekly.

When he came back, he handed her a glass of chilled wine and two tablets. He lit the gas logs in the fireplace while she drank two healthy swallows of the wine with her aspirins.

The wine was good. And after the disappointment, vexation and downright pain she had endured during the evening, Caroline was in the mood to be reckless.

"Did you have a bottle of chilled wine in your bathroom, too?" She held her glass toward the fireplace and watched the flames dancing in the pink blush of the beverage.

"In my bedroom."

"Mmm." She found the idea interesting. He hadn't planned to stay. He had asked her to dinner at the spur of the moment. He had spent the evening avoiding anything intimate or even personal. And yet, he had wine chilling in his bedroom. "Mmm," she said again.

Duke left the fireplace and sat facing her on the corner of the solid-looking wooden coffee table.

"Mmm what?" he asked, looking her in the eyes. His lips turned up in a half-formed grin.

Caroline widened her eyes innocently. "Oh, nothing."

"Do you like the wine?"

"It's very good."

"I guess I'll have a glass, too." He stood. His fingertips brushed the hair that fell over her shoulders. "I like your hair tonight. It looks good when you wear it loose like this." After an endless moment that had Caroline's stomach turning cartwheels, he began to walk toward his room. "Do you need anything while I'm up?"

"No. Thank you. I'm fine."

She took another drink of wine and tried to steady her nerves. Since they had returned to the suite, the difference in his attitude was like night and day. If she'd known a simple twisted ankle could accomplish so much, she might have been tempted to arrange an accident on the way to dinner and save herself a lot of grief.

Duke came back into the room carrying a dripping wine bottle and a glass of wine. He had shed the sweater, and the cuffs of his white shirt were undone and rolled comfortably back almost to his elbows.

He set his glass on the coffee table and the bottle on the carpet. Then he walked to the kitchenette. "There should be a wine coaster over here somewhere, don't you think?"

"I think I've seen one." Caroline closed her eyes and tried to remember where she had seen the wine coaster last week when she had been familiarizing herself with the kitchen. It was low, behind something on a shelf. The image popped into her mind. "It's to the left of the stove. Bottom cabinet, on the shelf behind the insulated coffee-pot."

Triumphant, she opened her eyes and saw Duke standing at the counter reading the message the front desk had taken when Bill O'Malley had returned her call. From warm and jovial, Duke's mood suddenly seemed to turn icy.

He laid the message slip down when he realized she was watching him. "It's nice to see you're keeping in touch with the people back home." His smile was automatic and insincere. "Where'd you say that coaster was?"

She told him again, and while he retrieved the coaster, she debated with herself about mentioning the morning at the overlook. There was only so much that words could do, and she wasn't sure that words would be enough.

She hadn't meant to hurt him that morning, but she had. She hadn't meant to hurt him thirteen years ago when she told her grandparents the truth, but she had.

They had both gone on and built separate lives, but that didn't make the heartache they had suffered any less. Through no fault of their own, they were both once burned and twice shy.

"Here we go," Duke said, resettling himself on the edge of the coffee table. He refilled Caroline's glass and set the bottle in its coaster beside him on the table. "To a glorious evening."

He touched his glass to hers and they both drank.

"With no more mishaps," he amended when the toast had been drunk. "How is it looking?"

He set his glass down and leaned over her ankle, stroking his hand gently over her foot and up the side of her leg.

"It doesn't feel too bad," Caroline said, fighting the urge to pull away from the tickling tingle of his fingers.

"It certainly doesn't. It doesn't look bad, either." He glanced up at her face, his hand still stroking her ankle. "There's just a little swelling. Take it easy for a few days and it'll be as good as new."

"Thank you." If he didn't move his hand soon, she was going to go out of her mind.

"It's funny, isn't it? How little control we have over the things we do."

Everything he did, everything he said, made her just a little more breathless than she had been. His hand left her ankle and moved up her leg, cupping her calf in his palm.

"I beg your pardon?"

"I didn't want to bring you here, but I had to. And after I did, I left because I couldn't stay away from you." His hand continued on, following the curve of her leg until his fingers paused to brush lightly over the back of her thigh. "And then I couldn't even do that. I had to come back. I had to be with you."

He slid his hand around to the front of her leg, and his thumb caressed the tender flesh along the inside of her thigh. "The wine and the fireplace. I planned to weaken your will and seduce you."

Involuntary tremors ran through Caroline with every twitch of his fingers. He was angry. He was hurt. She could understand the way he had acted. It didn't matter. She wanted him on his terms, on any terms.

"Planned?"

"Yes, planned. That's not what I want to do now." He withdrew his hand.

"What do you want now?" She could feel herself being drawn toward him. Whatever he wanted, she didn't want to lose him now. She hadn't spent two weeks waiting for a sign that he still cared to lose him when they were so close.

He shook his head slowly. "I want to know what you want. I want you to tell me what you want."

She leaned forward and reached out to him. "I want you."

He still held back. "That's not enough."

She had come too far to let pride stop her now. "I want you to make love to me."

Without another word, he picked her up and carried her into her room.

Duke lay awake in the dark room. Caroline's head was on his shoulder. As he listened to the gentle sounds of her sleeping, he felt a tenderness well up in him that he didn't want to feel.

The angry passion that had driven him earlier was gone, and lying there now with her so soft and warm in his arms, he was ashamed of the seduction that had been more ruthless than tender.

Every time they made love, it only seemed to end in pain, and he'd sworn it wouldn't happen again. He hadn't meant to make love to her tonight, but the note from Bill O'Malley had been more than he could stand. Hurt and angry, he had lost control, and now there was nothing left to do but harden his heart and leave.

If he was still with her in the morning, it would never be over. The longer they were together, the more he fell in love with her, no matter how hard he fought it. There was a sweet innocence about her that cast a spell over him and left him longing for more in spite of all her betrayals.

Leaving her now wasn't easy, but it was something he had to do. Careful not to wake her, he slipped his arm out from under her and climbed from the bed. Alone in his own room, he lay between cold, lonely sheets and tried not to miss the warmth of her body next to his. He tried to ignore the perfumed scent of her that seemed a part of the air he breathed. He tried not to feel the aching need in his heart.

Miserable but determined not to give in to his own weakness, he told himself she was nothing but trouble. That was all Caroline had ever been to him, and it was all she would ever be to any man who came near her. As he finally drifted off to sleep, he felt sorry for any man who loved her. He even felt sorry for poor old Bill O'Malley.

When Duke opened his eyes again, it was to find the light of dawn bleeding weakly into the room. Confused, he listened for the sound that had awakened him. A few seconds later, he heard it. A child was crying somewhere in the house, and the terror in the sobs set his own heart to pounding.

Still half asleep, he threw back his covers and staggered toward Kimi's bedroom. He stopped halfway across the living room to rub his eyes and clear the panic that clouded his thinking.

Something was wrong with the room. This wasn't his house. This wasn't even his suite. He looked around again, focusing finally. When he remembered where he was, he realized that Kimi wasn't the one crying. It wasn't a child. It was Caroline, and that somehow made the sound even more chilling.

Hurrying, he rushed through the door of her room, then stopped again abruptly when he saw her huddled against the head of the bed, whimpering between each racking sob. Her hair was wet against her head and tears ran in rivulets down her cheeks.

Her eyes were open and staring straight ahead in glazed, terror-stricken sadness. A pillow was cradled in her arms.

Murmuring gently, Duke pulled aside the sweat-soaked sheets that clung to her and slipped into the bed beside her. Curling his still nude body against hers, he took her in his arms and pulled her against his chest, careful not to wake her too suddenly. Very softly, he began to croon a lullaby in her ear the way he used to do with Kimi when she would cry in the night.

Still clutching the pillow in one arm, Caroline twisted in his arms and buried her face against his chest. He could feel her heart racing while her sobs grew more and more desperate.

She moved restlessly against him, her fist clenched, fighting an invisible foe until finally she moaned, "I'm sorry," and pushed violently away from him.

Her head thrown back, she cried out, "I'm sorry!" once again, and her eyes fluttered open. She stared at him in confusion, unfocused but obviously awake.

"I... What?"

She ran her fingers through her wet hair, then drew her hand away and looked at it with shock. Horrified comprehension dawned on her face, and Duke knew she realized what had happened.

"Was this your nightmare?" he asked gently.

He still held her in spite of her attempts to break free, and he could feel the tremors that were going through her like the soft fluttering of a bird's wings.

Caroline closed her eyes and the tears came again, slower than before. "I'm sorry," she whispered again.

"Sweetheart—"

"No," she cried, her tears coming faster. She jerked away from him, but he followed her. His arms still gently encased her, protecting her from the unfathomable sorrow that raged in her.

"Please," she begged, "please, let me go."

"I've already done that once tonight, sweetheart. I'm not going to do it again."

He couldn't help thinking that if she hadn't been alone, it might not have happened. And whether he was right or not, it didn't affect the way he felt. Knowing that she was vulnerable, he had left her there. To protect himself, he had sacrificed her. He didn't know what it would take to make him forgive himself.

Caroline curled forward, hiding shame and despair that were almost more than she could hold inside. She remembered falling asleep in Duke's arms, so sure the dream was gone, so sure that she was free to love him without fear.

Not only had the dream come back, but Duke had seen it. He had seen her. He had heard her cries, watched her fear and felt the cold sweat that was the price she paid for daring to love him.

"Caroline, baby, please. Talk to me. Tell me what it's all about."

Duke's voice was so soft, so loving. She wished she could do as he asked. She wished it would help. But all she really longed to do was to climb into a shower and scrub until the shame and fear were gone.

She loved Duke, but that wasn't enough. Until she could sleep without nightmares and wake without the sound of her own cries in her ears, her love for him was hopeless.

"It's no use." She straightened and was surprised to find a pillow still clutched tightly in her arms.

"What's no use?"

He gently tugged the pillow from her grasp and laid it aside.

"Us." She pulled a damp sheet up to cover her. "No matter how much we try, things only get worse."

"No," Duke argued fervently. His hands caught her shoulders and turned her toward him. "No, you're wrong, Caroline. This is the first time in our lives we've ever really been alone, with no one else around to get between us. This is our chance. Right now."

Too tired to fight her shame and too miserable to hope any longer, Caroline shook her head. "No, it's too late." She had thought when she found her father, it would help, but it hadn't. Nothing helped.

Duke's eyes burned into her. "Trust me."

"Trust you? I don't understand."

"That's okay. Just trust me and come with me. I promise you, you won't be sorry."

Still confused, she felt a tiny spark of hope come alive in her in spite of everything. "I have to shower before I do anything else."

"Great." He smiled. "Think you could use some breakfast?"

"Could we order up?"

"I'll have a feast waiting for you when you get out of the shower."

It was amazing how far the prospect of clean water and hot food could go toward restoring wounded spirits, Caroline thought as she wrapped the bed sheet around her and not quite limped her way to the bathroom.

Maybe he was right. Maybe if she just trusted him one more time everything would work out. After all, miracles did happen.

At the bathroom door, she stopped and turned around. "Duke?"

He looked up from the telephone, the receiver in one hand and the index finger of his other hand poised to dial. "Yes, sweetheart?"

"When I get out of the shower, remind me to tell you about my father."

"Your father?"

"Yes." She smiled, thinking of miracles. "I found him."

"Happy?" Duke asked. He tightened his arms around her and pressed her closer to him. The comforter that partially covered them slid lower.

"Blissful." Caroline smiled up at him and ran her hand over the muscular contours of his shoulder and down his flexed biceps to his elbow. "Just blissful."

The door to the bedroom was closed and bolted against the world outside. They lay nestled together in the Henry VIII bed under the rosy glow of the tiffany lamp in the windowless room built into the side of the mountain.

"Was I right?" he asked.

"Oh, yes, dear." She turned a fraction of an inch and kissed the shoulder where her head lay. "You were so right."

"You know, I hate to nag, but we never *did* discuss why you left town so suddenly all those years ago."

Caroline shifted her position to stare at the ceiling. It all seemed too long ago and unimportant now. It was almost funny to think that just a few months earlier, she had thought it meant so much.

"Can you remember that far back?" Duke prodded.

She laughed. "I'm trying."

"Let's see," he said, helping her along. "We made love for the first time. It was wonderful. We had our whole lives ahead of us. You would be eighteen in about six more months, and when I took you home, we were happy. We were in love, and I didn't see you again for thirteen years."

She reached for his hand and held it tightly between both of hers. "It still sounds so sad, doesn't it?"

Instantly protective, Duke turned toward her and cradled her to him with the arm she was lying on. "I'm sorry, sweetheart. I didn't mean to make you sad."

"I'm not. Not really. How could I be—" she raised their hands for them both to see, her left hand and his, side by side, with their matching bands "—when I have so much?"

"When *we* have so much," he corrected gently, and rested his cheek against her hair. "Now, are you going to tell me what happened or aren't you?"

She laughed again. "Okay, okay. Let's see. Well, I never told you, but in all of my nightmares, I was pregnant. I was terrified of getting pregnant like my mother did, and after I got home that night, I started worrying about it."

"About being pregnant? Because of what we did that night?"

"Yes. I guess I was really worried, because the dream I had was bad and it woke up my grandmother and grandfather. I was crying, and the dream seemed so real, and I thought I really was, and I told them."

"Told them," he repeated. "What? That you were pregnant or about us?"

"Both. And they had me packed and on my way to my mother's and a boarding school by the time the sun was up. They said they'd put you in jail for rape because I was underage if I ever tried to contact you." Her voice dropped to a whisper that was shaded with tears. "They wouldn't even let me write to Ariel for a long time, and when I finally could, I found out you had left town."

Duke held her tight while they both mourned what had been taken away from them. "We have each other now," he finally said. "That's what matters."

"Maybe we *were* too young then, or maybe I was, anyway. Maybe if I'd been older, I would have realized you wouldn't leave me just because I got pregnant."

He kissed her forehead, then her temple. "I would have married you in a minute, but it wouldn't have been because I got you pregnant. I made sure you were protected, sweetheart. I've always made sure you were protected."

Caroline laughed and turned her head to gaze up at him. "Oh, yeah? Then explain *this*." She put her hand on the gentle rounding of her stomach.

"Oh, *that*," Duke said, unabashed. "That was an accident. I wasn't myself that night."

She laughed again. "A likely story."

"I married you the next week, didn't I?" he murmured in her ear, pulling her close again while his hand joined hers on her stomach. "I'd have married you sooner if you hadn't wanted your father to perform the ceremony."

"It was nice," she said defensively, still smiling. "My mother, my stepfather. My father, my stepmother. My grandmother. My stepdaughter."

"It was a circus."

"What can I tell you? That's my family." The words were said jokingly, but she felt a swell of pride at the sound. Finally, she had a family. And soon, there'd be one more to add, the best one of all.

What she had once feared most was now a treasure most precious, growing and blossoming inside of her, and all her dreams were sweet.

"So," Duke asked again, "are you happy?"

"Oh, yes." Caroline turned on her side once more, her head still on his shoulder as she snuggled her body against his. "Blissful."

* * * * *

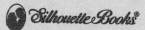

Silhouette Special Edition

presents

SONNY'S GIRLS

by Emilie Richards, Celeste Hamilton and Erica Spindler

They had been Sonny's girls, irresistibly drawn to the charismatic high school football hero. Ten years later, none could forget the night that changed their lives forever.

In July—
ALL THOSE YEARS AGO by Emilie Richards (SSE #684)
Meredith Robbins had left town in shame. Could she ever banish the past and reach for love again?

In August—
DON'T LOOK BACK by Celeste Hamilton (SSE #690)
Cyndi Saint was Sonny's steady. Ten years later, she remembered only his hurtful parting words....

In September—
LONGER THAN... by Erica Spindler (SSE #696)
Bubbly Jennifer Joyce was everybody's friend. But nobody knew the secret longings she felt for bad boy Ryder Hayes....

SSESG-1

SILHOUETTE·INTIMATE·MOMENTS®

IT'S TIME TO MEET
THE MARSHALLS!

In 1986, bestselling author Kristin James wrote A VERY SPECIAL FAVOR for the Silhouette Intimate Moments line. Hero Adam Marshall quickly became a reader favorite, and ever since then, readers have been asking for the stories of his two brothers, Tag and James. At last your prayers have been answered!

In August, look for THE LETTER OF THE LAW (IM #393), James Marshall's story. If you missed youngest brother Tag's story, SALT OF THE EARTH (IM #385), you can order it by following the directions below. And, as our very special favor to you, we'll be reprinting A VERY SPECIAL FAVOR this September. Look for it in special displays wherever you buy books.

Order your copy by sending your name, address, zip or postal code, along with a check or money order for $3.25 (please do not send cash), plus 75¢ postage and handling ($1.00 in Canada), payable to Silhouette Reader Service to:

In the U.S.

3010 Walden Ave.
P.O. Box 1396
Buffalo, NY 14269-1396

In Canada

P.O. Box 609
Fort Erie, Ontario
L2A 5X3

Please specify book title with your order.
Canadian residents add applicable federal and provincial taxes.

MARSH-2

Silhouette Books®

Silhouette Special Edition

proudly hails

WOMEN OF GLORY

from Lindsay McKenna

Soar with Dana Coulter, Molly Rutledge and Maggie Donovan—
Lindsay McKenna's WOMEN OF GLORY. On land, sea or air, these
three Annapolis grads challenge danger head-on, risking life and limb
for the glory of their country—and for the men they love!

May: NO QUARTER GIVEN (SE #667) Dana Coulter is on the brink
of achieving her lifelong dream of flying—and of meeting the man who
would love to take her to new heights!

June: THE GAUNTLET (SE #673) Molly Rutledge is determined
to excel on her own merit, but Captain Cameron Sinclair is equally
determined to take gentle Molly under his wing....

July: UNDER FIRE (SE #679) Indomitable Maggie never thought
her career—or her heart—would come under fire. But all that changes
when she teams up with Lieutenant Wes Bishop!